monsoonbooks

CW00621678

THE STRANGLER'S W/

Richard Lord is the autho   oks.
His first full-length books were non-fiction titles, including the highly
successful *Culture Shock! Germany* and the less successful *Success in
Business – Germany*. He entered the field of non-fiction short stories
with *Insider's Frankfurt*.

For the last six years, he has been concentrating more and more
on fiction, especially crime fiction. His short stories have appeared
in five anthologies as well as in the now defunct Amazon Shorts
program. One of his short stories, "The Lost History of Shadows",
was adapted as a mini-series for Singapore's Mediacorp television.
This followed the adaptation of his earlier story, "A Perfect Exit", as
a one-hour TV film.

Lord also has a solid track record as a playwright, with over a
dozen professional productions of his one-act and full-length plays.
Two of his plays were broadcast as radio plays by BBC World Service;
the second of these, *The Boys At City Hall* … was a BBC Highlight
of the Month.

Having lived in Germany for well over a decade, Lord developed
a fascination for Central European culture that infuses *The Strangler's
Waltz*. It is projected as the first volume in The Vienna Noir Quartet,
a four-book series of crime fiction set in Vienna from pre-World War
I to the 1938 *Anschluss* with Nazi Germany.

Books by Richard Lord

The Strangler's Waltz
Crime Scene Asia (editor-contributor)
Crime Scene Singapore (editor-contributor)
The World Outside The Window (contributor)

Culture Shock! Germany
Insider's Frankfurt
Success in Business – Germany
Countries of the World – Germany
Festivals of the World – Germany
Germany for Gourmets (English translation)
Cultures of the World – Switzerland (2nd edition) (co-author)

The Strangler's Waltz

Vienna Noir Quartet (Vol.1)

Richard Lord

monsoon

monsoonbooks

First published in print in 2013
by Monsoon Books Pte Ltd
71 Ayer Rajah Crescent #01-01
Mediapolis Phase Ø, Singapore 139951
www.monsoonbooks.com.sg

ISBN (paperback): 978-981-4423-50-2
ISBN (ebook): 978-981-4423-37-3

Cover design by Cover Kitchen.

National Library Board, Singapore Cataloguing-in-Publication Data
Lord, Richard A. (Richard Alan)
The strangler's waltz / Richard Lord. – Singapore : Monsoon Books
Pte Ltd, 2013.
pages cm. – (Vienna noir quartet ; vol. 1)
ISBN : 978-981-4423-50-2 (paperback)

1. Murder – Investigation – Austria – Vienna – History – 20th century
– Fiction. 2. Detectives – Austria – Vienna – History – 20th century
– Fiction. 3. Vienna (Austria) – History – 20th century – Fiction. I.
Title. II. Series: Vienna noir quartet ; vol. 1.

PS3612
813.6 -- dc23   OCN853632736

Printed in the United States

"If I speak of Vienna, it must be in the past, as a man speaks of a
woman he has loved and who is dead."
Erich von Stroheim

"Austria is a laboratory for the collapse of the world."
Karl Kraus

Introduction

That winter of 1913 had been vociferously harsh, the kind of weather that brought the natural melancholy of the Viennese seeping to the surface. Temperatures had slumped below zero (Celsius) shortly before the solstice and stayed locked there through most of January and February. Christmas was deep-white and frigid. Snow fluttered down with the confetti on New Year's Eve, but stayed around much longer. Through the first half of March, rancorous winds whipped off the Danube and swirled through the wide boulevards of Vienna, its narrow lanes and twisting alleys. Anyone who spent more than 15 minutes outdoors was sure to slink back in with brain freeze.

When the snow departed, something much worse – freezing rain – swept in. Broken bones became commonplace as the smaller streets turned into makeshift skating rinks.

The surface of the Danube froze over in the first week of January and stayed frozen through late February. In fact, an unusual number of people drowned in that period. The authorities weren't sure if these unfortunate souls had been seduced by the gleaming ice on the river and tried skating or even crossing the river without the convenience of a bridge ... or if these were just normal suicides, their numbers raised because of the harsh weather and infectious melancholy.

But this was Vienna, in those final years of Habsburg Vienna, a city which was happily, deliriously bipolar. Sure, melancholy was rampant, but this did not impair the ardent embrace of life's sweetest pleasures by those same people infected by melancholia. For a cultural split personality was a defining trait of Viennese society in that period.

This split was manifested in various ways. For instance, that melancholic posture of many Viennese was usually alloyed with a refined sense of *Lebensfreude* (the Austro-Hungarian version of *joie de vivre*). The Viennese could find reason for frolic and fun even in bad news. One prime example: in that brutal winter of 1913, the upper crust of Viennese society still held their celebrated pre-Lenten costume balls, where drink, dance and dalliance all flowed freely.

These balls were often themed events and one of the more popular bashes that year was a "Bankruptcy Ball", where participants celebrated the recent plunge of the economy that sent many formerly successful people into the maelstrom of insolvency.

At the ball, this monetary misfortune was parodied with women whose costumes flaunted the credits up top, debits at the bottom; thin men were asked to dress as deposits, corpulent men as withdrawals; and the posh restaurant at the hall, renamed Debtor's Prison for the occasion, was decorated with fake foreclosure notices and other signs of financial ruin.

And while Vienna was, on the surface, a sexually puritanical society, it also featured a string of elegant, high-end brothels and one of the highest rates of streetwalkers in Europe. More, premarital and post-marital affairs were evidently commonplace. A wealthy and well-situated Viennese gentleman who did not have at least one mistress was an exception who drew admiration or wonder ... or perhaps suspicion.

In that year of 1913, Vienna was the capital of the second largest contiguous empire in the world. (The Russian Empire was the largest.) Its southwestern corner included a slice of present-day Italy, all of Slovenia and Croatia and Bosnia. The main body of the country was, of course, Austria and Hungary, a large scoop of Romania, all of the Czech Republic and Slovakia, extended in the east to parts of present-day Poland and even a sliver of Russia.

As the capital of such a diverse empire, Vienna also boasted one of the most diverse multicultural populations of any European city. Its streets, factories, shops, bars and cafés were filled with ethnic Germans, Hungarians, Serbs, Croats, Slovenes, Italians, Romanians, Poles, East European Jews, Czechs, and Slovaks. Strolling through any of Vienna's working class neighborhoods, one could hear a rich symphony of languages, accents and street-tempered idioms.

In fact, with just over two million residents, Vienna's population in 1913 was double its immediate post-World War I population, when the country had lost much of its empire and ended up as plain old Austria, a small, landlocked country in the heart of Central Europe. In fact, even today, the population of Vienna is significantly smaller than it was in the last years of the Habsburg regime.

Vienna in those days was also a city of stark contrasts. For instance, within the city, one could find opulent mansions and large, luxurious apartments a short tram ride away from some of the worst slum dwellings of any major European city. Not surprisingly, the city was no stranger to class conflict.

There were also, to be sure, numerous frictions, resentments and prejudices amongst the various ethnic and social groups in the city. The ethnic Germans, who formed the majority of Vienna's residents, were most prone to these negative influences. There were a good many so-called pan-Germans, who wanted a more ethnically pure Austria and even dreamed of union with the German Reich and other lands with overwhelming German populations. These pan-Germans had their own newspapers and included some powerful politicians on their side.

Anti-Semitism was also rampant in Vienna at this time. The city boasted some of Europe's most successful and influential Jewish citizens – in fields as diverse as science, finance, heavy industry, newspaper and book publishing, and politics – and yet also suffered from much overt anti-Semitism. In fact, one of Vienna's most beloved politicians, the long-serving mayor Dr Karl Lueger, was an outspoken anti-Semite. And here, too, we see another example of the city's peculiar bipolarity: Lueger often inveighed against the Jews and their nefarious influence in Vienna, but he also had a number of Jewish friends and even appointed Jews to important positions in his city government.

(One of the famous historical figures who appears in this novel shared this trait: he was in those days a pedestrian anti-Semite, but some of his closest friends in Vienna were Jews and he respected and trusted his Jewish clients more than any of the others he dealt with in his business.)

This rich stew of a society was held together by the Habsburg monarchy, which had ruled Vienna and its environs for centuries, eventually extending the reach of their domains to become the leaders of a massive empire. It fact, it was the figure in the Hofburg Palace – the official residence of the Austro-Hungarian emperor – who kept the whole thing together in relatively peaceful circumstances.

That figure was Emperor Franz-Josef, who, at the time of the events in this story, was 82 years old, halfway to his 83rd birthday, and in the 65th year of his reign as emperor. Partly because of the longevity of his reign and partly because he then seemed like a cranky but affectionate grandfather figure, Franz-Josef was admired, respected, sometimes even loved by many of his subjects throughout the empire. His influence was strongest in Vienna, however, where his presence was dominant and his likeness in photos and paintings almost ubiquitous.

An inveterate reactionary in his social and political views, "old Franzl" had outlived most of his former political enemies by 1913 and had been steadily withdrawing from national and city politics for a number of years. He now served more as a unifying figure, holding together all the groups and forces in the country.

Many on the political left still despised the emperor for his past transgressions and his occasional forays into contemporary politics, while the anti-monarchy press often suggested he was a doddering old man, perhaps even senile. But his public appearances showed a remarkably robust octogenarian and solidified the affection for him amongst many of Vienna's ethnically diverse residents.

As the Karl Kautsky quote at the beginning of this book reminds us, Austria in the first decades of the 20th century was a laboratory for the end of the world. But Vienna in those years was also the incubator for the modern world that we now inhabit.

Much of how we today see the world, of how we react with each other, of what our dreams are – as well as our fears – are the product of the intellectual and artistic ferment prevailing in Vienna in the first few decades of the 20th century.

In those first decades of the last century, Vienna was known worldwide for its amazingly rich intellectual and cultural life. Much of modern psychology and other branches of medical science; economics; architecture; social and political theory; linguistics; philosophy ... modern decadence were started, developed or brought to their fullest fruition in Vienna. The city was not only a world capital of painting, theatre, music (in both classical mode and startling modern innovations); it was also a crucible for revolutionary politics which would soon reshape Europe and the world beyond.

Amongst those who lived in Vienna either short-term or

permanently before and after the First World War were many of the personalities who forged the modern sensibilities of the world we've inherited. Two of those who influenced the modern world in very important ways turn up in this novel as major secondary characters – even if the significant roles they play in the novel are not quite as important as the roles their real-life models played in the political and intellectual life of the last 100 years.

Another major feature of Viennese life in the first decades of the last century was the vibrant newspaper culture. Printed newspapers had been around in Vienna for over two hundred years, but as the 20th century began, there was an explosion in the number of daily and weekly newspapers along with the readers and reporters for those newspapers.

The mushrooming of newspapers set off a fierce competition between the various journals as they tried to outdo each other to push up circulation numbers and poach readers from the other publications. Truth was often the first casualty in the newspaper's heated war for readers: sensationalism ruled and facts were trimmed, disguised or simply discarded in the rush to fashion attention-grabbing stories.

As the sensationalist press could also claim the most readers in Vienna, their influence was enormous: many Vienna residents viewed their city, their world through the distorting lenses of the popular press that was churning out trash in able to keep their readership numbers up.

Much of this change was fermenting or already well underway in that last full year before the world plunged into the slaughter pit of the Great War.

Indeed, the empire and Vienna's place as one of Europe's most powerful cities were both endangered as the year 1913 rolled in.

Just over a year after the events in this book, the heir to the Austro-Hungarian throne, Archduke Franz-Ferdinand, and his widely admired wife Sophie were assassinated in Sarajevo, Bosnia. Ironically, the royal couple had made this trip to show the enduring power of Habsburg rule in one of the empire's outlying urban redoubts, but a group of Serbian ultra-nationalists decided to use the trip to make their own political point.

The assassination and Austrian demands on Serbia for recompense and justice are often cited as "the causes" of the First World War. That's too reductionist really, but certainly the murders of the royal couple and Vienna's decision to take strong retaliatory measures threw the fatal match into the political tinderbox that was Europe in those years. The result was a devastating conflict that would culminate with the destruction of not just the Austro-Hungarian Empire, but also the Russian, Ottoman and German empires. In this case, Habsburg pride led to a total Habsburg fall ... from power.

Intriguingly, many Viennese in those last years leading up to the war lived with a premonition of a major catastrophe about to hit their city and their country. They seem to have sensed deep within that the world they'd known their whole lives was about to come to an abrupt end.

The celebrated Viennese compulsion to enjoy life probably flowed from this premonition. So, until the catastrophe of the war arrived, the party raged on. And at no time was the party running at such a fever pitch as in the middle months of that last prewar year.

Yes, that winter of 1913 was unusually harsh, but it served as the overture to a spring and summer that were breathtaking in how they once again transformed the city of Vienna. *The Strangler's Waltz* may be a fictional work, but it employs a raft of the historical facts behind the rise and sudden decline of one of Europe's – indeed the world's – most fascinating cities. It's a tale of how a great city which carefully cultivated its split personality was suddenly jolted into confronting its darkest side as terror began stalking its normally charming streets and scarring the self-assurance of a unduly smug nation.

1

Finally, after four months of battering Vienna, winter broke. An enervating thaw set in. Spring-like weather filled the city: warm days paired with pleasantly cool evenings. The outward changes immediately brightened the mood of many Vienna residents; they felt they were finally being rewarded for having made it through a particularly harsh test of wills. As they saw it, winter had tried with all its force to break them, but they had won.

The gaunt young man with a disconcerting gaze had come to despise winter. For him, it signified the cruelty of death. Beyond the death imposed on nature, this animus had a personal side for him: his father had died on a brutally cold day in early January and his beloved mother had died four days before Christmas. So this mid-March thaw was, for him, all too welcome.

Returning to the center of town after what had been the equivalent of a long and busy day, he felt exhaustion weighing on his shoulders, making his limbs achingly heavy. Tucked under his arm was a ragged leather case stuffed with a sheath of his paintings, watercolors. He had spent much of that afternoon with a long-time customer. He had gone there hoping to sell him forty of his watercolors, which would have set a new sales record for him. To his disappointment, the owner of the shop had been in a sour mood so he ended up buying fewer than half. A lot fewer.

This was just one of the things on the young artists' mind as he ambled down Mariangasse. He was also mulling over an offer from a friend to make a trip to Prague, where he was assured he could sell more of his paintings in a week than he would in a whole month in Vienna. A further concern was the discussion in parliament about relaxing restrictions on eastern migration into the capital.

Tugging at his scarf as he moved along, the young man was so absorbed with his swirl of thoughts that he didn't hear anything until he was almost at the corner of the small alleyway halfway to Schafsgasse.

That's when he first heard those strange sounds. They seemed to be coming out of the alley. Ugly sounds, like someone gargling. He stopped to listen more intently. There it was, but now it sounded like someone taking a harsh gulp. The artist took three cautious strides to the edge of the alley. Now he heard some kind of scraping sound, like a heavy barrel being dragged along a gravelly road.

As he was right at the top of the lane, the sound changed. It was now the sound of heavy footsteps, moving rapidly. He turned to look down the alley and … was knocked down by a burly man rushing out of the alley but throwing a quick look back as he emerged.

The burly man seemed just as shocked by the collision as the lean artist. His hesitation following that jolt allowed his victim to scramble quickly back to his feet. The two stared at each other for several seconds; the younger man's stare was filled with blunt confusion, the older man's with raw disdain. The artist was still locked in that stare when the other man pushed him to the side, then turned and bolted down the street.

The push was forceful. The artist just managed to maintain his balance and keep himself from crashing to the ground again. He had to grab onto the side of the corner building to regain full balance. He then turned to look down the alley. About twenty meters from where he stood, he saw a figure lying on the ground. A female apparently.

Now his attention was fully seized and he loped quickly to where the figure was sprawled behind a trash can. Though he wasn't expecting anything too pleasant, what he did see came as a gut-wrenching jolt. It *was* a female, and she was lying there motionless. At first, he thought she might just be drunk, passed out; maybe what he'd heard from the street was some kind of argument between her and the burly man. But a closer look showed something much more serious.

Her eyes were open, staring blankly into a further distance that could be shared with no one. As the artist crouched down for an even closer look, he noticed the purple spread of bruises across the throat. He reached out, about to touch her, but then pulled back, suddenly repulsed. No touch was necessary: it was clear to him that the woman was dead.

Standing up slowly, he continued staring at the face for a full two, maybe three minutes. She was quite attractive, even in this position, this state. Heavily made-up with bright lipstick and alluring eye shadow accentuating the size and shape of her eyes. He then scrutinized her dress, which was rather seductive, slutty almost. He swallowed hard, though his mouth was suddenly dry.

Shards of impressions started fitting together into a deduction. A dead woman, neck severely bruised; the burly man hurrying from the alleyway, staring at the young man with fear, then pushing him away roughly; the man's hurried departure. It was horribly obvious: the man had strangled the woman, then fled the scene. Young Adolf Hitler had just witnessed the immediate aftermath of a brutal murder.

He jerked his head upwards and started looking around. He wasn't sure what to do. Should he try to find a policeman, or tell whoever he ran into on the street about the grisly discovery he'd just made? But just a few seconds of reflection convinced him that neither option would be wise. He himself could well become a suspect here. And his position as a poor, struggling artist with a reputation for rapid flashes of temper and even a few minor scuffles would possibly make him a prime suspect.

No, the safest course of action for Hitler would be to follow the lead of that burly thug and leave the scene as quickly as he could. Hearing footsteps down on Seidengasse, he decided to exit via the other end of the alley. But first he used his foot to push the woman's body closer to the wall. He wanted to be sure that anyone else who found the body that night would have to be looking for it, or at least walking the full length of the alley.

He then loped to the Burggasse exit, slowing up only as he neared the corner; no need to draw attention to himself. As he peered down Burggasse, he saw three people, young like him, about fifty meters away. But coming in his direction. He crossed the street, shifted the leather case to his right side, and started walking in the opposite direction from the trio.

He bent his head downwards and off to the side. That way, even if one of them glanced over, they'd never be able to identify his face later. But they were all too drunk and too absorbed with each other, singing and laughing as they passed him by across the road. He pulled his head back up and, looking down a dark street lit by pale lemon lighting, he tried to imagine what lay ahead. But what had just happened was so disturbing that all he could imagine was that by the time this ended, everything in his life might be thrown totally upside down.

He picked up his pace.

2

The body wasn't officially discovered for another three hours. The unlucky person who found it was a one-armed beggar who had gone to the trash can to scavenge for anything useful he might find there. Seeing the dead woman, he at first just stared, transfixed as much by her beauty as her coldness. Then, as he came out of his trance, he started screaming. And screaming. He kept on screaming for several minutes until people in the apartment building across the way came down to pummel him for waking them up. Instead, they joined in on the gruesome discovery.

When the police arrived, they began their interrogations immediately. It was clearly a case of strangulation, and that's how they proceeded. As the one who found the body was a one-armed man, they were able to rule him out quickly. The rough estimate made for the time of death would also have diminished any suspicions about the man who had found her. Actually, the second one to have found her, though police were fully ignorant of that key fact.

*　*　*

Back at the hostel for homeless men that had been his temporary home for three years now, Hitler was too shaken to attempt any sleep. The exhaustion that had possessed him earlier, before he ventured down that alley, had pretty much faded. His limbs and neck were still heavy with exhaustion, but his mind was racing. The problem: it was racing in every which-way, with thoughts and emotions scraping against each other as he tried to find a focus on the events back there off Mariangasse.

He had gone to the commons room just off the entrance when he arrived at the hostel. After just sitting there for a few minutes, trying to pull his thoughts into some kind of cohesive thrust, he closed his eyes and breathed deeply for a few minutes. When he opened his eyes again, he had some sense of emotional balance. Or at least he had an idea that made some sense.

Pulling out his sketchpad from his leather case, he opened to the first empty page, about three-quarters back in the book.

And then slowly, fastidiously, he drew a sketch of the dead woman's face as it was etched there in his memory. But in his sketch, she wasn't dead. She was asleep, a seductive smile on her face, as if swept up in a dream of a romantic encounter.

When he finished the sketch, Hitler sat back and stared at it for a short time. Finally, he smiled. It was if he had redeemed her from being the victim of a murder, had somehow revived her with the skills of his hand.

More, this was a real breakthrough for him: he was seen as an artist who could only copy the work of other artists. He had never been successful drawing or painting from real life, not even inanimate objects like bridges or buildings. But here he had produced a wonderful sketch from the image in his own head.

He stood and paced about the room a bit, taking deep breaths every few steps. Then he sat down again to sketch the face of the man who had stormed out of the alley. He thought he would have much more trouble with this sketch, but he was surprised to discover that it, too, came without much difficulty.

When he was finished, Hitler stared at the face with contempt. He hated this face, even though he knew so little about the man behind it.

Having finished both drawings, Hitler was still not ready for sleep, so he slipped the sketchbook back into his case, got up and stumbled out of the homeless center. As often when he was tossed in a jumble of emotions, he would walk around for a while, just in the immediate area, and try to pull the curtain down on the night's events.

His thoughts kept swirling – but always coming back to the dead woman, of course. He thought of other dead people he had seen: mainly his mother and his father. But those cases were very different. His mother had died of cancer after almost a year of excruciating suffering. "A merciful release" some of the neighbors, even his own relatives, had called it. But for Hitler, whose mother had been the fixed center of his life for so long, this sentiment was taken as a near personal attack on him.

His father had died suddenly. Out for a morning walk, he had dropped into a favorite inn for a glass of wine and died of a lung hemorrhage before the wine he ordered could be brought to the table. Hitler had not seen his father dead until the wake, and although he had despised the man for most of his youth, right up until the day of his death, as he stared down at the corpse in the open coffin, a veil draped over the lid, what he saw was a pitiful man who had killed himself with a daily dose of vile. Adolf, still a teenager then, had cried bitterly at seeing his once feared father reduced to a cold corpse.

But this woman in the alley was so much different. For one thing, she was so much younger, perhaps not much older than Hitler himself. And though he had always found a kind of hidden beauty in his mother, the woman in the alley was beautiful in an overt, even ostentatious way. He closed his eyes as he thought of that face again, trying through brash will to blank it out. But it remained, so he opened his eyes and continued walking down the lane, hoping to wear himself out fully and then collapse into sleep.

3

The police detail first called to the scene to investigate were junior officers assigned to night operations: the "red-eyed pulleys", as they were called. They had carried out all the sweep-up work, but were replaced by full investigators early the next morning.

The Viennese police force in those twilight years of the Habsburg monarchy had its own pet names for the various levels of police work. Every member of the force knew these terms and used them on a daily basis.

The scuffed-boots police who made street arrests and pulled in obvious or ostentatious criminals were called "hooks". "Pulleys" were those cops who did the preliminary work on more complicated cases, such as murder scenes, while "loupes" was the name for full-rank inspectors. That term came from the jeweler's loupe, the thumb-sized magnification device jewelers used to detect fine details. Not surprisingly, the "loupes" commanded the most respect among fellow officers.

(Those were not the only nicknames in the department; although they were unaware of it, senior officers who carried out most of their work from behind desks were called "the seat farts" by members of the other three groups below them.)

Because of several peculiarities surrounding this case, two of the more respected loupes in the Vienna force were assigned to the case: Karl-Heinz Dörfner and Julian Stebbel. Though both were seasoned veterans of the police force, they'd only been together as a team for half a year. And neither one was altogether happy about being paired with the other as an investigative team.

But the district commander had decided that it was a good pairing. The strengths of Dörfner complemented the strengths of Stebbel and vice-versa. Which also meant that the strengths of one made up for shortcomings in the other. Commander Willhof himself thought it was one of his more inspired pairings. Of course, Willhof was eased into retirement a short time after pairing up the two.

It would be another half-century before the phrase "good cop-bad cop" came into use, but that was the principle operating behind this pairing. Karl-Heinz Dörfner was bigger and more physical in many ways than his more experienced partner; he could be intimidating without even trying.

Julian Stebbel was shrewder and better able to trick people into revealing what they didn't necessarily want to reveal. Accordingly, Dörfner took the lead in questioning suspects or recalcitrant witnesses who were easily cowed; Stebbel stepped in when a witness needed to be wooed, a suspect needed the surgeon's-scalpel form of interrogation rather than the iron-fist method.

Dörfner was actually from a small town in Steiermark known for its resentment of most of what the modern world offered. But young Karl-Heinz quickly outgrew his affection for small-town life and those small-town minds that fit snugly on the dismal side of life's horizons. Stationed in Vienna as a young soldier, he remained in the metropolis after his compulsory military service had ended.

Because of a respiratory problem, Julian Stebbel had missed military service. A native of Innsbruck, Stebbel had completed his secondary education at a respected classical education *Gymnasium* in his home town before moving to the imperial capital, where he had slogged through two years at the University of Vienna before deciding to sample a career in law enforcement.

Their differing backgrounds were reflected in their personalities: as a rule, Stebbel spoke quietly and at a measured pace, as if testing each word before he let it out. Dörfner, in contrast, usually spoke at a rapid tempo; some might even say his speech too often ran a few steps ahead of his thinking. Julian Stebbel was clearly one of those who might say that.

4

Adolf Hitler rose early the next morning, something not at all typical of him. Other long-term residents of the Meldemannstrasse men's hostel knew there was definitely something wrong with their Adi. For one thing, he was lock-lipped quiet. You wouldn't want to say that Hitler was unusually quiet that morning. Hitler being quiet went far beyond the borders of unusual; it was more like mind-boggling. This was the fellow who had a strong opinion on just about any topic and was more than willing to share it with just about anyone. That trait had earned him the nickname of "the Linzer Lip" from his fellow residents.

On a typical morning at the Meldemann, a casual comment about the weather could launch the "Linzer Lip" into an impassioned screed. If it was miserably cold that morning, or if the day had started with dark sheets of rain, Hitler would give his take on that occurrence. More than often, he would find some way of dumping the blame for the miserable weather on the glut of Slavs in Vienna, or on some plot stewed by the Freemasons or secret cabals. If none of his Jewish friends at the hostel was around to be offended, he'd also lay an attack on the "Hebrew tribe".

But on that morning of April 12, Hitler had little to say about anything. When others greeted him or asked him something, his reply would be two, maybe three words. A few times, he merely shrugged, not having really heard what was said.

Those who knew him casually were afraid that he had the flu or some other contagious disease. They weren't really concerned about Hitler; they were more worried about how such a disease could spread quickly in a residence with over 500 men of shaky constitutions.

Those who knew Hitler better knew that he suffered from a chronic queasy digestive system; this, they suggested, was the cause of his strange demeanor that morning. He'd probably eaten something unhealthy the night before, they said; maybe he'd gone to that filthy *Imbiss* a few streets over and sampled some of their dubious meats. He'd be better after a few good shits, these guys decided.

Of course, they were all wrong. But the brittle artist was not about to share a hint of what was really troubling him that morning. He went down to the large dining hall and ordered a cup of tea, which he downed quickly. He then headed back upstairs, threw a few things into his bag, pulled on his overcoat and headed out into the yawning streets of Vienna.

He had decided to treat himself to breakfast at one of his favorite cafés that morning. Though he hadn't made the big sales he'd hoped for the day before, he still had enough extra cash from a good two weeks previously that he could afford the mild extravagance.

He took a table in a far corner of the Café Branntweiners, flagged down a waiter and placed his order. While waiting for his coffee and light breakfast to arrive, he bustled over to the newspaper racks and pulled down four of his regular reads. He first turned to the *Neues Wiener Tagblatt* and started quickly scanning the headlines. Though he was a ravenous reader of the papers, that morning, he was interested in one story only. Starting at the top, he moved down the page quickly looking for that story. Yes, there it was, in the lower right-hand corner: a neat cube of sentences about the murder. An unidentified woman, the report said, had been found in the alley off

Mariangasse, the apparent victim of a fatal assault. No other details were provided.

The same was true of the other three papers spread across the table. In fact, one of them could only devote a four-line smudge to the incident. Obviously, the story had come in too late to the editorial room. He was sure the afternoon editions would offer more extensive coverage. There he could learn more about the crime that had shaken him more than anything since the death of his mother.

* * *

"Hmm. Seems this fellow wasn't too concerned with good manners or the rules about how to treat ladies. No, indeed. It will be fun to get our hands on this swine and teach him some manners."

Dörfner and Stebbel were heading to the police morgue after first making the obligatory stop-off at their section of the Criminal Police Department. As they strode down the sickly green corridor leading to the morgue, Dörfner read from the preliminary report that he'd snatched from the team's in-tray. Now he read out what he took to be the salient items in the report to Stebbel.

"Victim was found in a tight-fitting dress with a deep neckline. Victim sported brash scarlet lipstick that had been thickly applied. Victim had heavily rouged cheeks. Eyes were shadowed in violet, with lines drawn from the corners to accentuate their size. She was heavily perfumed."

To the police, to most Viennese actually, each of these descriptions was part of a code which, put together, clearly spelled out W-H-O-R-E.

As Stebbel pushed open the morgue doors for his colleague, Dörfner suggested that their investigation was already two-thirds wrapped up. All they needed now was to find out why someone had murdered this unlucky streetwalker and who that killer was.

Doktor Gressler greeted the two inspectors; he knew just whom they had come to see. He led them to box 308 and, with the assistance of a medical student, pulled out the slab with the murdered woman's body on it.

The two inspectors stepped as close as they could to the cadaver and looked down, inspecting it closely. All the lavish make-up had been removed. But even without any make-up and with the bluish tint to her skin, they could see that the woman had been quite attractive, practically beautiful. They now wondered what perilous path had brought this lady to this final destination.

"We estimate the age as perhaps in her late twenties, maybe thirty, no more than that," Doktor Gressler said in the measured tone of the austere scientist. The two policemen simply nodded.

"Cause of death?" asked Dörfner.

"Oh, strangulation, definitely," answered Gressler. "Autopsy confirmed what the untrained eye would already have guessed. Killer did a thorough job of it too: he broke three bones in the neck." He leaned forward and pointed. "Here, here and here."

Dörfner nodded. "So our killer was powerful?" Dr. Gressler nodded. "Of course; the bastard."

Gressler then waved both of the inspectors closer. "Look at the neck bruises. Unusually broad. So that means our killer would have had wide hands. Wide across the palms."

Both policemen nodded. Stehbel was fully focused on the victim's face. "Anything else that's germane?"

Gressler nodded. "No significant signs of struggle. That's strange, considering the nature of the crime."

Dörfner untwisted his lips. "Probably means that she knew the bastard." The doctor started to nod.

"Or that he surprised her. Had his mitts around her neck and started the choking before she could fight back," Stebbel interjected.

"Yes, that's the other possibility," the good doctor responded.

"Anything else we should know?"

"Top of the dress was torn. Ripped apart actually. We suspect that was mainly necessitated by the act of strangling." Gressler then shrugged. "Oh, and semen in the vaginal tract."

"Any signs of rape?"

"None. None whatsoever."

Dörfner nodded brusquely this time. "So she was one of Vienna's horizontal ballet artists, hmm?"

The term puzzled Gressler. Even though he'd been working almost exclusively with police over the last four years, he'd never heard that one. "Excuse me?"

"A streetwalker. A lady of the night. A whore."

Gressler shrugged. He knew as a doctor he wasn't supposed to make such judgments, though he made them all the time in that corner of his mind where science was carefully excluded.

"I wouldn't expect to see a lady like this at one of our exclusive winter balls."

"No, I wouldn't either," Dörfner added.

Stebbel picked it up from there. "So, Herr Doktor, any idea of a … possible motive?"

"That's your sphere, isn't it, gentlemen?"

"Indeed it is. But I was just asking if you'd … care to speculate as to a motive." Gressler thought for a moment, then gave his head a slight shake, as if to say he hadn't thought about it enough.

"Robbery?"

Gressler took a deep breath. "If it was robbery, the criminal wasn't very good at it. He left those rings on her hand. I'm no jeweler or anything, but they looked like they were very valuable."

"Rings? She was wearing rings?"

"Three. And let me tell you, two of those stones would choke a medium-sized pooch. The one was this red beauty; you know, that one that shines a lot."

Dörfner jumped in here. "Is that a ruby you're talking about?"

"Maybe. Like I said, I'm no expert in that field. Thanks be to God, my wife has never developed a taste for anything too expensive in the realm of jewelry." He thought for a moment. "Maybe that's why I married her."

"So where are these rings? You have them here?"

"Up in your own department, gentlemen. Where they were taken early this morning."

"Of course. That's where they would be."

The doctor smiled. "And where they should be."

Leaving the morgue, they headed for the *paternoster* lift.

(Not a few people in the police headquarters building thought it appropriate that the *paternoster* went down to the morgue. The *paternoster* was an open carriage elevator system that travelled continuously up and down. It stopped for no man – and no woman – but defied those using it to hop on as it drew even with their floor and then to hop off again as they reached their destination floor.

For older people moving within a tall building – or someone like Dörfner, with his one bad leg – the *paternoster* was a challenge that involved serious risk every time they boarded or left the lift.)

Stebbel helped his larger partner as they climbed into the *paternoster* to take them back up to the fourth floor. Stebbel was picking at the scraps of evidence while Dörfner was already halfway to solving the case.

"OK, so we know that she's a whore."

Stebbel emerged from the cocoon of his thought. "That's just one of the things we don't know yet."

"Were you listening when I read out the foot soldiers' report?"

"*Ja*, but there were some things that ... don't quite fit together."

"Like what?"

At that point, they were just being pulled into the fourth floor, so they braced themselves and hopped off. Stebbel again helped Dörfner because of his bad leg.

"Well, for one thing, there was the semen in the vaginal tract. Prostitutes usually don't take a load from the last customer back onto the street. They ... douche thoroughly between clients so that there's no ... residue left."

Dörfner gave his signature guffaw. "What, you hang around to watch them cleaning up afterwards? I always settle up for whatever extras we've had, slap the money down and get out quick as I can."

Stebbel responded with an uncomfortable smile, showing Dörfner once again that he did not share his humor. "Just joking, you know; just joking."

Stebbel nodded. "Yes, of course. But I think the presence of semen makes it *less* likely that she was a prostitute."

"Well, we'll see. My bet is that she was doing the streets and offered her wares to the wrong guy."

By this time, they had reached the evidence depot. They knocked once, then stepped in just before the voice within invited them to do so. They told the head of the depot what they had come for, and minutes later they were opening the brown packet with three rings squeezed inside it. As they looked at the first ring, they were surprised, and the second one was even more surprising.

"That, Herr Colleague, is a ruby," Dörfner said in a near gasp.

"It certainly is."

"A generous chunk of rock it is, too." Stebbel nodded. "What's this other one?"

"An emerald, I believe. Handsome, isn't it? Not as prized as the ruby, but few girls would turn one down."

"No."

"And this third one's no piece of junk either." Dörfner held up a nicely ornamented, unstoned gold ring.

"So where do you think a prostitute would get jewelry like this?"

"Where? From a wealthy client, of course. Or three wealthy clients, I don't know. A woman who looked like that, she probably had no shortage of enthusiastic customers."

"Yes, that's the other thing that doesn't fit for me. A woman that attractive wouldn't be prowling the streets, she'd be working at a high-class brothel. She'd have the clients lining up to see her."

"Okay, so she maybe just arrived recently from the provinces. Was just getting the ... *lay of the land*, as it were."

Stebbel nodded but was only half-listening. Most of his attention was fixed on one of the rings, the one with no stone but rich ornamentation. Suddenly, a sharp smile filled his face. "Yes! Alright, we just got our first real break."

"What's that?"

"Galinsky."

"What??"

He turned back to Dörfner and showed him something in the ring's ornamentation. "See that, the way the lines curl: there's an L, then an A, and there's your G."

"Yes??"

"That stands for Leopold Albert Galinsky. The man who made these rings. Head man at Galinsky *Gmbh*, one of the city's top jewelers. The real craftsmen jewelers always try to initial their work in an unobtrusive way. *Comme ça.*"

"Anyway, we have got ourselves a lead. Now we need to speak to Herr Galinsky and see if he has any recollection of who these rings once belonged to. Or maybe who bought them."

"Right. Yes. So, should we bring him in?"

"Bring him in?"

"Yeah, have him brought in here. For the interrogation. Always knocks them off balance when they have to come in here. He might spill something he wouldn't otherwise."

"We're not interrogating him, Karl-Heinz. He's not a suspect. He's just an honest businessman who might be able to help us out significantly here. There's no need to put the gentleman on the defensive."

"You sure about that?"

"Quite. Look, we'll go over there to the Galinsky shop and speak with him on his home ground. If he can tell us anything, he will, I'm sure. He's a respected businessman and he wouldn't want to tarnish his reputation by refusing to cooperate with police investigators. Especially on a case like this."

"Alright, I see your point. Let's just hope that he doesn't choose to protect one of his clients who also just happens to be Madame X's client."

Stebbel chided him with his gaze. "If he tries to throw up a smokescreen, we'll know, won't we?"

"Yes, of course we will."

The two investigators then made the arrangements to take the rings out, signed the removal-of-evidence papers and made an appointment via telephone to see Herr Leopold Galinsky.

5

Upon their arrival at the jewelry shop, the two inspectors were greeted at the door by a well-dressed shop assistant. When they explained the purpose of their visit, the assistant nodded and went to fetch his boss.

Leopold Galinsky emerged from the back room less than a minute later. He was still in shirtsleeves as he stepped through the curtain, but he had a dress jacket clutched in his right hand. He stopped for a moment to pull on the jacket before proceeding to where the two inspectors stood. As he walked, he smoothed out his jacket and his tie to produce the proper appearance.

Galinsky had obviously been expecting the two visitors. He wore a friendly but cautious look as he offered his hand and greeted them with a melodious 'Servus'.

"So, how can I help you, gentleman?"

"Actually, we were hoping that you could give us some assistance identifying some items that were purchased here at your shop." Dörfner then opened the police department packet and carefully poured out the three rings.

"Would you happen to recognize any of these rings?"

Galinsky peered down at the three pieces on the counter for no more than five seconds before picking up the ruby ring. He then inspected it for another three seconds.

"This one certainly. It belongs to Frau von Klettenburg."

"Excuse me?"

Galinsky looked back up. "Frau Anneliese von Klettenburg." He then turned to another assistant standing at attention a short distance away. "Franzl, could you please fetch the book with the von Klettenburg accounts. It's the dark green book on the far right shelf."

"*Jawohl*, Herr Galinsky," the assistant replied before disappearing into the back room.

Stebbel was still trying to line up that name with a swirl of vague associations. "Von Klettenburg ... as in ...?"

"The wife of Karsten von Klettenburg. The privy counselor."

"Privy counselor?" Dörfner had a bit of smugness knocked out of him on hearing that this case might have a link back to the imperial palace.

"Not to forget, also one of our city's richest citizens. A big industrialist. Though most famous, I think, as the head of the Vienna Trust Bank."

"Absolutely stinking rich, in other words," said Dörfner.

"If you care to phrase it that way. Personally, I find that wealth has a rather sweet fragrance." Just then, the assistant re-emerged, clutching the accounts book. He had already opened it to the section with the von Klettenburg purchases and payments. This he placed in front of Galinsky before disappearing back into the other room.

"And the Klettenburgs, they were frequent customers of your establishment?"

"Yes, indeed. For a long time, in fact. Herr von Klettenburg's father and uncle were already clients back when I was a young man, just starting out in the trade." All this time, Galinsky's attention was divided between the inspector's questions and the scribblings in his accounts book. He reached over and picked up the other two rings, checking them against some entries.

"Yes, yes, just as I thought. All three rings belong to Frau von Klettenburg." He gazed back up at the inspectors. "I could give you the dates of purchase if you like."

"Later perhaps. But could you … could you describe the lady."

"Lovely lady. Always polite, warm … ready with a kind word."

"I was thinking more along the lines of a physical description."

Galinsky gave a soft laugh. "As lovely on the outside as within. Let's see … dark hair, shoulder-length, pulled to the side. Large blue eyes. High cheekbones, a fine aquiline nose. A strong chin, but not too strong, you understand. Everything becoming to a lady."

"Yes, I'm sure."

"Is there some problem regarding the Frau von Klettenburg?"

"She met with an unfortunate accident yesterday."

"*Ach, du liebe Zeit.* Nothing serious, I hope."

"She … succumbed to her injuries. She's no longer with us."

Galinsky reacted as if Stebbel had slapped him viciously across the face. Tears formed in his eyes, and for almost a minute, he seemed to have trouble speaking. When he did manage to get out some words, the first several were all limp, almost mangled.

"That's terrible. Just terrible." He then struggled to get out more words even as the tears increased in size. "And I'm sure Herr von Klettenburg must be devastated by the news."

"He hasn't been contacted yet. You see, Frau von Klettenburg was found lying on the street." Galinsky winced, as if this was the most ignominious fate a human being could suffer. And he still had no idea of the circumstances.

"That's why we sought your assistance, Herr Galinsky. She wasn't carrying any other identification and we weren't able to identify the body. Not until now."

"I see." Tears now started trickling down his cheeks. Dörfner tried to console him.

"Of course, we're still not absolutely sure it was this … Frau von Klettenburg. It's possible that it was somebody else." He turned to Stebbel to second the possibility. "Maybe a friend that she had lent the rings to."

"Lending rings like this? To a friend who looked just like her? I don't think we're in the realm of likelihood, gentlemen."

Stebbel stepped back in. "No, probably not. But we'll go now and notify Herr von Klettenburg and others. We still need to get a positive identification. But rest assured, we'll provide you with any information we have as soon as it becomes confirmed fact."

"Thank you, gentlemen. I would appreciate that." He had already pulled out a handkerchief and started brushing tears from his cheeks.

Having a good deal of important work to do now, the two inspectors bade their farewells and started towards the front door. Before they reached it, Herr Galinsky had moved quickly to the other side of the counter and hurried towards the policeman as he called out.

"Yes, Herr Galinsky?"

"I just wanted to say … that if you need any more assistance from me in dealing with this matter, please don't hesitate to ask. Don't hesitate for a moment."

Stebbel offered a sad smile. "Thank you for that assurance. We will certainly contact you should we need any more information." Galinsky then stepped around the two and opened the door for them. They both nodded their thanks and turned to step out.

"Oh, and please give my deepest condolences to Herr von Klettenburg when you break the news to him."

"We will. We certainly will."

And then they were back on the street and in a rush to return to police headquarters. There was much more work to do on this, but they were buoyed just to have made such progress so early.

6

As it happens, the two inspectors were not able to break the news to Karsten von Klettenburg: he was in Bordeaux just then, on a business trip. Some quick inquiries revealed that Anneliese von Klettenburg had two older sisters, but one was living in Prague, the other in Trieste. It made as much sense to try to contact the husband in Bordeaux as to notify one of the sisters. The inspectors hastily decided that the best path still open to them was to head over to the von Klettenburg residence and see if they could get more information there.

At the luxurious von Klettenburg home in the Hietzing district, the two inspectors entered a residence already in a state of decorous panic. As one of the servants explained, Frau von Klettenburg had gone out the previous evening and not returned. She had still not returned, the servant said in a semi-screech, and she had a piano lesson scheduled for two o'clock. The piano teacher was both bumptious and pretentious, and the servants were about to cast lots to see which one would have the thankless task of telling him that the lesson would have to be cancelled if Frau von Klettenburg did not appear soon.

The inspectors told them that it was very possible she would not be returning any time soon. At that point, Frau Barta, the most senior member of the household staff, marched in.

She quickly assessed what was going on, then elbowed her way to the front of the group and addressed the two policemen with the poised assurance of a senior servant.

"Excuse me, gentlemen, but would your visit have something to do with the whereabouts of our dear Frau von Klettenburg?"

Stebbel nodded and tried to keep his voice at a low and even pitch. "Actually, madam, it does; we were hoping that you might be able to ..."

At that moment, Frau Barta had turned to look at Inspector Dörfner. She interpreted his morose, eyes-lowered look immediately – and correctly. Before Stebbel could finish his sentence, she threw her hand across her mouth and gasped.

"*Mein lieber Gott, nein!*"

Stebbel threw a quick look at Dörfner, then tried to regain Frau Barta's attention. "Yes, we were hoping that you might be able to help us with an investigation that possibly involves the lady in question."

Frau Barta turned and whispered something to the other servants gathered in that tight circle. This stunned the servants, and though pressed for more information, the two policemen still held back the key fact. Instead, they peppered the group with more questions.

They soon discovered that a sister-in-law, Constanza, lived right down the street. One of the servants ran across to fetch her, and within a short time, the sister-in-law, Frau Barta and two of the other long-time female servants, along with the two inspectors, were all bundled into a police vehicle and raced back to the headquarters.

(In Vienna, 1913, it was always considered absolutely preferable to have male corpses identified by males, female corpses by females. Only one decent exception was recognized: for spouses. Where possible, as here, this gender divide was scrupulously held to.)

During the ride, Stebbel and Dörfner finally revealed the purpose of the trip. Any emotions held in check until that point finally burst through. The group was already weeping and moaning when they reached police headquarters. This, the two inspectors realized, was going to be one of the more unpleasant identifications.

At the morgue, the four witnesses were further advised of what they were about to see and how they might deal with it. This was standard police practice, though it almost never seemed to soften the blow.

The sister-in-law and all three servants immediately identified the corpse as their much-loved Anneliese. One of the servants swooned and another one asked if she might use the toilet. An orderly took her by the arm and they did a three-legged trot to the Ladies.

Afterwards, the four were led out of the room in shock and wrenching sorrow. A police department doctor and nurse were waiting just outside the doors to offer some awkward grief counseling to the witnesses.

Karsten von Klettenburg's sister Constanza said she would contact her brother and break the news to him. Dörfner and Stebbel offered all the assistance they could provide to the other three ladies and they all nodded numbly. The inspectors had no idea if the three were registering anything being said right then. But before taking their leave, they did take down the full names of the identification party and secured permission to get in touch a few days later to ask questions about the murdered woman.

Having left the four mourners in the safekeeping of the doctor and nurse, the inspectors headed back up to their office. As they waited for the *paternoster*, Stebbel gave a world-weary shrug.

"Well, at least we know a little more than we did this morning. For one thing, our victim was not a prostitute."

"No. I guess I was totally off the mark on that one," Dörfner conceded. Then, after a few moments pause, he added, "Still ... Why was a woman like that walking around in that district, late at night, dressed the way she was and with all that choosey-floozy makeup?"

Stebbel did his best imitation of the nasal-toned Dr. Gressler: "Answering that question, gentlemen, is your sphere, isn't it?"

Dörfner responded with a look that was a mix of amusement and frustration. He took one more quick glance at the preliminary report, thinking he might see something important he'd overlooked earlier. He was no more enlightened when the *paternoster* carriage arrived and the two climbed in. As they started their ascent, Stebbel tapped the side of the car, indicating that his mind was already burrowing into the case.

"And there was one other thing that doesn't fit here."

"What's that?"

"Those three rings she was wearing. Not one of them was ..."

With this small prompt, Dörfner himself saw the point. "A wedding ring!"

"Yes," said Stebbel. "So why was she out for the evening, dressed up like that, but without her wedding ring?"

"That's sticky and unpleasant, I'll tell you that."

"Of course, it could be that the wedding band was the one ring the killer did take from her. Maybe that was the only thing he was really interested in."

"Or else, he pulled that one off, was about to go for the other three when he was interrupted by somebody and decided it was time to haul his ass out of there."

"Also possible." They hop-stepped off the *paternoster*. "Or we could go with the easiest explanation of them all."

"Which is?"

"She wasn't wearing one. She just decided to go out last evening without her wedding ring."

Dörfner face twisted into a depressed expression and, as always when frustrated, he rubbed the back of his head with a full, open palm. Everything had now become so much messier.

7

The inspectors sat down across from each other to write up a report on the von Klettenburg case with everything they'd gathered up until that point. They handed their handwritten remarks to the secretarial officer, who typed out the report. Their next stop was to the district commander, to apprise him of the known facts of the case.

District Commander Gustaf Schollenberg was aghast when he heard that the victim was Anneliese von Klettenburg. "I can't believe it. Such a beautiful young woman. So charming, too. I danced with her, what, two years ago at one of the pre-Lenten balls. A benefit for the police department."

The two inspectors expressed their sympathy that the commander had lost someone he knew and had obviously admired. They then handed him a copy of their report and provided some fine details not listed in the report. At one point during the rundown of these additional details, Commander Schollenberg looked like he was going to retch. But that quickly morphed into a grimace of low-boil anger.

"Okay, none of these details – the sordid ones I mean – can get out. Even Herr von Klettenburg must be kept in the dark about some of this; at least for now. Understood?"

"Of course, Herr Commander."

"And I certainly don't want the jackals in the press getting even a scrap of this. I expect both of you to make that crystal clear to everyone in your division who has had any contact with this case. Crystal clear. If I see any one of these sordid details mentioned anywhere in the press, there will be consequences, gentleman. Severe consequences." He paused to take an imperious snort. "I think we all understand what's meant here, don't we?"

"*Jawohl*, Herr Commander," they both said, one right after the other.

The D.C. then banged his fist on the desk as a trailing thought came to him. "But they will be asking questions. Dozens of them. The husband sits on the privy council, for heaven's sake. So we need some damn thing we tell the press, the police commissioner, those weasly politicians. We can't say that she died of a heat stroke."

Stebbel was ready to cover this one. "A robbery. Or rather, an attempted robbery that went awry. Frau von Klettenburg resisted, she fought back, and the thief strangled her to stop her from defending herself."

Dörfner then jumped in. "And he must have heard someone coming just at that point, so he ran off before he could get the best stuff."

The commander mulled this over for a short time, then nodded. "Yes, that's it. That sounds very good. That's the story we tell everyone. An attempted robbery that went all wrong. Horribly wrong. Good work, Stebbel."

"Thank you, sir. Inspector Dörfner and I had discussed this earlier."

"Alright, that's all for right now. This copy is for me, isn't it?" The two underlings nodded, then turned to leave as the commander dismissed them with brusque "thank you" punctuated with a nod.

At the door, they heard him bark out another afterthought, "And please be sure you find this perpetrator *very* soon. The best way to heal the wounds of her husband and all her family and friends is to tell them that the culprit has been caught and will soon pay for this crime with his own life."

The two inspectors again voiced their obligatory agreement, dipped their shoulders in limp bows, and made their exit.

Back in the cramped, oversized cupboard that served as an office for the two inspectors, Dörfner and Stebbel went over their session with the District Commander. It could have gone worse, they both agreed. Much worse.

"Old Scholli seems to be happy with that story about a robbery going awry," Dörfner said.

"He's easy to make happy, as long as you don't make things complicated," Stebbel replied. "But when you think about it ... a botched robbery might be the truth."

"Yeah??"

"It's as good an explanation as any other."

This time, Dörfner merely nodded, but his mouth was twisted in a gesture of uncertainty. Stebbel elaborated.

"Our killer corners a wealthy woman in a lonely lane, tells her to hand over her money and jewelry. She starts making noises, so he throws his mitts around her throat to shut her up. She starts to fight back, maybe scratches him, so he squeezes harder to show his displeasure. A minute or two later, she's dead, he's scared, and then someone opens a window or door not too far down the lane, so he runs. It all works."

"So what do we do now? Start dragging in all the muscular thieves running around Vienna?"

Stebbel shook his head. "We wait for more clues to surface. Who knows, maybe the killer did manage to grab something off the poor lady before he got scared. If some valuable item of hers turns up, we've got our next lead."

* * *

As a languid April twilight settled across Vienna, the streets started filling up with the office workers heading home after a long day of work along with those just heading off to work. Amongst the latter was the corps of streetwalkers who would line the shadowy side of the Ringstrasse across from the Vienna Opera House or the side alleys in the theatre district.

But most of these women were heading into Spittelberg, that singular section of town that had become the capital's prime red-light district. For Vienna's often ridiculed Morality Police Division, Spittelberg was a hands-off zone where the sex trade had become a free market paradigm that might warm the hearts of the Vienna School economists just coming into renown at that time. But for a small group of policemen in the Homicide Division, it was the scene of a baffling murder that needed to be solved as quickly as possible.

* * *

It was the shallow side of midnight. Hitler should have been tired, already in bed even, but he was still filled with energy. Nervous energy, the kind that propelled him into his best work. He was again caught up in copying work – but this time he was not copying models from some other artist, but his own work. Hunched eagerly over his desk, he was making copies of the two sketches he had done the morning after the murder.

The woman's face was now seen from different perspectives: from slightly to the left, slightly to the right, arched from above. And then straight on, as if the perspective of one lover looking entranced into the eyes of the other.

He then took on the sketch of the killer. This time, he tried to delve more deeply into the psyche of the man and capture that. He dashed out one drawing, then another, each one calibrated to explore another shade of the man's personality, the hidden lines of cruelty within the face.

When he was finished, Hitler spread all the sketches out in front of him. He inspected the work with what came as close as he could manage to a critical eye. His assessment: the work was brilliant, and he himself was clearly a major artist. That great promise he always knew he possessed was now being realized.

And as he readjusted the position of some of the sketches, he could hear music playing … in his mind. It was the crescendo of a favorite Wagner piece, a strident surge signaling a moment of triumph, a moment of great triumph. He slapped the desk and whispered, "Yes, this is why fate brought me to Vienna. This is where I prove that art is a powerful weapon!"

8

Senior Inspector Rautz entered the room where the district's other seasoned inspectors had assembled for their Thursday morning briefing. Though the room was not very large and the eleven junior inspectors all turned and looked at him at he entered, Rautz still lifted his chimes to his chin and tapped out a signal with a tiny hammer.

"So, gentlemen, if you will just lend me your ears for a short time … Your attention please, gentlemen, your attention."

He looked around the room and when everyone there was looking sufficiently uncomfortable, Rautz smiled and began his spiel.

"A body was fished out of the Danube early this morning. A male body, 38-years-old. Our first impulse was to rule it a suicide. The deceased had motive for such an act. That's all I'll say for now. So we might be tempted to just file it away as a suicide. Except …."

Rautz looked around the room again, his way of soliciting even more attention. He then pulled at both sides of his moustache, as if he had hidden the other facts there and was now about to pull them out.

"Except that the dead man had a large bruise on the back of the head, right side. Now this large, ugly bruise suggests that our unfortunate fellow had been intentionally hit on the head by somebody and then dumped into the Danube for a fatal swim.

"But there is, of course, another possible explanation for that big, ugly wound: Our man did commit suicide by jumping into the river, but on his way down, he hit his head on the side of the bank, on the stone wall there, and that was the cause of his injury.

"So, suicide or murder? Well, if we want to pursue the possibility of the latter, some of you here in this room will have to carry out a long investigation with almost nothing to start on except that bruise and the victim's identity.

"But I want you gentlemen to help me decide if we should go forward and investigate this case as a murder. Mind you, it will take a lot of hard work to come up with any resolution. If there is, in fact, a resolution at the end of the whole thing." The senior inspector then turned to the next oldest officer in the room. "Herr Stegmeier – are you looking for some new assignment to keep you busy?"

"No, Herr Inspector. I have enough to occupy me right now."

Rautz nodded, then asked two or three others before turning to Dörfner and Stebbel. "So, Herr Dörfner, Herr Stebbel. Are you two looking for some additional work?" Stebbel put his hand up as if politely refusing a second portion of potatoes at a dinner party.

Rautz then asked two other inspectors, before smiling mischievously as he shook his head. "So, it *was* a suicide. Just as I thought. Thank you, gentlemen, for helping us close out this case. This is the kind of thing that warms my heart: a clean and efficient division that solves most cases very quickly and neatly, without headaches of any sort. Thank you, thank you, thank you."

Rautz then read out a few department notices, asked for questions, and dutifully gave inadequate answers to the first four questions that were tossed at him. Finally, Andreas Glotz raised his hand and asked who the suicide was and why the department reckoned it was a suicide.

"The dead man was one Leopold Scherling. A successful businessman. *Formerly* successful, I should say. In exports or something like that. Anyway, he filed for bankruptcy at the end of

January, and I imagine he hadn't been in a very cheerful mood since then.

"The fellow had every cause to kill himself. He was already drowning in debt, so I guess he decided he might as well be drowning in the waters of the lovely blue Danube." Rautz then laughed at his own lame joke and about the half the room joined in – after a tense interval of silence.

The senior inspector ended by asking if there was any more business and, getting no reply, he called the meeting to an end. As the juniors filed out of the room, Dörfner turned to Stebbel and Glotz, walking just to his side. "That Scherling fellow – I wonder if he went to that Bankruptcy Ball they threw during the Carnival season. Should have given him a free ticket, the way I reckon." The other two loupes shrugged and slipped through the meeting room door. They all had much work to attend to.

9

The two inspectors had started putting together a portfolio on the von Klettenburg family to see if they could discover anyone who would want to kill the wife. Perhaps, Stebbel suggested, it was someone wanting to get back at the husband for something he'd done as a privy counselor. Dörfner was much more in favor of the theory that it would have been one of his business activities. "I'm sure that a rich banker is never at a loss for mortal enemies."

Stebbel started working the privy council angle. As he discovered, von Klettenburg had only been a member of the privy council for four years. In fact, there was quite some surprise when he was selected for that body. Most speculation was that he had lent the government, in particular the emperor's office, large amounts of money. The privy council appointment was his reward for: first, his generosity, and second, his patience when the government had its usual delays in repayment.

But one colleague, Hecker Knoll, then recalled another account making the rounds: that von Klettenburg had used his key business connections to help the emperor's mistress secure her latest flat – a sprawling, elegant apartment at the edge of the theatre district.

Inspector Knoll then elaborated, "*Tja*, I heard he arranged for her to get the place, helped get her moved in, and all without a sniff of the palace in the transaction. That's why he was granted the seat on the council."

Stebbel smirked. "So hiding Franzi's mistress qualified as his 'contribution to the good of the empire'?"

"Not too unlikely," threw in Inspector Andreas Glotz from the other side of the police archives room. "But evidently, he's not too much of a nuisance over there. I heard he never turns up at any of the council meetings."

This brought a chortle from Dörfner. "I'll bet if you took him to the Hofburg and gave him two hours, he'd never even be able to find the Privy Council Chamber."

"Probably not. No, the only thing von Klettenburg and all those swells like him really care about is having the title '*Geheimrat*' to swing around. (*Geheimrat* being German for privy counselor.) The title lets them get the best tables at fancy restaurants or those special seats at the theatre and opera," added Glotz.

They all nodded. Vienna was one of those cities where the table where you sat was a prime factor in whether you enjoyed your meal or not, so anything that secured one of the best places was an honor worth having.

Stebbel and Dörfner were more relaxed after this little bit of mockery. One characteristic typical of police inspectors in the last years of the Habsburg monarchy – actually of all those in middle-level positions of any kind – was that they always preferred to piss up rather than down. But being a little more relaxed did not bring them any further along in solving the murder. And they knew that for many reasons, they had to solve it as quickly as possible.

* * *

Further investigations turned up very little about Karsten von Klettenburg that could help the inspectors open a crack in the case. He may not have been a model privy counselor, but he was an exemplary businessman. The son of a wealthy family whose wealth on both sides went back a few generations, he had started his working life in the bank that his father and uncle ran. In fact, he started high up in the hierarchy and quickly moved to even higher positions.

When his father and bachelor uncle passed on, Karsten inherited not only majority interest in the Vienna Trust Bank, but also several mid-sized factories and other businesses.

Strikingly wealthy and mildly handsome, he was one of Vienna's most prized bachelors until he finally took a bride at the age of 34. Anneliese Tiel was twelve years younger than Karsten and the object of many young Viennese men's desire before she went to the altar with the wealthy Herr von Klettenburg. She had no known enemies, and if any of her spurned suitors had felt betrayed or cheated by her marriage, that was almost ten years earlier and there were no indications of grudges cultivated into homicidal obsessions among those suitors.

Both Stebbel and Dörfner agreed that if they were going to find a cogent motive for this murder, it would probably have something to do with the business operations or immodest wealth of the husband. Now all they had to do was find the needle in that row of haystacks.

10

The requiem mass for Anneliese von Klettenburg was held at St. Stephan's, the imposing Gothic cathedral in the heart of Vienna's Old Town. As if that itself was not honor enough, Vienna's prelate, Cardinal Gustav Piffl, officiated at the ceremony. In fact, had it not been a funeral, the ceremony would have qualified as one of the major social events on the early spring calendar.

Those attending the elaborate ceremony included many of the major figures in Viennese finance, industry, secular and Church politics. The Emperor was not able to attend, but his nephew Friedrich-Otto, fifth in line to the throne, was there to represent the imperial family. (As some wag in the popular press reported the next day, "The Emperor had sent his regrets and his nephew. He should be even more regretful about the latter.") And as to pay honor to the guests and the venue, Herr von Klettenburg had engaged a full orchestra to play Mozart's *Requiem* throughout the ceremony.

Inspectors Stebbel and Dörfner had arranged to be assigned to the crowd-control detail for the event. Actually, this assignment was a cover: they were not there to maintain order and see that everything flowed nicely, but to do surveillance on those attending the funeral. As Stebbel had argued, a keen-eyed inspector can often pick up important clues at a murder victim's funeral.

The mass went on for just under two hours, including a round of eulogies by friends and family members. During this time, the large police contingent outside the cathedral had poked holes in the boredom by playing cards and trading juicy stories. Finally, the service ended, and they were back on duty.

Cardinal Piffl and his cordon of acolytes led the funeral cortege out of the cathedral. Right behind them were many of the top people in the city's political establishment and the sole member of the Habsburg clan. As Archduke Friedrich-Otto passed by in his pompous uniform, topped off with a feathered helmet, Dörfner turned to those around him, pointed at the archduke and said, "Didn't anyone mention to that gink that this was a funeral, not a costume ball?" Two senior officers laughed out loud, while the younger hooks on assignment covered their mouths in embarrassment as they joined in.

Right behind this group of temporal powers came another group of clergy, three of them swinging gold-encrusted censors as they marched. And right behind them was the ornate casket that bore the body of the murder victim.

Immediately following the casket was the victim's family, led by her husband, arm-in-arm with Anneliese's elder sister. Behind them were the younger sister and the sister-in-law, other relatives, and then members of the household staff. Frau Barta, the senior staff member, led this group, flanked by two other maids. The younger women were bawling loudly, and Frau Barta had her arms around both of them, trying to offer some comfort. Of course, her store of comfort was low as she herself was crying inconsolably.

As the family and group of servants passed by, Stebbel studied the faces. One thing that struck him immediately was the widower's face. Herr von Klettenburg bore a stoic look on his face; at one point, he even flashed what seemed to be a look of slight annoyance at the whole affair.

Stebbel wasn't sure if he was misreading this demeanor or not.

Maybe, he thought, that's the way members of his class are taught to comport themselves at funerals, even when the deceased happens to be one's own spouse. Perhaps for these types, full expressions of grief are reserved for the tight family circle. Or even just private moments.

Most of the other family members were not withholding tears and moans; the domestic staff was shaking with grief the whole time. But Herr von Klettenburg *was* the head of the family, and a privy counselor, so maybe he saw maintaining a wall of stoicism as his duty.

Following the family came a long parade of friends, business associates, and hangers-on. Even District Commander Schollenberg managed to get himself in on this group. As he passed Stebbel, he turned and nodded and the loupe thought he could even detect a slight smile on Schollenberg's face. He imagined this was to indicate that, although just a glorified cop, he had made the guest list.

As the last stragglers made their way out of the cathedral, Dörfner left his post and sidled up to Stebbel. "What do you think, Inspector? Did you see any murderer in there?"

"Not that I can discern. But I've been looking for little clues, not some big revelation that will help us solve the case right here."

"Okay. So, what do you say – the Café Dilgas is right around the corner. Let's go there and start comparing notes."

"Yes; not a bad idea."

"Come on; Dilgas has this excellent apple strudel, and if you get there before noon, it's still warm."

"Karl-Heinz, I've been in Vienna twice as long as you, but I don't think I know half as much about its cafés as you do."

"I've made them my special area of investigation. And, as you know, I am a relentless investigator." Stebbel nodded.

The amount of new and useful information the two inspectors were able to glean from the funeral crowd was exhausted after two minutes of discussion. But Dörfner's spirits had been lifted just by the detour to a favorite café. It even put him in a philosophical mood, which did nothing at all to brighten Stebbel's own mood.

Dörfner ordered a single pear schnapps to accompany his strudel and coffee. After downing the schnapps, he made a gesture of unbridled approval.

"You know, this whole morning, that's what makes Vienna Vienna. First you've got a completely over-the-top funeral, and then the comforts of the Vienna café. Nothing captures the city better."

"A funeral and an apple strudel? That's Vienna?"

"Don't forget the dark brew and the schnapps. OK, let me explain: back when I was in the army, one of my senior officers – a full-blooded *Wiener* – he told me that there's no other city in Europe that's a better place to live than Vienna … and no better place to die. He told me, 'those Viennese, they've made a real art out of living. And they've made dying into an even better art.' And you know what – right then, I said, that's the place for me."

"So why did you decide to stay in Vienna? The living or the dying?"

Dörfner mulled this over for all of five seconds. "I think it was both actually. But I decided to devote myself to getting the living part right and leave the dying to others. You know, those who are much better at it than me. Let me just investigate the dying."

"From a safe distance, yes?"

"Exactly." Dörfner then added a self-satisfied grin. "I figure that's the best way to arrange things. Clean and efficient – just the way old Rautz likes to have things." He then raised his hand to signal the waiter; that insight called for another piece of strudel, this time with a thick blanket of vanilla cream.

Stebbel looked outside. A light rain had started to fall on the

Wollzelle street. "I hope they have a big canopy out at the cemetery."

Dörfner shrugged. "It works nicely for the swells who can't manage tears. They can pretend the raindrops express their pain."

Stebbel gave a light snigger, then lifted his cup and gazed into the remaining coffee. Now too cold to enjoy, it did serve as a mirror of his mood at that moment: a stagnant muddle with slight overtones of frustration.

11

Adolf Hitler woke up somewhere in the pit of the night with a dull headache. He thought that he'd just had an anxiety dream and that's what had woken him, though the headache alone would have been enough to do the job. As he sat up in his narrow bed, staring through darkness, he realized what the problem was: these nocturnal headaches were usually unleashed by some untreated fears or a feeling that something that needed to be done hadn't been done yet. This time, it was both.

This realization was enough to dull the headache after a short time and Hitler slid back into sleep. He woke a bit early for him the next morning – though the regular time for most of the hostel's residents – washed and dressed, trundled down to the mess hall for a light breakfast and then set out.

He needed this early start because on this morning, he wasn't heading straight to the city center to meet clients and attend to the other duties of a struggling artist. There was now a more another important task he had to attend to.

Vienna's main railroad station in those days, the *Westbahnhof*, was too far from the Meldemannstrasse hostel, so Hitler first needed to catch a tram. But he wasn't going to the station itself; he swung around to a small lane near the imposing structure.

As it wasn't yet 10 a.m, the lane stank, as usual, of stale urine and spilled drink. Hitler tried to ignore the smells as much as possible, though he had always been sensitive to unpleasant odors. But he had important business on this lane and wasn't going to let the stink deter him that morning.

He hurried to the sleazy pub near the corner of Apollogasse. Although it was early, the pub was already open. He walked in and said that he needed to see Egon Ricks. One of the scruffy-looking men leaning against the bar told him that Herr Ricks was not around; in fact, they hadn't seen him for over a week.

But Hitler knew the duties of the gatekeepers at this establishment; he told all three men at the bar that he was an old friend of Herr Ricks from his days at the hostel. He then gave them his name and assured them that Herr Ricks would be glad to see him. After exchanging skeptical looks with his two colleagues, the first man nodded, told Hitler to wait a few minutes, then shuffled off to a back room.

A bartender appeared from another room, took his post, and asked Hitler what he wanted to drink. He didn't really want anything, but he knew the rules of the house; he ordered a mineral water.

The bartender was just pouring the water into a foggy glass when the first man re-emerged and told Hitler he could go into the back room. Herr Ricks was "ready to receive him". The scruffy fellow chortled at his own ironic phrasing, then guided Hitler to the door.

Egon Ricks was still lying on a beat-up mattress in a murky corner of the back room. He had obviously just woken up and was still doing some wake-up stretching. But he smiled when he saw Hitler. Then, not without some trouble, he rose to a sitting position and gave Hitler a welcoming wave.

He asked the young man if he was still staying at the hostel and when told that he was, he asked how things were "at the Meldemann". Ricks himself had been kicked out of the hostel a few times, for fighting and other offenses, and finally earned himself a permanent ban. But he had taken Hitler under his wing in the young man's first months at the hostel and given him a lot of practical tips about how to get along in the center, as well as how to survive in the underbelly of Viennese society.

As he had always been kind and helpful to the young artist, Hitler was sad when Ricks was expelled for the final time. But he had run into Ricks on the street about a year later, and the two stayed in touch since then. Hitler still found that Ricks could be very helpful, especially when it was not possible to stay completely within the stiff confines of the law.

"So, Herr Rembrandt – did you bring me a painting to put up in my little palace chamber here?"

"Oh course, mein Herr. It's a work I did especially for you. I couldn't think of a better person to present it to." He then reached into his leather case, pulled back a few sheets, and then slipped out a painting. The watercolor of the Kronprinz Rudolf Bridge was actually one of about a dozen renditions of the landmark Hitler had recently painted, but he presented it to his old comrade as if it were a unique product. Egon Ricks took it graciously, examined it and smiled broadly.

He then made it to his feet with some difficulty. Except for shoes and a street shirt, he had slept in his clothing, so there was no need for embarrassment as he stood. He held the watercolor up to the light, then searched for a suitable place to hang it. He finally chose a place near the door and said he would have to get a nail later to affix it "to its honored spot". He then put it on a table from where he also grabbed a pack of cigarettes and a matchbox. He offered Hitler a stick, but the young artist politely turned down the offer. Ricks lit his own cigarette, and after the first drag, got down to business.

"So, Adi, is this just a social visit or can I help you with something?"

Hitler gave a sheepish smile. He suddenly realized how dry his throat and mouth were and wished that he had been served that mineral water before he entered this back room. He swallowed twice, then got it out. "I need a weapon."

"A weapon?"

Hitler again nodded. "A knife. A battle knife. I mean something that's the right size for defending yourself." He then held his hands about six inches apart, to indicate the size of the knife he was considering. "I think there may be somebody after me. I need a knife so I can defend myself if I get attacked."

A look of total surprise filled Egon Ricks' face. It was followed within seconds by a look of pride. It was almost like a teacher's pride that a star student had learned his lesson well. He had mentored this young man in the laws of the street, had shown him the ropes, and now this scraggy fellow was ready to go out there and take care of himself. He took two long drags of his cigarette, then nodded sagely.

"A knife, is it? Why not a gun? I can get you a gun, no problem – though that will probably take me a few days."

"No, I don't want a gun. No gun, thank you. Just a knife big enough, sharp enough to protect myself."

"Sure … of course. Anyway, the gun would probably cost more than you could afford right now." He took two more drags of his cigarette, then told Hitler to wait there while he went to see what he could do.

As he moved into the main room of the pub, a new arrival there barked out, "Egon! I can't believe my eyes – it's barely 10 a.m. and you're already up and about. What, did the whore you brought back last night snore too loud?"

"Go to hell, Kremmer. No, I just received a surprise visit from a dear relative. All the way from Linz. What do you think, he just arrived at the *Westbahnhof*, and the first thing he did, before anything, was come to see his Uncle Egon."

This loud pronouncement, and the lies at its core, embarrassed Hitler. He was even more embarrassed when the new arrival, joined by the three others at the bar, turned and stared in at this "nephew from Linz". He smiled sheepishly, then turned away, as if he suddenly needed to explore something at the other side of the room.

Ricks, meanwhile, had slipped into the side room from where the bartender had emerged earlier. Hitler continued studying things of no interest to him just to keep from looking out again into the pub itself. He was breathing shallowly, wondering what he could say if one of them came to the doorway and started asking him questions about his "uncle".

But the only one who came was Ricks himself, who returned after about five minutes that seemed like an hour. He was holding a faded grey towel that he dropped onto the table next to Hitler's watercolor. It made a loud clang as it landed. Hitler quickly realized why.

"This was the best I could do at such short notice," Ricks said as he spread the towel open. "See if any of these is what you were thinking of."

Hitler stepped over to the table to examine the wares. There were four knives there, of different shapes and sizes. One of them seemed to be a butcher's knife, with a heavy handle and a long blade.

As Hitler studied the four knives carefully, Ricks took the last drags from his smoke, then dropped it right onto the floor and stubbed it out with his foot. Hitler picked up one of the four knives. Though it was actually the smallest of the four, it seemed just right for his purposes. The blade was long enough to go right through someone of Hitler's girth and could still put a significant notch into even a burly man. As the blade was also reasonably thick, it was enough to kill or seriously wound just about anyone. More importantly, the handle fit nicely into the soft artist's hand. He gave it a test thrust into the air; it felt good, reassuring actually, when he clutched it.

Most importantly, he measured it against his jacket pocket and saw that it would just fit into that space. Hitler turned to Ricks and told him this was the item he was interested in.

Ricks nodded. "I would usually charge someone five kroners for that piece. But I'm giving it to you for three. This painting you gave me more than makes up for the difference in price. I'd even let you have it for two, but I'm a little short of cash at the moment." He paused there. "By the way, can you pay me right now?"

Hitler nodded. He reached into his pocket, pulled out a small purse and removed the three kroners in coins. He handed them to his old mentor. He knew that this extravagance meant he would probably have to skip at least one meal for each of the next few days. But it was well worth the sacrifice, he told himself. What did it matter if he was well fed and that killer should confront him on the streets and decide to silence him?

Following this transaction, Hitler told Ricks that he had to hurry downtown as there were a number of clients there who wanted to discuss purchasing his paintings, maybe even commissioning him to paint something. Ricks said he understood and ended by making "Adi" promise that he wouldn't become a stranger. He wanted him to drop in again from time to time – but, he stressed, at a decent hour next time.

Hitler and Ricks then shook hands, Hitler gathered up all his belongings, including his new purchase, and rushed out of the bar, nodding politely to the men out front and wishing them a pleasant day.

As he hurriedly made his way back to the *Westbahnhof* (from where he would catch another tram), Hitler reached into his pocket and fumbled with the knife. It felt good, quite good, and he was proud of himself that he had had the guts to go there and procure the weapon.

It was the perfect choice, too. Weapons were strictly forbidden at the men's hostel; possession of a weapon meant immediate expulsion with probably a permanent ban attached to it. Bringing in a gun, or even a large knife, would risk the end of his residency there.

But this piece was perfect: if someone from the administration there found it, Hitler would claim that he needed it for his work as an artist ... to slice paper, maybe other materials. Sometimes he even needed such a knife to reshape a corner of a picture frame, he could say.

No, this weapon would not get him into any trouble. More importantly, it might be able to get him out of some trouble. Serious trouble.

12

The day after the funeral, Inspectors Stebbel and Dörfner went to interview Karsten von Klettenburg. As suggested by the widower, the meeting took place at his *pied á terre* in the center of town. He did not wish to meet at any of his business offices, as he thought his personal tragedy should be kept separate from his business dealings.

Shortly before three, the two policemen arrived at a striking building on the southern stretch of the Ringstrasse. Waiting for them just inside the ornate front door was one of von Klettenburg's servants, a dour fellow trying to look cheerful. He escorted the visitors to the lift and attempted a smile as he pressed the button for the fourth floor, which was also the top floor. (This structure, unlike police headquarters and most other public buildings, had a full-service lift that allowed a complete stop at every floor.)

As they stepped out of the lift, another servant met them. This fellow bowed so deeply, Dörfner felt he was trying to kiss his own navel. The bow ended, he guided the two visitors to the von Klettenburg flat.

They followed the servant inside to the study, where Karsten von Klettenburg was waiting for them. He had been poring over the set-up on a chessboard, which he eased to the side before rising and politely indicating that the visitors should take their seats. He then turned and pointed to the board.

"It's a re-creation of the famous seventh game of the Lasker-Schlechter title match." He duly noted that the reference made no impression on either of the inspectors.

Stebbel took a quick perusal of the room and noticed two other chessboards on a shelf to the right, and one on a shelf to the left. "It would seem that you're quite the chess enthusiast, *Herr Geheimrat.*

"Yes, it is one of my special passions actually. And as you have noticed, Inspector, I'm also a fond collector of beautiful chess sets. Strange as it may sound, I feel they impart a sense of permanence."

Both inspectors smiled politely. Stebbel had flirted with chess while at the *Gymnasium* and later at university, but never poured much of himself into the game. The only time Dörfner had ever touched a board or chess pieces was when he burst in on a match to make a roughhouse arrest of a Serbian agitator.

"I find that chess is also a very useful game for someone like myself. It's excellent training for the business world. In fact, I believe that a successful businessman should always be a good chess player."

Stebbel nodded towards the arrangement on the desk. "Did your wife also play the game?"

"Yes. But not very well."

On that note, the formal interview got underway. The first few minutes followed the standard script: full introductions, extending condolences, gratitude for seeing the two cops so quickly. Stebbel then jumped to the pivot in the script by saying they realized that the *Herr* must have many things to do at this time, and they didn't wish to steal too much of his time. A round of nods later, they got down to the less pleasant matters.

Von Klettenburg himself delivered the opening. "I want to assure you gentlemen that I'm ready to give you all the assistance I can. I want to see this monster who murdered my beloved Anneliese arrested and subjected to the full measure of justice our great country provides. I trust you gentleman will see to the first stage of that."

"We appreciate all your help, Herr *Geheimrat*," Stebbel replied. "And we hope to reward your trust with the capture of this ... person."

"More like a fiend than a person, I'd say. But please, please, ask me any questions you think might help here."

As if on cue, Dörfner flipped open his notebook and started running down the questions.

"Herr *Geheimrat*, did your wife have any enemies, or anyone who might want to settle a severe grudge?"

"Enemies? I can't imagine anyone who would want to be her enemy. She was such a lovely person ... so gracious, so generous."

Stebbel then stepped in. "But a grudge maybe. Could she have ... unintentionally offended someone, a servant or a shop assistant who then wanted to do her some harm as retribution?"

"Again, gentlemen, I just can't imagine anything like that happening. As I said, my late wife was overwhelmingly gracious. She was an uncommonly sensitive person, always finely attuned to the needs and feelings of others. And, of course, generous. Generous to a fault, one could almost say."

"Did she express any fears, any uneasiness of late?"

Stebbel finished the thought. "Well, what we mean is ... did she feel that she was being followed, her movements tracked maybe? By ...oh, let us say a thief who saw her as a likely target for an assault and robbery. Did she have any fears about the streets, going about the city?"

"Sorry, gentlemen, none that I know of. I wouldn't say that such fears were not there, but if so, she never chose to share them with me. But that was my Anneliese: she never wanted to burden me with worries about something that might simply be a misunderstanding. She knew how many other things I had to worry about, and she would never throw some additional worries onto the pile."

He paused and pursed his lips slowly. "Now I wish she had been a little less cautious in talking about such things with me and others in our circle. Perhaps if she had, this tragic event could have been prevented."

"Don't blame yourself, Herr von Klettenburg. Regrets are usual when something like this happens. It's all too easy to think that our own mistakes, something that we've overlooked, contributed to the final tragedy. But it's rarely the case that such cautions could have prevented the crime. The criminal would have just sought another way to get to your wife and do whatever he wanted to do."

"Thank you. But I still torture myself with the thought that …" He trailed off, swirled his head to the side and slapped the desk harshly.

Dörfner turned to Stebbel who gave him a slight nod, signaling that they could now move to the rather awkward stage of the interview.

"Was your wife acting strangely of late, Herr von Klettenburg?"

"Strangely?"

"What I mean is, acting out of character. Saying strange things. Showing an interest in things that might not be so … respectable. Maybe overlooking caution where caution is clearly called for." He stopped and took a deep breath before throwing out the next question. "Did she perhaps go out and not explain where she was going? Or give an account of where she had been that you didn't find entirely credible?"

Von Klettenburg stared first at Dörfner, then at Stebbel; his patrician stare had a clear measure of distaste to it. Dörfner responded perfectly. "We don't mean to be in any way offensive, Herr von Klettenburg. And we certainly don't wish to go poking into your private affairs. But when such a horrible crime takes place, it's our duty as police inspectors to pursue every possible avenue. Even those that are *barely* possible."

"Yes, yes, of course. I see that you are both fine gentlemen and that you would never engage in anything gratuitously offensive."

He then sighed as he tapped his upper lip. "All I can tell you is that at this moment, I cannot think of any behavior my late wife exhibited that could fit any of the descriptions you just threw out there. But I will try to examine the darker recesses of my memory and see if anything like that surfaces. If I do think of something, I will certainly contact you right away and share it with you."

It was now Stebbels' turn. "We would appreciate that, Herr von Klettenburg. On the very unlikely chance that any such thing ever comes to your mind, of course."

"Of course. I think we all understand the situation quite well, gentleman. And let me again remind you that we are all working on the same side with this. As I already assured you, I will do everything in my power to help you find this murderer and bring him to justice."

The two policemen again thanked von Klettenburg and wrapped up the interview neatly. They then took their leave and were escorted out the door and into the lift by the servant. Back on the ground floor, they managed to make their own way out the front door as the dour servant stationed there earlier had disappeared.

They flagged down a cab to take them back to police headquarters. As they rode, they traded their impressions of the interview. Stebbel's uneasiness about von Klettenburg's demeanor as he walked out of St. Stephan's was in no way weakened by having now met the gentleman personally and questioned him. As he they rode along, he turned to Dörfner, "Did our *Geheimrat* strike you as a bereaved man, someone suddenly widowed, and widowed in such a horrible way?"

Dörfner brushed it off as typical of von Klettenburg's class. "These people, they have different ways than the rest of us. They like to keep their emotions wrapped up tight. Or at least, they don't want to show their emotions to people like us." Stebbel gave a skeptical shrug. "They're trained most of their lives to act this way, don't you know. The way they're brought up, if one of them got caught in a burning building, he'd probably walk out slowly, never letting his panic show, maybe even stopping along the way to admire a painting or something."

"OK, you might be right, but I still think there was something missing there. I realize this thing about the upper classes maintaining a façade, but with von Klettenburg, I had this feeling there wasn't much under the façade."

Dörfner shrugged, then glanced out the window to see how close they were to police headquarters. He was anxious to get back into a universe of people like himself; the very wealthy always made him feel uncomfortable.

"*Ja*, maybe. I don't know. I guess I really don't know how people in that class function. But I'm pretty sure he'll give us all the help he can."

"I hope so."

"Absolutely. He obviously wants this thing solved, and solved quickly. No matter how bereaved he is, or not, the whole mess has got to be a stinking embarrassment for him. He wants the mess taken care of."

"Oh, I have no doubts about that: he clearly wants the mess taken care of."

Just then, the taxi turned into the Burgring and headed for the police headquarters, four streets away.

There was, however, some parade slithering along just outside the Palace of Justice, so the whole area was blocked off to motor traffic. As a result, the inspectors had to climb out and walk the last three streets.

"Another one of those damned visiting dignitaries," Dörfner hissed. "I don't know why they don't just stay where they belong."

"Is your leg alright?" Stebbel asked. "We can maybe – "

"No, no, I'll be alright. Just the time lost really." He rubbed the back of his head hard with his full palm. "God damn dignitaries; not good for anything but making everything inconvenient for the rest of us."

Dörfner walked with a noticeable limp – a result, he claimed, of a combat injury from his military days. When asked to give details, he told everyone – including Stebbel – that it was the sort of thing soldiers don't like to talk about. Everyone left it at that.

But one day, a friend of Stebbel's whose job gave him access to the police department's personnel files provided the details of that "combat injury". Dörfner was, indeed, shot in the lower leg, but it wasn't enemy fire. He was stationed in eastern Galicia, and members of his battalion would fight the evening boredom in that God-forsaken outpost by drinking heavily and sometimes playing a game they called Morons' Csárdás.

The rules of that game were as simple as they were stupid. One soldier would shoot towards the lower legs of another standing about ten meters away. That soldier would move to dodge the bullets, kicking up his legs in imitation of the popular Hungarian Csárdás dance.

Often the soldiers would play in pairs, a drunken marksman and a "dancer" in each pair. The marksman would shoot at the other team's dancer, then *his* armed partner would shoot at the legs of the one standing next to the soldier who had just fired. A favorite variation would be for the dancer and the shooter to switch roles: after firing, the marksman would hand the gun to his partner and would then prepare to start "dancing" himself.

And like the Csárdás music and dance itself, the action would start out slowly, then speed up, until the dancing soldier had to start dancing his way clear of ringing bullets every few seconds. The game ended when each side had fired two full rounds, which was deemed the right amount for a good game.

It's not quite clear if Dörfner was so drunk that night that he couldn't kick his legs up at the right time, or if the shooter was too drunk to come close while still trying not to hit him. Whichever it was, one bullet caught Dörfner right in the flank of his left leg. He let out a sharp scream and fell to the ground.

Fortunately, the excess alcohol he had consumed helped him bear the pain until a doctor could be found and brought to the infirmary where the wounded dancer lay, a clumsy tourniquet strapped around his leg. A week later, he was reassigned back to Vienna to complete treatment for his wound.

The injury was not crippling, but it was still enough to earn Dörfner an early discharge from the army. Ironically, he was given a citation upon his release with a commendation saying that he had taken his injury during the course of "meritorious action".

When Stebbel asked his friend with the personnel files why the army had issued such a citation, he was told it was standard practice in the Austro-Hungarian military for soldiers injured doing stupid things like that. Apparently, the military did not want Russian operatives to get a clear notion of what fools the military of the Dual Monarchy was stationing out near the Russian border.

But the citation certainly helped Dörfner's application to join the Vienna police service move quickly to approval. As Stebbel's friend in the Personnel Office said, "It just proved that he had the necessary stupidity to become one of us."

13

The distinguished looking gentleman in an elegant blue suit arrived some ten minutes before the appointed time. He approached the desk sergeant at the reception and said, "Excuse me, but I was asked to come in and speak with Inspectors Dörfner and Stebbel." He then presented the sergeant his card. The sergeant pulled over the Visitors Sheet and copied the name exactly as it appeared on the card: Professor Doktor Sigmund Freud.

Freud declined the offer of a seat on the visitors' bench and stood surveying the office while the two inspectors were informed of his arrival. Then the honored doctor was escorted in by the sergeant.

The session took place in the main interview room, the one used for special guests. The chairs in that room were finely upholstered and stuffed to the point of extreme comfort. And the man about to be interview certainly qualified as a "special guest". Freud was at the peak of his fame and influence then, and it was an honor just to have him appear at police headquarters as a witness.

Hours before the meeting, the two policemen had agreed on a strategy about how the session would proceed: Stebbel would serve up most of the questions, while Dörfner would just poke in a follow-up here and there. Otherwise, Dörfner would serve as backdrop to the Q&A, a visual reminder of how serious the whole affair was.

Freud had now settled into his seat. Stebbel smiled at him. He was struck at how ramrod straight the great psychiatrist sat. More, he had placed his left hand on the arm of the chair, at its knob, in fact; his right hand was laid easily on his right thigh, the fingers slightly arched. He looked like he was posing for a photo, perhaps a photo to appear in the inside flap of his next book. And it looked like a pose he had working on and struck hundreds of times already.

The celebrity doctor and the police inspectors traded greetings and other amiable formalities. Then they started in on the real business.

Stebbel started out carefully. "Doktor Freud ... we called you in here because we hoped you could help us with the case of Anneliese von Klettenburg."

"Yes; the officer who presented the summons to me had already mentioned that fact."

"We happen to know that Frau von Klettenburg was one of your patients."

Freud nodded. "This is true."

"So what we wanted to know ..."

"Excuse me," Freud interjected. "But I'm curious as to how you came to know that."

"We were given access to Frau von Klettenburg's appointments book. Also, her chauffeur reported that he had driven her regularly to Berggasse 19, and then waited there until Frau von Klettenburg re-emerged an hour later."

"Ah, I see. It's ... reassuring to know that our guardians of public safety are so thorough."

"We try to be thorough, Herr Doktor. And sometimes we succeed. Now, what we would like to know is anything that can help us break the case. For instance, did Frau von Klettenburg reveal any fears that she had, or talk about any enemies, or anyone who was unusually jealous of her?"

"I'm afraid I can't tell you anything about that."

Dörfner took this answer as his invitation to poke into the questioning. "You can't or you won't?"

"In my case, the two meld into one. I'm quite sorry, gentlemen, but anything that Frau von Klettenburg told me during our therapy sessions must remain tightly locked secrets."

"Excuse me?"

Freud offered a wincing smile as he shook his head. "Anything that might have been said is protected under the rules of patient-doctor confidentiality."

Dörfner was not about to accept that easy way out. "*Ja, ja*, that's all quite wonderful, admirable even, but here we're talking about the vicious murder of a thirty-one-year-old woman. You can't tell me that your 'rules of confidentiality' hold up in a situation like that."

"I can and I will tell you that the rules hold no matter what the circumstances. As this unfortunate lady's doctor, I'm like a priest bound by the seal of confession."

Dörfner's face twisted into a scowl. "Doctor Freud, you're a Jew, aren't you?"

"That's correct."

"So how do you dare compare yourself to a *priest*?" Freud's left hand lifted off the arm of the chair momentarily, but he rested it back there almost immediately.

"As has often been said, and frequently written, we psychiatrists are doctors to the soul. So the comparison is not, I don't think, inappropriate. As your priests work to heal and save the souls of their flock, we try to do the same with our patients."

Still, Dörfner would not retreat. "Fine. So while you were busy saving her soul, you couldn't help save her life. Now I think you owe it to her to tell us everything you know that might help us catch her killer. And if you don't cooperate, we'll get a pile of subpoenas thrown at you that will force you to testify."

Freud drew a sigh, as if he were instructing a not-so-bright medical student. "I think you'll find that every court in the country will support me on this. Patient-doctor confidentiality is a highly protected principle." He then turned his gaze away from Dörfner to Stebbel. He seemed to intuit that Stebbel was the one more likely to sympathize with this, that there was a connection between the two of them.

His instincts were, as usual, spot on. Stebbel stared at Freud for a few moments, then turned to his partner. "I believe Doktor Freud is right on this point. As much as we might regret it, that patient-doctor covenant keeps him from telling us something that might help us move this case forward."

Freud nodded in gratitude. But Stebbel then played the last card in his hand. "Is there anything that you *can* tell us, Herr Doktor? Anything that doesn't fall under your medical seal of confession?"

"All I can tell you is that Frau von Klettenburg was a lovely woman, in temperament as well as outward appearance. I was deeply struck by her death. As I imagine almost everyone who knew her was."

Stebbel picked up the loose string in that sentence immediately. "*Almost* everyone?"

"Again, I have hit the borders of what I am allowed to share with you, gentlemen. I truly regret that I can't tell you any more. But you must realize the nature of my medical practice. A very special kind of practice. If I did give away any of the secrets Frau von Klettenburg revealed to me, the word would spread quickly. You know the power of gossip in a city like Vienna. If I told you any of the things my unfortunate patient told me, I would be finished. No patient would ever again trust me. I'd have to close up my practice in six months – at most. Because absolute trust, gentlemen, is the life's sap of my profession."

It was clear that the interview had stumbled into a dead end. There was no sense in prolonging the tussle of wills. The three men in the room concluded with the same kind of anodyne, amiable phrases they had begun the session with. The inspectors' hope – that they had found a source who could give them a key to solving the case – was left sprawled on the floor, a cracked shell. They'd have to find some other way to start to bore into the mystery of Frau von Klettenburg's murder.

*　*　*

A short time later, Stebbel was parked at his desk, noting down in the casebook the details of the futile interview they'd just conducted. Dörfner glanced over his shoulder to see what he was writing.

"You know, I don't really trust those people. Not at all."

Stebbel did not look up, as he did not want his partner to see the sour expression on his face. He was sure this was an anti-Semitic remark. And he had never told Dörfner that his own grandmother – a woman he adored as a child – was Jewish.

"And by *those* people, you mean the …?"

"Scientists."

This time, Stebbel did look up. "You don't trust scientists?"

"Some of them, sure. People like Dr. Gressler, or that Ehrlich guy who cured syphilis, the people who invent automobiles, electric lights, airplanes. But this Freud guy: no. Definitely not. His kind of scientist, they're just …"

"Psychiatrists."

"*Ja*, that's the name. I don't know, I just don't trust them. They're going into places science shouldn't go. You know what I mean: digging into the minds of people, their souls. It's just not natural."

"Isn't that something like what we do? When we're trying to ferret out criminals? We burrow into their minds, their souls. Try to understand all those dark places."

"*Ja*, maybe. But that's different. We're trying to catch bad guys. People like this Doktor Freud, he's just doing it for ... research. And he's looking into something that should stay private. It's perverse, you know. Anyway, I just don't trust what he's doing or why he's doing it." Stebbel couldn't think of any better response than a shrug.

Halfway to his side of their shared desk, Dörfner turned and added one note. "And as you know, Herr Colleague, in our profession, distrust can be an essential weapon."

* * *

That next evening after he'd been lightly raked over by Dörfner and Stebbel, Freud sat in his study poring over the pages of the file on "Stella 3". He read carefully, and with every page that grabbed his special attention, he'd pluck the page out of the file and lay it to the side, though in the same order it appeared in the file. Next to this sheath was a sturdy manila envelope, big enough to hold the whole file if necessary. But Doktor Freud was not planning to slip in all of those pages, only the most pertinent ones.

"Stella 3" was his case name for Anneliese von Klettenburg. The pages he was removing were those which revealed much of the inner workings of her psyche, as well as information about her personal life that Freud felt could not be shared with anyone else – even if they were investigators looking into her murder.

It was easier for Freud to choose pages he needed to take out than those which could remain in the official file. For instance, he decided he could keep in those passages where Frau von Klettenburg talked about her headaches – their intensity, duration, how they sometimes got so bad she would start pounding the sides of her head with her fists, as if she could drive out the pain that way.

He also decided he could leave in those sections where she spoke about her physical appearance, especially her fears that her physical attractiveness was slowly ebbing away as she started moving into her thirties. This was ridiculous, Freud thought: she was still the kind of woman other women in Vienna would grow envious of at a simple glance, while men would continue desiring her for years to come.

Still, she spoke about putting on weight, finding streaks of grey hair, lines appearing under her eyes and the ridges forming between her nose and mouth. Such excessive fears were nothing that a society *dame* like Frau von Klettenburg would ever wish to share with too many people, but it was nothing that could ruin her reputation, have people in her class shun her if it were known. Probably every other wealthy woman in Europe who had entered her thirties and was moving on to her forties had similar anxieties.

The problem was that the fairly innocuous passages were often on the same page as something quite embarrassing. And so they had to be taken out, along with the pages where the darkest journeys into the lady's psyche were described in startling detail.

After Freud had gathered all the pages he did not wish to be seen, he eased them into the large brown envelope. When they were all nicely fitted in, the envelope bulged like a New Year's Day carp.

He then took tape and sealed the envelope tightly. Taking up the scissors, he cut off the extra lapels of tape and placed them neatly into the wastebasket on the left side of the desk. At the top of the envelope, he wrote, in a very careful hand, "Stella, for later".

He then rose and called out to Lena, the kitchen maid, to tell her that she could now serve his hot chocolate. When she arrived minutes later toting a tray, he handed her the envelope.

"Lena, Doktor Marklin will be coming by soon to pick up some correspondence. Put this envelope in there with the other articles. When he arrives, could you please hand it to him and tell him that I will see him tomorrow. And be sure to extend my deepest gratitude to him for picking this up."

"Certainly, Herr Doktor."

He then turned and took a sip of the chocolate. "Delicious, Lena. You are a true artist when it comes to making chocolate."

After Lena left, Freud sat back and ruminated as he sipped his chocolate. Marklin was someone he could trust thoroughly. He would take care of those sections that had to remain private. Should the police find some way that they could order Freud to hand over his file on the murdered woman, all they'd be able to find there would be anxieties over headaches, grey hairs and sneaky wrinkles.

One day, he promised himself, he would definitely write an account of his work with Frau von Klettenburg and have it published. Giving her a false name, of course. Hers was doubtlessly one of the more fascinating cases he had dealt with in recent years. And what made that case all the more interesting is that some of the darker bits in her story may well have led directly to her murder.

Freud gave a slight wince: it was truly a shame that he could never share these darker bits with the police. But they had their own uses of dark truths; he himself had a professional duty to keep such dark truths safely in the dark.

14

The von Klettenburg murder case was looking more and more like a permanent dead end – something the Viennese police had quite a few of in those last years of the Habsburg dynasty. A popular witticism in many European capitals was that if you really needed to commit a terrible crime, try to do it in Vienna; your chances of getting caught there were not all that good.

At the end of a day where the only visible progress involved shifting papers from one desk to another, or from a desk to a file, the two investigators decided to wrap things up. Dörfner headed off to a popular wine tavern, while Stebbel returned home and sat at his dining table with a glass of brandy to keep him company.

Stebbel's home was a rather spacious, elegant flat in the Währing District, considered a plum area for the mid-level bourgeoisie. One major advantage of this apartment, in Stebbel's view, was that it was situated a comfortable distance from both police headquarters and the general noise and clutter of downtown. As such, it let him think of the apartment as a refuge.

Such a residence was, in fact, something that a regular police inspector with only six years in that post couldn't even hope to afford. But Stebbel had inherited the property from an uncle and aunt, a childless couple that had long considered the young Julian almost like their own son.

Shortly after he married, Julian and his wife Irina moved in and the flat underwent a wall-to-wall renovation. Irina insisted that almost all the furniture and trinkets the aunt and uncle had left Julian be removed and replaced with more fashionable furnishings and fixtures. (Stebbel subsequently spent a few years paying for all of this.) The dining table, a classic beauty, was one of the few items to survive the renovation campaign. Which is perhaps why it remained one of Julian's favorite places in the apartment.

Many would consider this dwelling an ideal place to live, and it was the envy of many of his acquaintances. But Stebbel, who now lived there alone, often felt like a stranger in his own home. He felt as if the main occupants were actually ghosts, and he was just there as a boarder, residing at their pleasure.

Those ghosts were not only his aunt and uncle, but also his wife. In fact, it was only six months after Irina had led the take-no-prisoners renovation program that she herself left.

Yes, it was quite a comfortable, attractive place, and Stebbel had no intention to give it up. But without his wife and drained of any sense of past intimacies, the flat lacked the feel of "home" for him; it was more like a retreat than a place where he felt he truly belonged.

Even so, gazing out of the large living room window into the deep Vienna evening with its sea of lights, he felt glad to be where he was, in this city, this part of that city, and in a world in which he could still make a little bit of sense of everything. Or of most things. And these were important features for a police inspector.

15

Exactly ten days after Frau von Klettenburg was murdered, a similar killing took place, only a few streets over from the scene of the earlier crime. This time, the victim definitely was a prostitute, a 19-year-old girl from Galicia who had been selling her wares on the streets of Vienna for the past few months. She, too, had been strangled, the neck streaked with bruises, a few bones broken. The young police officer who had been the first on the scene wrote in his report that "her eyes stared heavenwards, as if confounded at what was happening to her. Maybe imploring the Almighty for some explanation."

The case was originally assigned to Inspectors Klaussen and Plaschke, two typically sluggish department veterans, but Stebbel and Dörfner asked that they be allowed to take over the investigation. As they argued before Inspector Rautz, the similarities between this case and the von Klettenburg were strong enough that it could well be the same murderer, probably with a similar motive. Rautz quickly agreed with them and switched around the assignments. Stebbel and Dörfner now had a second strangulation on their hands. Again, it involved an attractive woman alone at night, seductively dressed and … Yes; and what else?

This investigation had far fewer complications than the von Klettenburg murder, of course. For one thing, the victim was a prostitute, a profession that always carried a heightened risk in a city like Vienna.

The victim's family were all back in Galicia and were totally in the dark about what was happening in the diligently dissolute capital of the empire. The young girl, Maria Kolenska, had told the family she had taken a job as a servant in a large house. The work was not hard, she wrote them, and she was earning more now than she ever could have imagined back in her hometown.

Stebbel and Dörfner talked to whatever friends of the victim they could find, along with some of the other girls who didn't count as friends, but knew Maria because they plied the same trade on the same streets. But nothing the loupes were able to uncover gave them any really useful information. On the third day after undertaking the street interviews, the two slipped into a café near headquarters to go over their options.

"I'm really thinking more and more that our killer was a pimp," Dörfner said as he sunk his fork into a piece of curd cheese strudel. "He killed this young thing for whatever reason pimps kill their whores. And with Frau von Klettenburg ... well, the way she was dressed that evening and everything else, he probably thought that he had chanced upon some exciting new talent and wanted her to join his stable. When she refused, he decided to make his point a little more strongly."

Stebbel nodded. "It's also rather likely that she would have said something nasty to him. In her polished accent, too. This would have enraged the brute, and he decided to teach her a lesson." Dörfner's mouth was stuffed with strudel, so all he could do was nod energetically.

"Or it could have simply been a matter of mistaken identity. The pimp thought this *was* one of his streetwalkers or someone who owed him something, and by the time he'd strangled her, he realized his mistake."

Dörfner took a large slurp of coffee to wash down the remaining strudel. "You know what – I think it's time we went to see the Turk."

Stebbel agreed. "He's probably the best one to help us out of this corner. But why don't you go by yourself to see the Turk. You always seem to have a much greater sense of rapport with him."

Dörfner nodded. "We share a love of fine ... conversation."

16

The Turk's real name was Redizade Bahadir Sakir Efendi. Turkish indeed, but only half Turkish. His mother was French; his parents had met while the mother was on an exotic holiday in Turkey with her sister, an aunt, and an older brother. A whirlwind courtship followed, and then Mademoiselle Louise Lascelle married Redizade Tamur Hoca Efendi in a civil ceremony in Istanbul. Their only child's stunning good looks were one of the many gifts bestowed on him by his two slightly wealthy parents, who were known as a very handsome couple. His given name was Bahadir, but to the French side of his family, he was simply "Bernard".

Born in Istanbul, Bahadir spent his early years there and in Paris. At the age of ten, his parents had sent him to an English boarding school, hoping that he would quickly acquire skills in speaking English along with the veneer of an English gentleman. But the main thing that he acquired there – actually mastered – was a penchant for cheating and breaking rules.

He eventually managed to get himself kicked out of the boarding school, but only after he had learned the skills that he would build his later career on.

He then proceeded to engage in a number of business failures in Istanbul and other places. Because of family connections on his Turkish side, a somewhat tarnished Bahadir was finally able to secure a respectable position in the Ottoman Embassy in Vienna. Arriving at the embassy in the early spring of 1909, he almost immediately found his footing. His principle duties at the embassy seemed to be fulfilling a number of nebulous assignments, but these he saw as pretty much side affairs.

In truth, his main activities in Vienna involved pimping, drug dealing and underwriting the shady to criminal activities of others. He used his position at the embassy as both a cover and a conduit for these illegal activities. It wasn't long before he had amassed quite a tidy nest egg. Along the way, he also managed to bed some of Vienna's most beautiful women, all of whom were quickly snared by his sultry good looks, his courtly manners, and the air of seductive danger that hung about him. Also, the fact that he could lavish some of the milder drugs on them before and after their liaisons.

Playing off his name with his French family, he always told his Viennese friends and paramours to call him "Bernhard", but the police he had contacts with invariably referred to him simply as "the Turk". And he had quite a few contacts in the Viennese police force.

*   *   *

Dörfner contacted the Turk and arranged to meet him at an unimposing shop he owned on the Tichtelgasse. The shop sold a jumble of Turkish textiles and textile products, but it was mainly a front for his illegal activities. Most of the visitors to this shop were either cops or criminals.

Dörfner strolled into the shop ten minutes before the appointed time, thinking he might be able to catch the Turk off guard. He kicked aside some bolts of Turkish linen that had fallen to the floor and headed straight for the back room, where he knew all the serious business took place.

He was halfway there when another man stepped out and placed himself in front of the open doorway, like a sentry. This man was thin but muscular, with dark hair and glaring eyes set off by a ruddy complexion. Dörfner didn't know this fellow, but immediately determined that he was the gatekeeper to the Turk's inner sanctum.

As the inspector got closer, the sentry took a couple of steps forward himself. He positioned himself as if he were a feral animal getting ready to strike. His glare rose a few degrees as Dörfner neared. Dörfner gave his perfected guffaw-snort.

The inspector had taken out his police I.D. plate before entering the shop and he now held it in his right hand, at his side. As Dörfner had just about reached the door of the back room, the sentry took another stride forward. At just the right moment, he swung his right arm up and slapped the I.D. plate into the other man's face. As he did, he barked, "Inspector Dörfner of the Vienna Police Department. I have an appointment with your boss."

The movement was not only perfectly timed, it was also perfectly placed: the plate landed right in the sentry's nose and upper lip, stunning him. He fell backwards and spat out an obscenity. Dörfner smiled broadly, proud of how well he had timed the mild assault.

The other man recovered, and though sniffling from the blow, he reached for the upper left hand side of his coat. But Dörfner grabbed him with both hands before he could grab whatever he was going for. The inspector, taller and bulkier, pushed the man against a counter and said, "Do you understand German, my good man? If not, I can always try to get my message through using hands and feet."

But that's as far as it went, for just at that time Redizade Bahadir stepped out of the backroom. He clapped his hands like someone who had just received a surprise gift. This, despite the fact that he knew Dörfner was coming by. He then turned to the gatekeeper.

"Vlatko, this is my old and very dear friend, Inspector Dörfner.

He's the man I have been expecting here." Vlatko did not seem to brighten much at this news. Bahadir turned to Dörfner and smiled. "Just like you, Inspector Dörfner does take a little time to warm up to people, but once he does, he can prove to be a very valuable friend."

At this, Vlatko and Dörfner looked at each other warily and exchanged truce nods. Satisfied, Bahadir snapped his fingers and pointed towards the front of the shop. Vlatko nodded and headed off in that direction, still rubbing his nose and lip. As he did, he found a smudge of blood coming from the lip.

Bahadir then turned his full attention to the inspector. "So, my friend, you are still as ruggedly handsome as ever. But you are looking just a little bit peaked. Are you sure you are getting enough sleep?"

Dörfner sighed. "Not over the last few weeks. These murder cases, you know. The two ladies."

"Oh, yes. Of course, of course. Let us go back into my office and discuss this further." He threw a quick look towards the front to see that Vlatko was properly occupied, then extended his hand to ease Dörfner into the back room.

"You have arrived at just the right time, my friend. I was just about to take my afternoon tea. And, of course, some delicious Turkish pastries. I know you will enjoy them; they arrived just this morning, direct from Istanbul."

Moments later, the two men were sitting on opposite sides of the Turk's imposing mahogany desk. The Turk deftly poured tea from a shining silver pot with a long spout into the traditional diminutive Turkish tea glasses. He then slid across a silver plate with an array of sweets on it.

"Please, my friend, help yourself. I especially recommend the baklava. It's originally Turkish, you know, not Greek. And I am told by a very religious man that pastries such as these are served to you by the *houris* the day you arrive in paradise. So, please – give yourself a small foretaste of paradise."

Dörfner choose four of the delicate pastries and eased them onto a smaller plate Bahadir had set down in front of him. At that point, his host raised his glass of rich, amber-colored tea. "So – *zum Wohl!*"

Dörfner reached and grabbed his own glass. The small vessel disappeared between the three fingers he used to clutch the glass. He hoisted the tea. "*Zum wohl.*" They both finished the tea in two sips. Bahadir then refilled both glasses.

"So, Inspector, how can I help you?"

Dörfner then explained how he and his partner had run into a series of dead ends in their investigation. They needed to speak to the second victim's pimp. But none of the people they had interviewed could tell them who it was.

"I see. Well, let me make inquiries and see what I can discover for you. I will certainly make every effort I can to find this information."

Since Dörfner did not wish to share any details of the two murder investigations, the two swung back into gossip and small talk. There was a discussion about the nature of Turkish pastries. When it became all too clear that the meeting was about to come to an end, the Turk slipped in his own appeal.

"Oh yes, I almost forgot: now, I know that this is not a matter for the Homicide Division, but you might want to pass along the information to your colleagues who are responsible here.

"It has come to my attention that there is a shipment of some value coming all the way from Persia. Now, as I understand it, a man will be arriving by train this Thursday at the *Westbahhhof*. This man will be carrying a large, bright red valise. In that valise will be ample amounts of both opium and heroin. Very nasty things, as we both know."

"Now when this gentleman arrives, he will be greeted right there on the platform by a 'long-lost cousin'. These two cousins have, of course, never met before. They will exchange a code, and embrace each other. Then the arriving man will turn and go off in one direction while his "cousin" will pick up the red valise with all those nasty drugs and he will start to walk off in another direction entirely."

Dörfner nodded. "So, a delivery of contraband drugs."

"It would seem so. And it …it pains me to say that the man who will receive these illegal drugs is one of my own countrymen. But that is the truth here. And I thought that your colleagues in the illegal drugs department will want to know about this."

"I'm sure they will. Thank you very much."

The Turk nodded. "You're welcome. I see it as my duty as a resident guest in your wonderful city."

And then, fifteen minutes after he'd first entered the shop, Dörfner announced that he had to get back to headquarters. He rose, but Bahadir got up even before him, stepped around the desk and escorted him all the way to the front door of the shop. Then he put his hand around Dörfner's arm and gave him a friendly clutch.

"So, just remember: this Thursday, the train coming in from Varna. Scheduled to arrive at 6:45, though it is almost always late. And in the meantime, I will do everything I can to find out who was this poor girl's pimp. We can discuss it again towards the end of the week."

Dörfner smiled and nodded; he knew how these deals with the Turk worked. When the drug mule and dealer were arrested on Thursday, the Turk would tell Dörfner who Maria's pimp was. It was pure *quid pro quo*.

The Turk was a highly valued informant, but his information always resulted in some profit for himself. For instance, when he ratted out some fellow drug dealer, it was almost always to remove a competitor from a field that was very profitable for the Turk himself. By cutting the supply of opium and heroin in Vienna, the Turk could increase his own prices for these items. And he already had very handsome profit margins on these items as serious drugs were becoming very fashionable among the Viennese avant-garde.

The Morality police were well aware of this devil's bargain they were involved in, but they readily accepted it. Their rationalization was that by snaring Bahadir's competitors in the drug trade, they were removing large amounts of these dangerous items from circulation.

And even the fact that the arrests ultimately helped Bahadir's own business did not trouble them much. After all, they reasoned, by allowing the Turk to hoist his prices for the drugs, they assured that only those with a comfortable store of disposable income would be able to afford them. This kept the drugs out of the hands of the poorer classes, those who stood to become the worse victims of drug addiction. Morality cops and top politicians all liked to think that wealthier Viennese would use the drugs responsibly, as a form of recreation.

The inspector and his "good friend" shook hands and went back to their respective duties. Early Thursday evening, the train arrived from Varna, a man alighted with two light bags, one of them bright red in color. As predicted by Bahadir, he was greeted by another man, who moments later walked off with that red valise. Six policemen then descended on the pair and arrested them both. Early the next morning, a message arrived at police headquarters for Inspector Dörfner: his friend in the textile trade had ascertained the information he requested.

Dörfner and the Turk met again at his shop early that afternoon. At this meeting, the Turk handed Dörfner a sheet of paper with a man's name written on it in precise script. Below the name were several places where the inspector and his colleagues would be likely to find this man.

The Turk then added some information. This man was not actually the dead girl's main employer. He was the on-site agent for the employer. But he was responsible for the day-to-day activities and so he was, in fact, the best person to speak with in order to get the information sought. And then the Turk appended a request of his own.

"Please, if possible, don't be too diligent in your interrogation of this fellow. I mean, diligent in a physical way. It is my understanding that he is a very reliable and valuable worker and that his employer has a high regard for him. He would not want him to lose any work days due to an unfortunate injury.

"I also understand that this employer has already spoken with the pimp and told him to cooperate fully with the police and to tell the inspectors everything he knows about the girl and her situation." He then took a long breath. "You can rely on everything this man Hochner tells you."

Dörfner read the code immediately. The Turk himself was Maria's pimp, but he had wanted to hold back any information until his drug-dealing competitor was taken out of action. Dörfner also accepted that the sub-pimp would give them all the information they needed, as it was now a matter of honor to Bahadir that the police receive anything that might help them move their investigation forward. Dörfner expressed his gratitude, and the Turk acknowledged this with a warm smile.

17

Early Saturday morning, Gerhard Hochner was awoken by heavy pounding on the door of his room. He fell out of bed and staggered to the door, where two tall and beefy policemen were waiting. Hochner simply nodded; he knew what they were there for. His boss, Redizade Bahadir, had given him adequate warning and details on what he should say. Hochner asked the policemen to give him about ten minutes to get ready. They nodded and stood to the side. But when he tried to close the door, the beefier of the policemen blocked the motion with his beefy arm. Hochner nodded in resignation and turned to wash and dress.

Not quite an hour later, Hochner was at police headquarters, sitting in the interrogation room with Stebbel and Dörfner. He peered out from aching eyes, their dark pupils in the middle of deep red sloshes.

"A long evening yesterday, was it, Herr Hochner?"

"Well ... Friday. You know what Fridays are like."

"Especially in your business."

Hochner offered a lopsided smile. "Especially in my business."

And that was the full extent of the pleasantries. After that, the grilling started; a light grilling, but a grilling nonetheless. Hochner told the two loupes everything he knew about Maria Kolenska. They asked further questions, some of which Hochner could answer, some of which he couldn't. Neither of the inspectors felt he was lying, or even swallowing the truth on any of these points. The pimp even seemed upset about the young woman's death.

"She was ... innocent. I mean, really innocent. Even after a few months in the game. At the end of every month, she sent a little money back to her family in Galicia. And she kept on telling her friends that she only intended to work for a year or two, then she was going to use whatever she could save to go back and help her parents buy a shop. It was going to be ... well, some kind of shop. They owned a little shop when she was a kid, but then they lost it somehow."

Hochner let out a shallow laugh. "When she was a kid? She was still a kid. She even had this toy lion that she kept in the room where she ... entertained her clients. And there was always something ... little girlish about her." He took a deep breath. There seemed to be wide glints, from tears perhaps, in the red of his eyes. "No, gentlemen, she had no real enemies here. Whoever killed her had no good reason to do it."

Stebbel and Dörfner knew at that point that the interrogation was coming to an end. They asked a few more technical questions, just to tie up the matter. And then they escorted Herr Hochner to the door. Stebbel even opened the door for him. But just before he stepped out, Hochner turned, looked both inspectors in the eyes and spoke strongly.

"When you do catch this swine, please make him suffer. Make him suffer a lot for what he did."

The two inspectors agreed to see justice done. Then a young policeman walked up, greeted Gerhard Hochner and guided him to the *paternoster*.

Back in their own office, Stebbel and Dörfner discussed the interview. Both agreed that Hochner seemed quite sincere. For a pimp anyway.

They didn't see any reason to proceed further.

"So it wasn't the pimp," said Stebbel. Dörfner hesitated a few moments before answering. His answer was a simple "no" in agreement. He didn't think it added anything to pull in the Turk at this point. They focused on one thing that Hochner had said: that she had no real enemies here in Vienna.

That squared with everything her streetwalker friends had said. It seemed that the killer had chosen Maria at random, that she had simply been an unlucky victim of a sick mind.

This conclusion was doubly troubling for the two inspectors, as it probably meant that Anneliese von Klettenburg's murder had also been something random. If so, there was no logic, no matter how dark or twisted, behind it. Both crimes were simply the tumble of fate's dice and left no traces of motive other than the killer's desire to inflict humiliation and death on two attractive young women. When they went in to see the district commander at the end of that week, they were forced to report this conclusion and tell him what little progress they had made, or were likely to make. Like hamsters trapped on the wheel in a cage: no matter how hard they labored, how wildly they turned the wheel, they were getting nowhere.

* * *

The tension in the office was thick that morning. It didn't take long for it to combust.

"Why didn't you tell me Maria's real pimp was the Turk?"

Dörfner had let this slip out in a blah-blah session with Inspector Glotz, and Glotz casually mentioned it to Stebbel.

"I didn't think it was ... helpful at that point."

"Karl-Heinz, you know everything is sort of helpful at this point. Everything."

Dörfner was in the middle of a defensive response, when he stopped. He looked at his partner point blank. "I'm sorry. You're right. I should have told you as soon as I found out."

"Fine. But now I say we should bring the Turk in for an interrogation. He has to be considered a suspect."

"He wouldn't do something like that. Besides he's not strong enough, his hands are thin and delicate."

"Alright; but he could hire someone else to do it. We should bring him in for questioning. Just so we know we've covered everything."

"OK. Then why don't we drag in your friend Doktor Freud at the same time and question him. The way I see it, he's just as much a suspect as the Turk. Probably even more."

"Doktor Freud? Are you crazy?"

"No, he sits there listening to all these nasty things, the women telling him all their secret wishes, all their fantasies. And you know how he operates? I asked somebody: he has his patients lie there on a couch, just lying there spread out, telling him all their inner thoughts. So he's watching this beautiful woman, Frau von Klettenburg, lying there in front of him, session after session, and finally he can't control himself anymore. So one night he follows her, catches up with her, tells her he wants to have her, she refuses, maybe threatens him with exposure, and he has to kill her."

"Karl-Heinz …"

"And did you notice his hands when he was here? Pretty big, those hands of his. Enough to strangle a woman the size of Frau von Klettenburg."

"And what about Maria Kolenska? Why would he kill her? She wasn't one of his patients."

'Well, maybe he … he listens all day to women telling him these really sexy things, he gets himself all worked up, and he goes down to the district where none of the women will know him, the eminent doctor, and tries to find some relief down there. And Maria does something that gets him really angry, so he … loses control. Wouldn't be the first time a very respectable citizen commits a terrible crime, would it?"

"No, it wouldn't. But I cannot accept that Doktor Freud would be our strangler. I just can't believe it, and I won't embarrass myself by hauling him in here for a third degree."

"OK, so you get your 'excused-from-serious-interrogation' pass for the good doctor, and I get mine for the Turk."

Stebbel took a deep sigh. He knew that deals like these did not constitute good police work. He felt that eventually the decision to let both of these men off without investigation might hurt them, but he reluctantly agreed. This is what a partnership between two inspectors entailed. Which is why he wasn't all that enthusiastic about the idea of partnerships.

After a short time, he turned back to Dörfner and fixed him with a stare. Dörfner wanted to respond, with either a burst of words or an even more rigid stare, but knew that he couldn't. The subtext of that stare told him once again that Stebbel was the senior partner; this had been established by the district commander when he first teamed them up. So instead of a stare or a torrent of words, Dörfner simply shook his head. Then, as usual when he was trapped in frustration, he rubbed the back of his head with his open palm.

Stebbel knew that he could now dictate the full terms of how they were to proceed. But he also knew that a police partnership, like a marriage, meant making compromises that cut deep into your soul. He folded up his stare, turned slightly to the left and nodded.

"Alright. We don't bring in either Doktor Freud or the Turk." He rode a long breath. "Not for the time being anyway." Dörfner took his hand away from the back of his head and stifled a smile.

An hour or two later, after tensions had cleared, Dörfner presented Stebbel a peace offering: a small packet of chocolates that he knew his partner was fond of. He then turned the topic to the days ahead.

"You have any plans for the weekend, Steb?"

"Nothing solid. A friend has tickets for the theatre on Saturday; some comedy. But I was thinking of getting away, maybe a couple days in a *pension* outside of town. I guess I'll wait until Friday afternoon, see what mood I'm in then."

"Yeah, that sounds good. Look, you want to do me a favor? You're the senior partner in this team. Could you assign me to full weekend duty. Maybe going around Spittelberg, questioning the local talent, even doing research here."

"How is that a favor?"

"It will give me a good excuse. You see, my wife wants me to come down to Steiermark for the weekend. One of her uncles is having his 70th birthday and there's going to be this big family celebration for him. I just do not want to go there."

"So you want me to be a callous senior partner, assign you to duty, and rescue you from that family obligation?"

"Exactly."

"Alright. Herr Inspector, you are hereby ordered to cancel all personal plans for the weekend and devote yourself to further, unspecified investigations of the strangler murders."

"Thank you, Herr Inspector. I knew I could rely on a fellow grass widower."

That was another similarity between Dörfner and Stebbel: they were both grass widowers – or, as German-speakers say, *Strohwitwer*. *Strohwitwer* are married men whose wives are away for a while, giving them a license to behave a bit more like unmarried men. Or more than a bit more.

The term is still used more frequently in the German-speaking world, but was particularly widespread in the Austrian Empire of the time, where divorce was, until 1934, not legally possible.

The wives of grass widowers could disappear for the weekend, or be visiting the family for a week, a few weeks, even a month. But both Dörfner and Stebbel were long-term grass widows. Frau Dörfner was back in her hometown in Steiermark, Austria, while Frau Stebbel was many miles away in Slovenia.

Irina Stebbel was a native of Slovenia, which at that time was still a far southwestern protuberance of the Austrian Empire. A beauty, with dark hair framing an oval-shaped, becomingly pale face, she had moved to Vienna in 1903 to study Mathematics at the university. That's where she met the still charming Julian Stebbel, as suave and polished as any Viennese swell, even though he himself was from Innsbruck.

The two fell in love quickly, and at the end of Irina's first year at university, they married. Sometime in her second year of studies, she took a leave of absence, from which she had never returned. For the next few years, both Stebbels kept saying she was going to rejoin the university soon, but eventually it became all too clear this would not happen.

Her leave of absence, recommended by a physician and approved by the university authorities, resulted from what was described as a "nervous condition". Starting in their second year of marriage, Irina's behavior had become steadily more erratic.

She was finally diagnosed as being "neurasthenic". This was a catch-all term in that toddler period of psychology for any illness that was not too overt or violent. The doctors saw Frau Stebbel's case as a classic form of the illness: she suffered from chronic physical and mental fatigue and often found herself locked in the dark cell of depression.

While two of her doctors felt that she should stay in Vienna and be admitted to a clinic there which specialized in the treatment of "neurasthenic females", her husband and her own family decided that it would be better if she returned to Slovenia to be treated in an institution there, not far from her hometown.

Julian took the long, wrenching journey with her and then stayed at her side for two weeks. At the end of that time, he insisted that he had to return to Vienna and his own university studies, which had been disrupted by her illness. He would return during the term breaks, he said, and when he finally took his first degree, he would bring Irina and her younger sister back to Vienna with him.

Stebbel officially dropped out of university and started his career with the constabulary the following year, and except for repeated trips to Slovenia, he did not resume his married life with Irina. In recent years, his trips down to the Adriatic coast had become less and less frequent.

The marriage saga of Karl-Heinz and Hannah Dörfner was much more prosaic. Dörfner met his wife when he was 17 and she was 16. In a relationship fueled mainly by adolescent lust on both sides, they became very close – for a while. When he left Steiermark to do his military service, they made the typical young couple's commitments to each other.

Every time Dörfner received leave from the military, he would hop the first train back home and spend much of his leave time with his Hannah. Two months after returning to duty from one of these leaves, Karl-Heinz received a sloppy letter telling him that Hannah was "in the family way".

An engagement by mail followed and on his next leave, Karl-Heinz and Hannah were married in the local church. The priest officiating the ceremony had to keep from laughing a few times, which actually cracked up the bridegroom. The young man had to make several attempts to get through his marriage vows without mistakes or laughter.

Their son Eugen was born not a half a year later, and a daughter, Clarissa, followed the next year. When Dörfner received his discharge from the army and secured a post with the Viennese police, the family joined him in the imperial capital.

But Hannah Dörfner was a small-town girl through and through, and she quickly acquired a resentment of the big city where everything was available. Thoroughly unhappy, she wanted to return with the children to their hometown. Karl-Heinz was himself not very happy with married life, so he agreed to her request. He also promised that as soon as he made enough of a reputation in the capital that he could get a high-ranking job back home, he'd resign from the Viennese police and join her and the kids back in Steiermark.

But even as he made this promise, he realized it had little likelihood of ever being kept. Karl-Heinz had grown all too fond of Vienna and its many vices and had no desire to go back to the place that he had spent so much energy getting out of. He made frequent trips to see the family – far more regular than Stebbel's trips to Slovenia – but had no wish to stay longer than he did.

Neither of these arrangements was uncommon in the Austro-Hungarian Empire in its last years. No one in the police department or in Vienna's smart society found it strange or distasteful that Stebbel and Dörfner lived apart from the wives on a semi-permanent basis. In fact, their superiors in the department felt it was actually an advantage, as wives were known to hinder investigative work for top inspectors. As one senior official put it, "Wolves who travel with their mates rarely make the best hunters."

18

Adolf Hitler was again returning from a client in the city center. This time, though, he chose a different route. He was not going to go anywhere near that alley again after nightfall.

He had had more success that afternoon, selling half of the paintings he brought along. Now, as he trudged along, tired and cold, Hitler decided that he could splurge a little and catch the tram back to the hostel. He turned and headed back down Laxenburgerstrasse to the tram stop.

The streetlights on that stretch of Laxenburgerstrasse were out again. Already feeling less tired because of the decision to take the tram, he let his thoughts drift off into plans for redesigning a row of buildings in his district, just south of the hostel. Suddenly, his train of thought was snapped – he thought he heard footsteps from behind. Heading towards him.

He concentrated and started listening intently. No, he wasn't imagining anything; there clearly was someone coming up behind him. And the footsteps were heavy, like those a burly man might make. Hitler increased the pace of his walk just a little, then a little more. But even as he sped up, it seemed that the person behind him was also increasing his pace. How fast could a burly man walk?

Hitler's breathing became heavier and he peered down the street. How far was that damned tram stop? Were there others waiting there, or nearby?

Until that moment, Hitler had been reluctant to reach for the knife in his coat pocket. But now he was sure he needed it. He reached into his right pocket and felt around. But where was the knife? *Scheisse – had he lost it somewhere?*

His mind started racing now. Had he taken it out at any time during the day? Or the day before? But this was a hell of a time to make that discovery. He reached in once more, more deeply, and slipped his hand into a corner wedge. There it was. He carefully pulled it towards the top of the pocket. As he and his follower moved into a more lighted area of the street, Hitler took a full grasp of the knife handle. He was surprised at how good it felt, how reassuring. He could almost feel confident, though he was still scared. He could now hear the footsteps moving even faster, closing the distance on him. He clutched the handle more securely and eased it halfway out of his pocket.

Near the corner, he suddenly stepped back and off to the side. He turned on the person who was almost even with him by then. He stared fiercely, the knife ready to slash away. It was a man, a large man ... but it was not the killer he had collided with that evening two weeks ago.

The man turned and looked at Hitler, confused. Then he saw that this strange, frail fellow was holding something in his right hand and guessed that it was some kind of weapon.

Realizing this, his face stiffened with fear. He shouted out, "Are you crazy?" and started moving quickly in the opposite direction from where Hitler stood. This accusation angered Hitler, and that sense of anger flared in his face. He spat out a retort. "You'd better watch yourself, that's all. Don't go sneaking up on people in the dark."

The other man just shook his head and continued walking off, though now even more quickly, almost at a jog.

Hitler felt embarrassed at what had just transpired. But he also felt rather proud of himself. He realized that he had not been afraid to grab the knife when he felt threatened and, more importantly, that he had been quite ready to use that knife. In fact, he was perhaps seconds away from having thrust the blade into the man's midsection.

He was glad that he didn't have to use the knife in any sudden street combat, but he was also relieved to know that he could use if it were necessary. *Life was a struggle, after all, and only those who were ready and willing to take part in the struggle could expert to thrive.* He was now clearly one of them.

Then he realized that he was sweating, despite the light chill in the night air. He yanked an almost clean handkerchief from his trousers pocket and wiped his face. He took a few soothing breaths and looked around. The tram stop was within view. He would certainly have a good ride back to Brigittenau.

19

Less than a week after the murder of Maria Kolenska, a sudden chill swept back into Vienna. The temperatures that evening dictated that people bundle up a bit. This also meant that fewer potential customers made their way to the city's streetwalker zone. Some of Spittelberg's narrow streets were virtually empty, as only a reduced corps of prostitutes turned up for work that evening and the few intrepid men driven by uncomplicated lusts produced an unfavorable ratio for those women out there looking for customers.

One of the women, trying to make the evening financially worthwhile, made an unfortunate choice. Following a few rejected pitches, she approached one man who was not there for the standard offering, but had something much more sinister in mind. Within moments of making her sales pitch, she was dead.

It was again strangulation, similar in mode and traces as the two earlier murders. This was now looking more and more like part of a series, and the atmosphere was about to get very heated and quite unpleasant in Vienna's police presidium.

This time, the victim was a local woman, a former factory worker named Gertrud Prestel. Frau Prestel had been married for a few years, but her husband suddenly took off and left no forwarding address, only a stack of unpaid bills. (Some accounts had him going to America, others claimed he had moved to Sardinia and taken up sheep farming.) Not long after she had lost her husband, she also lost her job. And soon, she was looking at losing her flat as well.

To support herself, she had taken to the streets and been able to earn survival money by ardently offering her body to strange men with limited amounts of money to pay. Evidently, one of the strange men she was about to offer her body to abruptly pushed her against a wall and proceeded to brutally strangle her. At the police morgue the next day, Doktor Gressler noted that the neck bruises were quite similar to the two earlier cases, though this time, they were even uglier.

There was also a large purple bruise on her right thigh. Doktor Gressler surmised that the victim had put up some resistance, and the killer had rammed his knee against her thigh, then shoved her against the wall to finish his task. And although it was not Gressler's job to make such a leap, he was pretty sure all three murders were the work of the same man.

Stebbel and Dörfner listened to Gressler, glanced back at the victim's corpse one more time, then thanked the doctor for his work and his thorough report. They already knew that the serious problem on their slate had just become much more serious.

* * *

Stebbel sat at his desk, a morose glower on his face and a newspaper spread out in front of him. He reached for his coffee cup, but put it down without taking another sip. He'd already had enough bitterness that morning.

When Dörfner shuffled into the office a short time later, Stebbel looked up sympathetically. "Have you seen this?" he asked as he shifted the paper around for Dörfner to read the oversized headline.

"DOES VIENNA NOW HAVE HER OWN JACK THE RIPPER?"

Dörfner picked up the paper, glanced at the headline and the first few lines of the story. He then clucked disapprovingly and threw the paper back onto the desk.

"I wouldn't expect anything better from the *Neue Freie Presse*. They're just a bunch of greasy sensationalists. They love to stir up trouble and make a lot of money while they do it. You want to talk about dirty whores ..." he pointed to the paper, "these are the worst of them."

"Maybe so," said Stebbel. "But they have one of the largest readerships in the city. In all of Austria actually." He turned the paper around and glared again at the headline. "This is not good. And I'm sure we're going to find out very soon how not good it is."

Stebbel was quite prophetic. Half an hour later, a young desk officer came to tell them that District Commander Schollenberg would like to see them in his office at 10:45.

* * *

Sitting in the District Commander's office, Dörfner and Stebbel were trying very hard not to look as uncomfortable as they felt. District Commander Schollenberg was tossing out shreds of small talk to fill the anxious moments while they waited for Senior Inspector Rautz to join them. He finally arrived fifteen minutes late. As soon as he had apologized and taken his seat, Schollenberg leapt into the sole reason for this hastily called meeting.

With this third victim, the public was now becoming quite concerned about the strangler. The press was, of course, having a field day with the events, and that meant all the popular newspapers. And those two developments meant that Vienna's political leadership had also become very concerned. The politicians still had faith in the short memories of the Viennese, but if this string of murders continued up to or even close to the next election, it might mean some serious bruising at the polls for the ruling factions.

After running through the raw facts of the latest murder, the four policemen tried to fit it into some context. The district commander asked if Dörfner and Stebbel were sure that all three murders were the acts of one man.

Stebbel sat up in his chair to answer. "Not 100 percent sure, sir. We can't really be *that* sure until we have the culprit arrested and squeeze a confession out of him." Dörfner nodded vigorously in support of his partner.

"But there are very strong indications that this is the work of a single culprit. There are so many similarities, not the least of which is the fact that all three victims were clearly strangled by a very powerful man." Dörfner again nodded with his whole upper body.

The district commander was in no way mollified by this testament. He looked over at Rautz, who made a meaningless gesture, backed up by a few negligible words. Schollenberg then addressed all three of his subordinates.

"It seems this monster has fallen into a pattern. He seems to like killing young women out on the streets alone late in the evening."

Dörfner shifted uneasily. Stebbel responded.

"There is definitely a pattern here, especially if it is a single perpetrator. We can't speak about his motive yet, but I would venture to guess that he does get some kind of perverse satisfaction out of killing these women."

"All of which suggests that the bastard will strike again. Very soon again maybe. He chooses these women at random and kills them for the same reason those crazy mountain climbers scale some mountain: because they're there."

Dörfner now saw it as his turn to speak. "That does seem very possible, sir."

"Splendid, just splendid. Have any of you seem the front page of the *Neue Freie Presse* today?" He turned to each man in turn, but each one merely shook his head. Stebbel and Dörfner had seen it, of course, but they pretended ignorance; they didn't want to deprive Schollenberg of his indignation.

"Well, not to worry, I have a copy right here." He reached to a stunted table next to his desk and snatched up the daily. He stared down at the headline for a few moments, as if filling up with bile, then looked up and recited the headline in full histrionic. "DOES VIENNA NOW HAVE HER OWN JACK THE RIPPER?" He threw the paper back down on the desk. "And the rest of the article doesn't get any more soothing."

Rautz decided it was his turn to contribute something. "Sir, you know how the press is. They love to sensationalize everything. They have no respect at all for basic decency. They actually prefer melodrama to accurate reporting. I wouldn't worry too much about what they write."

"Oh, you wouldn't? But I certainly would. And I think you should start learning to worry about such things, Rautz. Because a lot of people in this city believe all the rubbish these papers print. And that can make life very uncomfortable for me, Rautz. And when my life gets uncomfortable …" He stared at the senior inspector, who finished the sentence for him.

"Our lives become uncomfortable."

"Indeed." He then turned away sharply from Rautz, as if disgusted by his very presence. His next words were addressed to the two junior inspectors.

"I want you to solve this case. As quickly as possible. Use all the resources in your division that you need. Have other inspectors assist you in the investigations. Tell them to drop any minor things they're doing at the moment and get involved with this. From this morning on, this case has top priority. We can even get some people seconded from other towns if that is needed." He then turned back towards Rautz and spoke with an undertone of intimidation. "Though I would hope that it's not."

He tapped both fists menacingly on the desk, then picked up that morning's newspaper again. "One thing we cannot have here, that we will not have here, is another Jack the Ripper spree. We cannot have dozens of women murdered here like they did in London."

Stebbel hesitated politely before correcting the district commander's wild exaggeration. "Sir, I think the number was much lower. Under ten murders by the Ripper, if I remember correctly."

"Oh, so maybe only eight or nine? What a relief. We can certainly afford to have eight, nine ... ten young ladies murdered on our streets." He took a breath, embarrassed by his own poor spew of irony. "How long did it take them to catch the Ripper anyway?"

Dörfner looked at his partner, before turning to Schollenberg and answering. "Jack the Ripper was ... never caught, sir. The murders remain unsolved to this day."

"*Ach, du lieber Himmel.* So that bastard might still be out there." He snorted down an angry breath. "But that was London, this is Vienna. They're all Freemasons and freethinkers over there. Here, we still hold fast to our traditional values, we practice old-time virtues. And *we* are going to find our strangler. And we will find him very soon and put an end to all this.

"I have faith in the skills of you three men, and I want you to use those skills excessively to catch this criminal. Catch him very soon, before he strikes again." He then took another deep breath, this one drained of much of that anger. "Have I made myself very clear, gentleman?"

"Oh, very clear, Herr Commander," Rautz said. "Very clear

indeed." The two juniors nodded in agreement.

"Good. Then the next time I see any one of you in this office, I expect it to be when I congratulate you on solving the case. Or at least when you give me a report of significant progress."

"*Jawohl*, Herr Commander."

Schollenberg then gave a mechanical nod, which told the three subordinates that they were excused. They all rose and left his office in decorous haste.

As Stebbel and Dörfner strode down the corridor, Dörfner gave his well-honed contemptuous snort. Then, referring to the District Commander, he said, "I wonder if that guy ever gets out of his seat anytime during working hours. He really should, you know – just to air out his ass a little."

Stebbel shrugged. "You should ask him the next time we drop in. I'm sure he'll be touched by your concern for his well-being."

"Yeah, that's just I'll do. Right after I win top prize in the state lottery."

20

Barely an hour later, six young policeman had gathered in the larger interview room with Dörfner and Stebbel. Dörfner was giving them a brief rundown of the case, underscoring everything they needed to know to become a part of the expanded investigation team. Stebbel stood off to the side, from time to time being called upon to back up his colleague when Dörfner turned for confirmation.

He was finishing up his spiel when a knock came on the door and Inspector Stegmeier shuffled in. He gave a short, deferential bow and took his place next to Stebbel.

Neither Stebbel nor Dörfner were happy to see him there. It was Senior Inspector Rautz's idea that he should join their team. As Stegmeier had years more experience than either Dörfner or Stebbel, it strongly suggested that Rautz was rapidly losing confidence in those two to solve this case. The unknown strangler seemed to be causing even more havoc in their police division than on the streets of Vienna.

But later that same day, fate smiled on Stebbel and Dörfner. Coming back from lunch, Stegmeier miscalculated his exit from the *paternoster* and landed badly. His right ankle went one way, the rest of his leg the other. Rushed down to the infirmary by four muscular policemen, he writhed in agony, swearing revenge on the *paternoster* the whole trip. *That damn thing, which he had never gotten along with, had finally broken his leg.*

It wasn't quite that bad. The infirmary doctor declared the ankle severely sprained and said Stegmeier should keep off it for at least a week.

Stegmeier himself decided to play it cautious and got the doctor to declare him medically excused for ten days. This, of course, meant that he wouldn't be around to pester Stebbel and Dörfner. And Rautz didn't think to appoint a replacement for the injured inspector – much to their relief.

The following day, it became clear that the six young officers chosen for the expanded investigation team added nothing to the investigation. Dörfner and Stebbel started assigning them errands that would keep them away from their own operations. This investigation was proving difficult enough on its own; they had no desire to have a pack of assistants who mainly served the purpose of getting in their way.

One positive change that came from the stepped-up campaign to nab the strangler: Stebbel and Dörfner were moved to a bigger office down the corridor, closer to Inspector Rautz's own office. Not only was this office much bigger, with a wider window, but it also came equipped with a telephone. This meant that the inspectors could make and receive calls without rushing to another office. (And there were only two other telephones in that corridor: one in Rautz's office, one at the reception.)

The packing, heavy lifting and assorting of the move was carried out mainly by the six new assistants. It took less than two hours from start to resettlement, and at the end of the move, the two inspectors were finally grateful to Rautz and Schollenberg for having assigned the young officers to help in the investigation. Progress of sorts was being made.

* * *

The funeral mass for Gertrud Prestel was a far different affair from that of Anneliese von Klettenburg. This time, for instance, there was no crowd-control detail, as there was no crowd. Inspectors Stebbel and Dörfner were able to slip inside the church and had no trouble finding an empty pew from where they could take in the whole ceremony.

The mass was held at the victim's parish church in the Meidling district. The church was small and malodorous, the ceremony depressingly simple. There were no eulogies, no Mozart, no ostentatious floral arrays. The priest, looking as worn-out as his church, gave a short sermon, which focused on the unbounded mercy of God, Who is willing to forgive and redeem us no matter how vile our transgressions. The obvious reference to Frau Prestel's trade was not lost on most of the two dozen attendees (which included four elderly parishioners who turned up for every notable event at the church, no matter what the occasion).

As it had become common knowledge what Gertrud Prestel did for a living, the priest was forbidden by the Vienna Church hierarchy to accompany the body to the cemetery and perform graveside rites.

The two inspectors did attend the burial. Part of the reason was sympathy for the deceased: they didn't want to see a simple woman who had been victimized by a cruel husband, a factory supervisor, a rigidly hierarchical society and, finally, a cold-hearted killer receive one final indignity. That didn't think it right that there should be so few mourners there to watch her body lowered into the grave.

But more important: they wanted to see if anyone turned up for the burial who had not been in the church. No one like that did turn up. And there were no faces at Frau Prestel's funeral that they could remember from the von Klettenburg funeral. If there were any important clues to be gleaned from the ceremony in Meidling and the burial that followed, the two inspectors missed every single one of them.

21

Three days after the crisis meeting with the District Commander, Stebbel was at his desk, sifting through some reports, when Dörfner strode in. He clapped his hands to get his partner's attention as well as to signal that he had good news.

"Herr Inspector – we just got a big breakthrough!"

"We did?"

"I just spoke with the Turk. The morning after the murder, I told him we needed special help. Well, he came through."

"Yes?"

Dörfner nodded energetically. "He had his people doing some thorough investigations. And you know what he found out? This Frau Prestel didn't actually have a pimp."

"She didn't?"

"*Tja*, she had one for a short time. But he ran into some trouble, the Turk wasn't specific, and he had to leave Vienna. After that, she was working on her own. For maybe the last six months." He clapped his hands again, as if he had just about wrapped up the case.

"And how is this such good news?"

"Come on, give a smile, it won't hurt you. No, this strengthens my theory: the killer is a pimp. He tried to get Frau von Klettenburg and this Prestel girl to join his stable. When they refused, he killed them. Or – alternative theory – he was angry that these two freelancers were poaching on his territory. He thought that they were selling their wares in an area that only his whores were allowed to work. He was protecting his interests."

"And Maria Kolenska?"

"He wanted her to leave the Turk and join his stable. She turned him down, so he killed her."

"The Turk? You mean Hochner."

"*Ja, ja*, of course; Hochner."

"Of course, there's another explanation." Dörfner raised his eyebrows to a near skeptical height; he was pretty much sold on his own two explanations.

"What do pimps do?" Stebbel asker rhetorically.

"They tell their whores where to go, how to keep customers satisfied and … then they collect their money."

"They also protect the girls. Of course, for them, it's more like protecting their investment. So if neither the first nor the third victim had a pimp to look after them, the killer had easy targets. Maybe that's why he went for them."

"And our second victim?"

Stebbel didn't skip a beat. "Maria was unlucky. Her pimp was off somewhere else and the killer found her all alone. Let's face it, lucky and unlucky is often the difference between being alive and being dead."

"But if it's all luck, if it's all random, then we're simply … back there spinning around, not knowing which direction to go."

Stebbel shrugged. Actually, his whole body signaled irritation.

"Steb, let me finish laying out my strategy here. We start hauling in the city's pimps. We take them into the sweat box and give them a serious going over. The killer may break, right there, or at least give us enough tell-tale signs that we can pin him as the main suspect and go from there."

Stebbel picked up a file lying on his desk. "Herr Colleague, I just discovered that there are upwards of 15,000 streetwalkers in this city. And those are just the ladies who have taken the trouble to register. So how many pimps are out there?"

"Each pimp has a stable, Herr Colleague. They're not one-to-one."

"But it's also not a thousand prostitutes to each pimp. We would have to grab ... hundreds of pimps to question, and then ..."

He trailed off and the look of resignation on his face told Dörfner he should postpone any further discussion of his strategy. In the uneasy silence, Stebbel started sorting the papers on his desk into several piles, as Dörfner rubbed the back of his head with a flattened palm.

Dörfner headed back to his own desk and slumped into his chair. He took a deep sigh that he didn't want Stebbel to either see or hear. But the senior could feel it; that's how charged the air was. Stebbel knew he had to break the tension.

"But that was good work ... finding out about Frau Prestel and her lack of a pimp. It is a step forward."

"But a very small step, right?"

"At this point, any step at least means that we're moving somewhere. And not just spinning."

Dörfner again rubbed the back of his head with his open palm. Both inspectors were all too tired of this repeated spinning; as Stebbel had said once, it was giving him mental motion sickness.

22

Doktor Sigmund Freud was taking his regular mid-afternoon stroll in the bantam park not far off the Ringstasse. He had just extracted a cigar out of the linen pouch he used for his portable smokes and lit it. As a plume of grey smoke lifted from the cigar, someone approached from his right flank.

"Doktor Freud! What a pleasant surprise!"

Freud turned to see Inspector Stebbel. He smiled.

"Ah yes, the good inspector. You know, I am too often misquoted as saying 'there are no accidents in life', but here I would dare say that this "chance encounter' is no accident."

"No, not really. We did some surveillance and found that you always take a pause from your work and come here to enjoy a cigar at 2:45. I'm told you could set your watch by the time you appear at the park entrance."

"I must learn to vary my routine then. I wouldn't want any of my enemies to start trailing me." He again smiled broadly. "Speaking of cigars, would you like one yourself?" He held out his pouch.

"I shouldn't."

"Not allowed to smoke while on duty?"

"Actually, it's because I have a respiratory problem. But one light smoke won't kill me, I don't think. Especially as I take it for fellowship."

"So, then. For fellowship."

Stebbel extracted a cigar and Freud offered him a flaming match to light it. As Stebbel took his first soft puff, Freud brought the match near to his chin and meticulously blew out the flame, as if performing a solemn ritual, then placed the match into a brass box where he consigned all such matches which had served their purpose.

"So, Inspector, as you also probably know, I can only devote a short time to these afternoon breaks, so we should get right down to business. I suspect you've come here on police business?"

"Mainly. First of all, I'd like to apologize for my colleague's behavior during the interview at police headquarters. Herr Dörfner is not really a master of tact and when he gets impassioned about a case, he … sometimes acts brashly and speaks without thinking what he's saying."

"Not to worry, Inspector; I was not too offended. Compared to what a number of my critics and enemies have written or said about me, I found your colleague's statements quite mild stuff really."

"I'm glad to hear that. I was afraid you might chase me away just because I stayed quiet while Inspector Dörfner insulted you." He paused to allow Freud to give a never-mind laugh. "And so, on to the other business."

"Please."

"I was hoping you could give us some assistance now. I fully appreciate that you can't divulge anything about Frau von Klettenburg, but now we have two other victims. And we're working on the assumption that the killer in all three cases is the same person." He stopped and turned. "This killer isn't one of your patients, is he?"

"I should certainly hope not!" Freud pulled his cigar away abruptly and used it to emphasize his next point. "I can assure you, Inspector, that none of my patients has confessed to me that he's been going around strangling young women."

"Good; then we might be able to make some progress here."

"This time, I will try to give you all the help I can."

"You're familiar with the three murders? The circumstances and such?

"I am. I've read everything I can about the crimes in the newspapers. And not the boulevard press either – the serious journals."

"Good. Some of the reports were wildly inaccurate."

"So I surmised. Let me tell you, Inspector ... as the first of the victims was not only my patient, but also a woman I had a great deal of respect and admiration for, I have been following these cases even more closely than is my wont. And I do generally have an interest in manifestations of a sick mind in crimes."

"So have you fashioned any theories about the killer in these cases?"

Freud pursed his lips tightly before commencing. "As you may be aware, the human mind is a series of labyrinths and caverns, connected by bridges that ... don't always connect. Sometimes because those bridges have been intentionally destroyed. So until I would actually have the killer sitting in front of me, where I could speak with him at length, it's all just a theory."

"Of course."

"But an *educated* theory. So, I would say that this killer is filled with a deep animosity towards women. That sounds all too obvious, I imagine, but this would be a special strain of animosity. I suspect that our killer has sexual problems, severe sexual problems. He may be ... how shall I put this ... unable to perform under normal circumstances.

"I would not be surprised to discover that he actually achieves sexual arousal when he gets his hands around the woman's neck. This is his version of physical intimacy. And the choking sounds his poor victims make, their enlarged eyes as they are strangled, he would take this as the female responses to their 'couplings'. This is the kind of man you might be dealing with here."

"I see."

"And you should also be looking for a man who had problems with his father. And then problems with his mother. He may have been abused by his father and turned to his mother for protection or solace. When she was unable to give him all he needed, he saw this as a betrayal. He would probably then feel that his mother was part of a pact with his father.

"He may have even caught his parents in the act of sexual intercourse and seen this as part of the unholy pact they had formed against him. So when he assaults these women and begins to strangle them, he feels he has usurped his father's role and is, at the same time, taking revenge on both his mother and his father." He flicked away five centimeters of ash and took a deep drag from his cigar. "It's all rather complicated."

"Indeed."

"And I imagine that all three victims resemble each other physically?"

Stebbel tried to recall the three faces along with the additional information he'd seen. "Not really. No, three rather different types, I'd say … though each one attractive in her own way."

"Oh."

Having just been jolted by this bump in his smooth theorizing journey, Freud felt it best to switch tracks to another subject.

"Tell me, Inspector, do you think you'll be able to catch this man? Before he strikes again?"

"We certainly hope so."

"And what if you can't? Or at least, not for some time?"

"God help us."

Freud took a long draw of his cigar, then blew the smoke out slowly.

"Do you believe in Him? God?"

"I should."

Freud smiled. "I'll take that as a gentleman's way of saying 'no'."

Stebbel turned to him and returned the smile. "Better to take it as a police inspector's way of saying he should believe."

Freud held up his cigar. "I should stop smoking as much as I do. But I don't believe it's ever going to happen."

"My relationship with God is a little more complicated than that. I still go to mass. Not all the time, but ... more than can be considered mere courtesy."

"And confession?"

"All the time. At least once every fortnight."

"Ah ... now that's very interesting. It shows again that religion still fulfills some important functions even for an intelligent modern citizen like yourself. The need to go and talk about one's problems to someone who is said to have magical powers."

"It's not that. Well, that might be part of it, but that's not the whole story." Stebbel drew a short drag on his cigar and let the next words ride out on the light cough that followed. "I'm not sure about God, but I still believe in sin. And evil. And guilt. And punishment."

Freud shrugged. "Except for the sin, that's very much what one would expect a good policeman to believe in."

"But for me, sin is the most important thing."

Freud pursed his lips and nodded. This was something that did not fit all that neatly into his skillfully constructed system. He was about to dissect the subject of sin more thoroughly, but first consulted his watch and decided this was a subject that would take more than the few minutes he could spare yet.

Stebbel, meanwhile, was already thinking of how he was going to deal with this when he filled in the casebook.

"So let's be clear: you really believe that this man could be getting sexual thrills out of killing these women. Killing them the way he does?"

A morose look filled Freud's face. "I am a doctor, you know. A fully qualified physician. Went through all the stages of medical training. And did quite well at every stage, I might mention." Stebbel nodded; he had no doubt that Freud had been an exemplary student.

"Now the reason I became a doctor was to heal people, to remove – or at least relieve – the suffering of my patients. But after some time, I came to realize that some of the worst suffering, the greatest torments, were lodged not in the body, but in the mind. And that's how I was slowly drawn into psychiatry."

"I can understand that," Stebbel replied.

"But always – always – foremost in my goals was to heal my patients. To relieve their suffering wherever possible. I thought it could be like carrying out a medical examination, coming up with a diagnosis, writing a prescription or recommending some physical therapy."

He shook his head sadly. "And some of what I do is just that, and at the end, I feel that I have helped the patients. But more and more, as I explore the human mind, I find things about the human being that I wish I had never discovered.

The two men stopped walking, and Freud turned to face Stebbel directly. "Inspector, I see things in the human soul that make me shudder. Literally shudder. I go to write something down, maybe a prescription, and I see it looks like a child's scribble because my hand is shaking so much."

Freud then wrapped his left hand around his right and the two started rubbing each other, as if trying to calm them just from the memory of these frightening cases.

"The horrible murder of Frau von Klettenburg. And now these two other victims, both younger than Frau von Klettenburg. How does one even begin to explain things like that? There's only way to explain it: something dark in the human psyche, something indelibly dark and destructive."

The doctor then swept his hand across the boulevard to indicate some of the more imposing structures gracing their Vienna. "Look at this wonderful civilization we've created here over the many centuries of the human enterprise. But there is something at the core of many of us, perhaps most of us, that would tear it all down if given the chance."

"You may be right, Doktor. I have seen some terrible, terrible things myself."

"I'm sure you have." He took another puff of his cigar. "So, Inspector, I hope some of what I've told you can be helpful."

"All of it is helpful," Stebbel replied. "I just hope that some of it will lead us quickly to the killer. Before he strikes again."

"I must confess, Inspector, I've been feeling deep tugs of guilt since our last meeting."

"Oh?"

"Yes, I keep asking myself if I couldn't have told you more, couldn't have offered some theory, some advice. Perhaps if I had come in earlier, with more information, these last two young ladies would still be alive."

"I wouldn't blame myself if I were you, Herr Doktor. There's probably little any of us could have done at that early stage. We even thought then it was all about Frau von Klettenburg, that she was a targeted victim."

Freud pulled out his watch and glanced at it. "Sorry, Inspector, it's not that I don't find our conversation rewarding, but my break time is almost over. My next patient should be arriving in ten minutes, so I have to get back."

"Of course; I understand completely. I'm grateful for the time and the help you were able to give me ... even though I arrived without an appointment."

Freud gave a gruff chuckle and took another puff of his cigar.

"Don't hesitate to 'drop in again' if you need some more help. I, too, want to see this killer caught and his string of crimes brought to an end. Very much so."

"And I appreciate your offer, Herr Doktor."

The two shook hands and Stebbel started walking away. He hadn't gone ten meters when Freud called out to him.

"One other thing, Herr Inspector."

"Yes?"

"Frau von Klettenburg had ... fantasies."

"Fantasies?"

"Fantasies that might not be considered that healthy." He suddenly looked away as if the recall of those fantasies had caused him physical pain. He turned, stepped out to the curb, and flagged down a taxi.

"Such as?"

"I'm sorry, I ... I can't tell you any more. I probably shouldn't have even told you that much." The taxi pulled up and Freud opened the rear door. "But I'll see what help I can give you. There must be some more that I can do. We'll talk again before long."

He climbed in; the taxi door swung closed. As the cab pulled off, Stebbel took two shallow puffs of the cigar while he savored that last revelation Freud had let slip out.

*　*　*

When Stebbel arrived back at his desk, Dörfner had still not returned from checking out the other people living in Gertrude Prestel's building. Glad for the respite, Stebbel slipped into the chair and pulled out his notepad. He wanted to copy the scribbled notes there into the larger casebook he had in his drawer. He found the casebook and began writing.

"Spoke to the eminent scientist Sigmund Freud this afternoon." As he finished writing that sentence, a broad smile slid across his face. He could just imagine Dörfner cringing when he read that 'eminent scientist" bit. He thought of underlining those two words, then decided not to stick it in too deeply.

"Doktor Freud has a rather interesting theory about the case. He speculates that our killer is driven by a deep animosity towards women in general. He suspects that the killer has severe sexual problems. In fact, in Doktor Freud's opinion, the killer may be unable to perform under normal circumstances. Freud told me he would not be surprised to – "

He stopped in mid-sentence. He had just hit another stump of theory. He quickly rose and stepped over to the large files on the cases. He hauled own the first file and brought it back to his desk. Flipping back to the first murder, he came to the autopsy report on Anneliese von Klettenburg. He pulled it out of the file, then flipped back to the other two autopsy reports. He pulled those two out as well and then scanned through all three. There it was. He again jumped out of his seat and headed towards the door.

A few minutes later, he was at the morgue door. He tugged anxiously at the cord that rang the bell. A few moments later, a morgue assistant opened the door.

"Yes, please?"

"I must talk to Dr. Gressler. Right away, please."

The assistant seemed confused. "I'm not sure if he's still here. If you can wait, I'll check and see."

Having been in the police department for almost a decade, Stebbel was familiar with this game. "Please tell him that it's Inspector Stebbel calling. The lead investigator in the serial murders cases. The strangler murders."

It was as if he had just clicked the 'On' switch in the assistant. The assistant nodded, then replied, "Actually, I think the doctor is still here. Let me see if I can get him. Would you like to come in and wait?" Stebbel gave a nub of a smile as he stepped in.

He looked around. The smell of various chemicals seemed to be stronger now, the entire atmosphere of the place even colder than on his typical visits.

The assistant had quickly disappeared into a rear nook from where, several moments later, Gressler emerged, looking polite and flustered.

"Inspector, how can I help you?"

"Herr Doktor, I'm so grateful that you could find the time to see me. I'll make it quick: I have a question about the autopsy reports on the three victims."

This knocked the doctor off his guard. "Oh? I don't think we made any mistakes there. What were you thinking of?"

"No, no, I'm sure you didn't make any mistakes. I was just struck by the fact that in the reports on the last two victims, there was no mention of semen in the vaginal tract."

"Well, I guess that means that we didn't find any."

"So there was none at all?"

"Well, perhaps a few traces, nothing more. We're not perverts here, you know."

"But if a report says that there was semen in the vaginal tract, that would mean … ?"

"A significant amount."

"Yes; good. A significant amount." He then tried to latch this to another thought. "Which would indicate that the victim would have … ?"

"She would have had sexual intercourse not too long before she was killed."

"Yes, I see. Yes … yes."

He again thanked the doctor for having seen him at no notice and left. He rushed back to his office and the casebook. The page was still open to where he had left off.

"Freud told me he would not be surprised to discover that the killer actually achieves sexual arousal when he gets his hands around the woman's neck. This is his version of physical intimacy. That could well explain why his victims are all prostitutes – or those he believes to be prostitutes – and also why there is no evidence that he has actually had sexual intercourse with these women."

He pressed in a full stop and set his pen down. He saw no need to add that Frau von Klettenburg was the exception: she clearly had had sexual intercourse shortly before her murder. This simply confused things, and he didn't want those who might read the casebook later to slide into the confusion. Let them solve the case completely, and then they could fill in all the gaps.

But those reflections and revelations coming out of Stebbel's chat with Doktor Freud were more like isolated flashes of light in an otherwise murky landscape. Nothing else the two inspectors were able to come up with helped them advance in a fruitful direction. Every "lead" was just a desperate grab at getting something meaningful. But at the end of every interview, every trip, every bit of research, they seemed to be exactly where they were right after the murder of Gertrud Prestel: not far from square one.

The way Stebbel now viewed it, this case strongly resembled the sketch of the troubled human mind as Freud had described it: any leads they had were just a series of bridges that didn't connect, that all stopped somewhere in the middle.

Even more alarmingly, the case was looking like a labyrinth, with the two inspectors just feeling their way blindly through the caverns of that labyrinth. And no matter how many paths they explored, after all their gropings, all their maneuvers, they seemed to always end up back in the same place: a cold place, smothered in shadows.

23

The day had been as busy as it was frustrating for Stebbel and Dörfner. It was mid-afternoon when the two returned from their latest round of pointless street interviews. Dörfner had stopped off at the toilet on the way to the office, so Stebbel walked in alone, mulling the day's events. The young policeman at the Reception desk signaled him over. He leaned forward and half-whispered the news.

"See that man over there?" He pointed furtively at a man perched on the visitor's bench. "He claims to be a witness."

"Witness?"

"To the murders. All those strangler things. He says he knows who did it."

Stebbel turned to view the man. "Oh, does he? Well, this should be interesting."

Just then, Dörfner trudged back in. Stebbel called him over.

"Karl-Heinz, we have somebody who claims to be a witness to the killings." He indicated the man with a slight jerk of the head. "Over there on the bench."

The desk-duty policeman, Henninger, added, "And his is the third time he's been in today. Every time I told him you two were out, he said he'd come back because he had to talk to you."

Dörfner looked at the thin man with the robust moustache. "Looks to be a little bit loony."

"He does indeed," replied Stebbel.

"Tell you though, some of the best information I've had as a police officer came from informants who were half loony."

"Well, we've not going to turn him away. Let's see what he has to say." He turned back to the young officer. "What's the fellow's name?"

"Hitler. He also claims to be from Vienna, but he doesn't sound that way."

"Well, please tell our Herr Hitler that the two inspectors handling the case will speak to him in a few minutes. We'll go and arrange a room." The two started to walk away, when Stebbel suddenly turned back.

"Oh, Henninger – don't tell anyone else in the department about this. We want to be sure how credible this guy is. We don't want to be raising false hopes, do we?"

"No, sir. I won't breathe another word about this."

A short time later, Hitler was led into Interview Room No. 3 by Henninger. Stebbel was already waiting there; Dörfner walked in right behind Hitler. Stebbel rose from his chair and walked over to greet the witness. He offered a hand.

"Good day, sir. My name is Inspector Stebbel, and you've apparently already met my colleague, Inspector Dörfner.'

The man nodded. "Hitler ... Adolf." He then shook hands with the two inspectors. Stebbel was mildly surprised at the firmness of his grip and the ease with which he carried out this ritual of greeting. Stebbel then asked Hitler to take a seat in the witness chair while he and Dörfner sat down on the other side of the desk.

"So, Herr Hitler, we understand that you were a witness to these killings of the young women."

"No, not all the killings. Just the first one. Frau von Klettenburg's murder." He then reached into his leather case and extracted his sketch of the killer. He placed it carefully on the desk. "And this is the man who killed her."

The two policemen looked at the drawing. It seemed to be a surprisingly good drawing, though they had no idea if it bore any resemblance to a real person.

"Do you know the man's name?"

"No. I just know that this is what he looks like." He then proceeded to recount the story of what had happened to him that night, the collision with the man as he came rushing out of the alleyway. Also, how he had gone home after that and sketched the man's face.

"But you didn't actually see him kill Frau von Klettenburg?"

"No. But when he banged into me, we looked at each other. Hard. And then I looked in his eyes. And I knew that he had just committed some awful crime."

"And how did you know that?"

"I am an artist. A committed artist. I can look into a man's face and see what lies deep within that man." Hitler then took a mild gulp. He thought of what a number of art teachers and one of the examiners who had turned down his application at the Academy of Fine Arts had told him: that he had a certain amount of technical skill, but his work was clearly missing something. He never got below the surface of his subject.

Stebbel then asked him what time this incident had occurred. Hitler did some quick reckoning. As he recalled, he was walking back to the hostel when the bells at St. John Capistrano church started tolling 10:00. So that would have put the collision somewhere between 9:30 and 9:45. Stebbel nodded and Dörfner just stared intently at Hitler. That was consistent with the estimated time of death.

They asked Hitler if he had seen the dead body. He hesitated for a moment ... and then lied. He told the inspectors that he was so shaken by the collision with that man with the ugly gaze that he quickly turned and headed home as quickly as he could. He didn't actually see the strangler's dirty work. But nonetheless, he was absolutely sure the man in the sketch was the man who had killed her.

The two inspectors glanced at the sketch once more. Finally, Stebbel decided that they couldn't just throw this lead back into the rubbish bin.

"Herr Hitler, we need more information about this man. Now a few floors below, we have what we call the rogues gallery. It's a collection of files filled with photos of most of the people who've been arrested in Vienna over the last ... oh, ten years or so. It includes people who have been convicted as well as those later released or found not guilty in a court.

"The big advantage for us is that these photos all have the name of the suspects pasted on the back. What we would like you to do is to go down there with us and go through these books. The chances are that the man you drew in this sketch will also have his photo in our files."

Hitler agreed immediately, and the two inspectors escorted him down to the rogue's gallery. There, the officer responsible for the files greeted them, then went to haul out the files. As the first files were presented to Herr Hitler, Stebbel and Dörfner said they would be back shortly, then left him there alone with the rogues gallery.

About half an hour later, Dörfner strolled back down to the gallery to see how the star witness was getting along. As he approached, he saw a sullen Hitler turning the page harshly, glaring down at the photo, then flipping over the next one just as harshly. Dörfner stood a short distance away, just observing Hitler for a minute. His own quick reading: this poor man was almost choking with a bitterness made that much more bitter by the fact that it had no outlet. Dörfner was no stranger to bitterness, including his own, but this seemed a unique, pure form of the affliction.

He was still observing the witness when Hitler suddenly seemed to become aware of his presence and turned brusquely. Dörfner was embarrassed at being suddenly caught out like that. He pretended to have been just approaching as Hitler turned.

"So, Herr Hitler – have you seen any face there you recognize?"

Where he had been rigorously polite upstairs during the Q&A in the interview room, Hitler was now curt and contrary.

"No, I don't know any of these faces." He then tapped the sketch, resting in the space above the files. "This is the killer here. This is the man you should be out there looking for."

"But this, this is just a sketch."

Hitler looked up with a cultivated glare. "It's a careful drawing by a trained and highly respected artist."

"*Mein Herr ...*"

"And I can assure you, Inspector, that this drawing is a more accurate representation of the man's appearance than most of these fuzzy, half-shadowed photos you've got in these books."

With that, he started swinging his arm wildly across the table, pushing two of the files to one side, two to the other, and one all the way off the table. That file went crashing to the floor. Hitler stood staring down at the file for several moments, breathing heavily. Then he seemed to press a button deep within, emptying out a stream of his anger.

"I'm sorry. That was an accident. I should be more careful here. This is government property."

He bent down to pick up the file. Dörfner also bent over to help him get the file and place it back on the table. Hitler then took out a slightly ragged cloth and carefully wiped off the file, front and back.

"Herr Hitler, I'm sure your sketch is a quite accurate representation of our killer, but it would help us even more if you could find that same face in our files."

Hitler just stared straight ahead and nodded. It was, however, the kind of nod that indicated inner resistance.

"Besides, the drawing belongs to you. We can't take it from you."

Hitler looked up. His mood changed fully. "It's a copy actually. I copied it from the original drawing I made. This one you can keep." He stood up and presented it to Dörfner with both hands. "I would feel honored if the police would accept this as my contribution to the capture of this criminal."

Dörfner took the sketch and gave a nod of gratitude. "Of course. We'll use this to every advantage we can."

Then he escorted Hitler upstairs and out the front door of the building. He breathed a sigh of relief, glanced at the sketch again, and hobbled onto the *paternoster*.

As he walked into the office, he saw Stebbel hunched over his desk, poring over an article as he sipped tea. Dörfner slid the sketch in front of him.

"A present. From our star witness."

"Our *only* witness. If he really is a witness, if he didn't hallucinate the whole thing." He picked up the sketch and took another glance. "Did you get any address from him, or any other details in case we need to contact him?"

"I did indeed. He lives over in that big men's hostel in Briggitenau. You know, the one the city built."

"That's where he lives today. Tomorrow, he could be somewhere else." The inspector then turned back to the sketch. Within seconds, Stebbel went from a glance to a close look, to an intense stare. He looked up at Dörfner briefly before turning back to the sketch.

"What is it, Steb?"

"This drawing … I know this face."

"Where from?"

"Yeah, that's just the problem – where from?" His stare became even more intense and then he put his hands to his face.

"Was he somebody we arrested? Someone I saw in here? How about our witness, Herr …?

"Hitler"

"Right. Hitler. Who did he match this up with down in the rogues gallery."

"Nobody. He got frustrated, gave up on the whole thing. I don't even know how many files he slogged through before he gave up. You want to find this guy, you'll have to go through the files yourself."

"I see. Thank you, Herr Hitler," he said with a generous sprinkle of sarcasm.

"Well, I don't have anything better to do this evening. I'll go down there after I finish this tea and see what I can find." He picked up the sketch in both hands and again glared at it. "I'm sure I've seen this face before though. Just have to find out where."

24

Though he stayed at the task for almost two hours and went through each file assiduously, Stebbel was unable to see anyone with even a vague resemblance to the man in Hitler's sketch.

After he slapped the last file shut, his eyes were aching and he had taken a headache. *The ceiling in this room is too low, the lighting poorly placed, and the ventilation stifling*, Stebbel complained to himself. He needed a drink even more than usual.

Stebbel took a tram to one of his favorite cafés, the Starnberg, and found a two-chaired table off in the back. When the waiter approached, he ordered a double brandy.

Brandy was his preferred drink when he was feeling low – not just for its taste and generous alcohol content, but also because he could stare at its amber swirl in the glass and imagine a pure beauty, with no complications.

Now holding the glass up and staring into it, he tried to sort out everything they knew about the murders so far. It didn't amount to much. Not much at all. He had to sadly admit that the sketch Herr Hitler had given them was the most valuable lead they'd received so far – and even that wasn't very helpful.

Or maybe it was. He quickly downed the remaining brandy, enjoyed its fiery tickling of his throat as it streamed down, paid and headed out into the pleasantly cool evening.

He made his way to the streetwalker district. Though they still didn't know if they could put any faith in the testimony of this Hitler fellow, Stebbel was thinking – hoping actually – that he might see that face in the sketch prowling the district. Perhaps the killer spent a few nights on reconnaissance missions before deciding where to strike next.

And what if he did see the man? After all, the only evidence they had was a sketch by someone who might himself be half insane. He could hardly haul the man in as a suspect just on the basis of that sketch.

And he wouldn't be able to haul him in by himself anyway. According to Dr. Gressler, the man would be rather big and quite powerful; Stebbel was no match for a man like that; he'd need to fetch other police officers to assist him in any arrest.

Stebbel ambled through the seven or eight main streets where the streetwalkers trawled for customers. He was approached by several of the ladies, each one offering him a wonderful time, but he spurned them all with a polite smile and a raised hand. He acted like he was turning down an offer of food by street vendors.

Some of the whores were rather pretty, Stebbel thought, most of them depressingly young, and all of them exuded a sense of desperation. But he spent more time studying the faces of the men prowling the streets looking for an easy round of sex than those of the ladies ready to supply the sex.

He had gone through all the main streets of the district twice without any success in finding that suspect face. He felt even more frustrated than when he'd finished going through the rogues gallery photos.

He was about to give up and start looking for a cab to take him home, when a young woman appeared out of the half-light on the Schrankgasse. There was something particularly vulnerable about her appearance; maybe it was her slight shape. But it was also her demeanor. In contrast to the other women he'd seen there, who were rather straightforward in peddling their wares, this one seemed demure. In fact, as he glanced at her, she looked away shyly, and then, as he was about to pass by her, she turned back and gave a hesitant smile before looking down.

Stebbel slowed almost to a standstill and looked at her intently. She blushed, he thought, and then spoke for the first time.

"Are you lost, *mein Herr*? Maybe I can help you find what you're looking for."

"I'm … not really sure what I'm looking for."

"Oh, what a shame. Well, are you maybe looking for some companionship? I can help with that as well."

Stebbel had stepped closer to the girl and was now within a few inches of her. As she finished making her offer, she tentatively reached out and touched his hand lightly with her fingers. It was almost romantic, like a young girl approaching a potential boyfriend for the first time.

"You look very kind, mein Herr. But also very lonely."

"That could be true."

"I understand loneliness. I've often been lonely myself. Would you like to come with me and we can help each other shed our loneliness?"

"How much?" Stebbel asked. But he said it in a way that didn't sound like the beginning of some crude business transaction; it was more like the sweet compliment of a man in the opening stage of infatuation.

She took a demure breath before answering. "Ten kroners for an hour. Is that … too much?"

"No. No, that's not too much. That's not too much at all." And again, it sounded not like a prostitute and her client agreeing to the terms of the purchase of sex, but like two mildly infatuated people getting to know each other a little better. The girl reached out and gently took Stebbel's arm, then gave him the warmest smile he had seen in … years maybe. He let her take him wherever she was going to take him.

After they had finished, Stebbel went into the alcove with the sink and washbasin and sponged himself off lightly. Just enough so that he wouldn't feel too grungy as he made his way back home. Then he pulled on his clothes. He turned and Carina, still mostly unclothed, gave him another smile. It was warm and seemed almost sincere. She said she would need to take some time to clean up and get ready for the rest of the evening. Stebbel bid adieu and left. As he stepped out on the landing, he heard the door close behind him and the click of a lock.

Walking the three flights down to the street, Stebbel passed two other "short-term" couples going up the stairs, the first about five steps in front of the second. Both men bent their heads down and turned to the right (away from Stebbel) so that they couldn't be seen. Stebbel also bent his head slightly, though he did try as much as possible to peek at the men's faces.

He was unable to catch much face, but neither of the two men appeared to be that big or that powerful. The two girls both gave Stebbel a highly friendly smile as they passed him; he took the looks as advertising for the future.

Back on the street, he turned and headed towards the busy Neubaugürtel, thinking that would be the best place to find a taxi. But halfway down the street, his guilt grabbed at him and he turned back. He waited outside the building where he's just had his liaison with Carina. (If that was even her real name, which Stebbel doubted.)

When she emerged from the building, she turned and headed off in the other direction. Stebbel called to her and when she stopped, trotted over. She gave him another warm smile.

"What is it, *mein Herr*? Do you miss me already? I thought with what you just gave, you'd be too tired for a while. Do you wish to go back upstairs?"

Stebbel smiled and touched her cheek gently. She didn't resist and after a few moments even put her hand on his. "Shall we, my friend?"

"No, it's just that I ... wanted to ask you something. If you don't mind." She shrugged to indicate she didn't mind too much.

"I just wanted to ask ... haven't you heard about this killer? Three women already – two of them in your line of work. The other seemed to be. This monster seems to be targeting lovely young girls who work the streets. Aren't you scared? Why don't you ... stop for awhile? Until we ... until this beast is caught"

"Should I also stop eating for awhile? Stop paying the rent on my room. Stop helping my family? I try to be careful. All my friends out here are trying to be careful. But as my friend Luisa said, "We could be struck by lighting walking down those same streets. But nobody stops walking around because of that."

Stebbel wanted to argue with her, wanted to do everything he could to get her off the streets until the killer was caught. But he realized that would be pointless. So he tried another tack to get her off the streets.

"How much would it cost to spend the whole night with you?"

"The whole night? For you, I would give a special price: 100 kroners. We could sleep with our arms wrapped around each other." She then flashed a coquettish smile. "And I promise you that I won't let you sleep the whole night through. I'll wake you several times, and I'm sure you will be very happy every time I wake you."

Stebbel was tempted, but he did not have anywhere near 200

kroners on him. Even if he had raced back home and pulled out his savings box from its hidden nook, he knew it would be considerably less than two hundred. He apologized and said he was just asking for some evening in the future. She understood and told him that he could always find her on one of these streets here.

She then turned and headed back the way she was going when he had called out to her. He watched her as she walked slowly, seductively. And still looking so innocent, so vulnerable. For a moment, he even considered arresting her on some trumped-up charge and tossing her into the safety of a police cell for the night. But instead, he just watched her walk away until she disappeared into the next narrow lane over.

* * *

Later, deep in the night, Carina was again out on the streets looking to sell her charms to whatever man was interested in leasing them for an hour or two. But as there was no one else around, she turned and headed into a dark nook. Suddenly a man approached out of the darkness. In a deep, soft voice, he greeted her: "*Servus.*" She smiled and asked him if he was lonely. "Very lonely," he replied.

The man was large, broad-shouldered, with powerful arms. Carina reached out to touch his arm gently, as she had touched Stebbel's earlier in the evening. But the man suddenly lurched at her, seized her throat in his two vice-like hands, squeezing tighter and tighter, he actually lifted her off the ground as he pressed his hands deeper into her neck.

She was choking, her lovely face caught in shock and pain, she tried to use her hands to pull his off her throat, but she was totally outmatched. The man pulled closer to her, his own face only inches away from hers now. It was him, the face in the sketch, the man who had been seen after the first murder. But now the face was filled with unbridled fury.

Carina's hands now dropped, as she knew resistance was useless. The man kept squeezing her throat, getting more and more and more forceful. Somehow, despite the force, she was still alive, still trying to somehow beg for mercy, but choking more and more. At that point, the man looked up, and for the first time noticed that there was a large mirror mounted on a post just above Carina's head. Without any relaxing of his grip, he stared up into the mirror.

And then he saw the face. It had changed – Stebbel now saw his own face, it was his face and his hands that were strangling this lovely young woman. Fear was hung as strongly in his own face as in the girl's.

Suddenly, there was a jolt. He must have hit her body against the post: the mirror came loose and started to crash down onto him. It was coming straight at his face and then it smashed into his face, breaking up into a hundred jagged splinters, and then he heard a screaming. Horrible screaming …

It was Stebbel's own screams, though they were nowhere near as loud as they had just been in the dream. He sat up in his bed, breathing heavily. It was a dream, all a dream, just a very, very bad dream. He felt that he was sweating now, though the bedroom was rather cool. Only gradually did his breathing slow down to normal. And only gradually did the ache in his head start to subside.

He threw his head back onto the pillow and closed his eyes. He wanted to look at the clock near his bedside, but was afraid to. He knew it was late. Much too late.

25

Dörfner was having some trouble with his leg that morning, so he was later getting to the office. That, and the fact that he had stopped off at a nearby bakery for a couple of fresh *Buchteln* sweet buns dusted with cinnamon sugar.

When he arrived, he found Stebbel at his desk, reading Freud's *The Interpretation of Dreams*. Dörfner strode by and stole a peek, then raised his eyebrows.

"That must be a good read. From our revered High Priest of Perversion, no less."

"It's an interesting book, Karl-Heinz. Some fascinating theories. If you like, I'll lend it to you when I'm finished."

"No, thank you. I already know what he says there." Stebbel raised his eyebrows skeptically. "If you dream about meeting a tall woman, you want to have sex with your mother; you dream about a smaller woman, you want to have sex with your sister; you dream about meeting a man, you want to have sex with your brother. And if you dream about flying, you want to have sex with a pigeon."

Stebbel just smiled and shook his head at this.

"Well, I'm right, aren't I?"

"I haven't come to that part yet. I'll let you know when I get there."

"I'll be looking forward to that. In the meantime, we've got ourselves three nasty murders to solve here."

"Yes, I remember something about that."

"So what do we do today? Where do we go from here?"

Stebbel just looked at him helplessly, then shook his head. This deflated Dörfner's light mood immediately.

Where could they go from there? Just sit around and wait for the next time the strangler struck.

* * *

The next murder was not long in coming. In fact, this one came less than a week after Gertrud Prestel was killed. The victim was again a streetwalker, and it occurred at the edge of the redlight district.

Friends in the street trade identified her soon after the pulleys had arrived at the scene: Sonia Dinescu, a Romanian girl from Bukovina, then a border district of the Austro-Hungarian Empire. By the time Stebbel and Dörfner again made the slow trek to the morgue, Dr. Gressler had assembled a roster of facts. He first read from a chart, running down the casual details, such as name, height, and body build.

"Listed age is 22, though I suspect she was lying about that. A lot of workers coming from the provinces do lie about their real age. Anyway, as you're about to see, she looks younger than what's listed in her records."

As Gressler and an assistant eased the slab out, Stebbel turned his back. He had seen enough of these murders. He would just listen to Gressler's rundown and let Dörfner be the visual witness.

"Same *modus operandi*. Almost certainly the same killer. Look at the arrangement of the bruises."

"Not as brutal this time though," Dörfner remarked.

"You're quite right. My guess would be that this one put up little or no resistance, so the killer didn't have to put as much energy into the enterprise."

Without turning to look, Stebbel gave his take. "Or else he's just getting better at his work, and he doesn't need to expend as much energy."

"That's another explanation. Anyway, the chances are extremely high that this is the same killer. The full autopsy report hasn't been completed yet, but I'll get that to you as soon as it's ready."

"Thank you, Herr Doktor. We really need every little scrap we can get."

Gressler's cool scientific demeanor softened a bit as the slab was pushed back into its darkness.

"It must be really difficult for you two, dealing with all these murders. A real string you've got here. And the press raising such a big stink about it. Blaming the police. It must really be difficult."

"It is. Very difficult." Stebbel then started walking away. Dörfner thanked the doctor and joined his partner, moving as quickly as he could with his gimpy leg to catch up. The only communication between them as they left the morgue was an extended look of helplessness.

A short time later, there was a knock at the door of the inspectors' office. It was one of their assigned assistants, announcing that they had a visitor: Dr. Gressler from "down below".

This was not only unusual – it was the first time Gressler had ever paid a visit to their office. Dörfner noted the occasion with a chirpy greeting.

"*Gruss Gott, Herr Doktor*! Did you finally decide to come up from the bowels of the building and enjoy a little bit of the view we enjoy all the time?"

"That as well, Herr Inspector. That as well." At Dörfner's

invitation, Gressler walked over to the window and gazed out. Their view was not onto the Ringstrasse, but was impressive nonetheless.

"Yes, a very inspiring vista. I imagine it's one small compensation for the difficult tasks you have."

He turned and stepped back towards the inspectors' desks.

"But the main reason I came up here was to personally deliver the autopsy report on our latest victim." He placed the report on Stebbel's desk. Dörfner stood and took his post at his partner's shoulder. "There's a very interesting discovery we made. If I may draw your attention to the middle of the second page, gentlemen."

The two inspectors started reading, trying to find what the doctor was referring to. They hoped whatever it was, it would allow them to make a big breakthrough. Stebbel quickly found something interesting, which he pointed out to Dörfner.

"You discovered opium in the victim's bloodstream?"

"A rather significant amount. Which suggests that Frau Dinescu had been indulging in the drug not long before she encountered her killer. And she must have been smoking a substantial amount. She would have been in a deep state of opium intoxication."

"And what would that mean?"

"Well, it explains why there wasn't as much bruising this time. She wasin such a thick opium haze, I wouldn't be surprised if the poor girl was smiling at her assailant until shortly before he put on the final squeeze."

"That must have made him feel good," said Stebbel. "And saved him some effort."

"I imagine it would have," the doctor said.

After another few minutes of discussion and explanation, Doktor Gressler said that he had to get back "to the bowels" to take care of a few other matters. The two inspectors thanked him for bringing the report personally and helping them push their investigations forward a little. Dörfner walked him to the *paternoster*.

When he returned to the office, Stebbel gave him the raised eyebrow salute.

"Opium," Stebbel said.

"I'm familiar with the substance."

"You know what I'm talking about. A prostitute using opium, that points the finger in one direction."

"The Turk?" Stebbel nodded. "Steb, the Turk's not the only pimp in Vienna. Or the only one in town with access to opium."

"Did I say something wrong?"

"I don't know, it just seems that you're anxious to pin everything on him. But I don't think that he has anything to do with this. For one thing, it doesn't make good business sense, and before everything else, the Turk is a businessman."

"Well, you go see the Turk and tell him that his business is in danger because of all the heat caused by these killings. And tell him that until we catch this killer, the heat will just keep getting worse and worse and worse."

"I will take care of that. And I'll ask him to help us in any way he can."

26

Dörfner met the Turk at a café near the Ottoman embassy. Before their coffees arrived, Bahadir raised both hands high and swore that he was not Sonia Dinescu's pimp. He also said he himself did not supply her with the opium. But he did have something juicy to give Dörfner: he had spoken to some of his "associates" and turned up three of Sonia's streetwalker friends who were with her the night she was murdered. And, as a bonus, the Turk had arranged for Dörfner to meet these three friends early that evening, before they started their regular shift on the streets. Stebbel could come along too, if he liked.

Bahadir smiled the smile of a man doing favorable calculations in his head. He knew he could add this to the "Favors" side of his ledger with the Inspector.

The meeting took place at a bar on the scuffed edge of Spittelberg. Knowing that whores had a flexible notion of punctuality, Dörfner himself arrived a little late. The ladies had not yet arrived.

The seedy pub reminded Dörfner of the dives he used to frequent during his army days. Just a few minutes waiting for the three friends to show up reminded him why he didn't miss those days and those dives.

Sonia's three friends arrived together. To warm them up *and* lubricate their tongues, Dörfner offered to buy them all a drink. They were ready to accept some cheap British gin, but Dörfner insisted that they order wine instead. It was, he said, a point of honor for him that he treat ladies well. (But when the barkeep held up the wines on offer, the inspector quickly pointed to the cheapest one.)

One of the friends, who went by the name of Estella, took the lead. She told Dörfner that Sonia had shown up for work already buzzing from an opium-smoking session. She was so clearly out of it, they told her she couldn't perform that evening. After a mish-mashed argument, they convinced her to go back to her room and sleep it off. They walked her to the corner of Siebensteingasse, then saw her head off to her place. And that, they all said with tears, was the last they ever saw of her.

Dörfner was beginning to doubt that this interview was really worth his time, not to mention his outlay on the three glasses of wine. This account was interesting, even touching, if you were in the right frame of mind, but it didn't lend the investigation any new worthwhile information.

But then one of the girls, Marta, added something that was potentially valuable: she had seen some strange guy prowling the area not too long before Sonia showed up for work. The other two girls immediately backed up her recollection.

She went on; she was standing alone then. This guy had started approaching her, but when the other two girls stepped out of the doorway, he stopped, turned and walked off. Most guys, the ladies all agreed, would come up and check out all three and see which one he might like to spend a little time alone with. But this guy seemed to be after something else.

"So what did he look like, this strange guy?" Dörfner asked. The answer he got hit him like an electric jolt.

"He was big ... pretty tall," said Marta.

"And burly? Like me?" As he asked that, Dörfner stood fully upright and threw his shoulders back. The three ladies studied his pose for several moments before one of them answered.

"Even bigger," Estella said, and the other two nodded in agreement.

"Anything else strange about this guy?"

"Oh yes," Marta said. "The singing."

"Singing?"

"Humming really," Estella added. He was humming as he approached Marta, stopped when the other two appeared, but started humming again as he walked off.

"And what was he humming?" Dörfner asked.

* * *

"A waltz?"

"That's what they said. He was humming some waltz tune. They weren't sure which one, but it was one of the popular numbers."

It was the next morning, back in the office, and Dörfner was reporting every detail of the previous evening's meeting – gleaned from either his notes or his memory.

"A waltz. This whole thing is like ... sport to him," Stebbel said in disgust. "He's playing a game, he's having fun. He's killing young women and it's all sport to him. Like dancing a waltz."

"I'm pretty sure it was our guy they were describing. They saw him, but they didn't know who he was."

"Did you show them the picture? Herr Hitler's sketch?"

"*Ja*, but it didn't do any good. All three admitted they didn't see enough of his face to make any reliable identification."

"Well, at least we know that he likes his waltz music. That should narrow it down to just under a million people here in Vienna."

"Sorry; I tried to get as much useful information as I could."

"No, no, you did good work there. I don't think anyone else could have done any better. And we did learn that he leaves the scene when the ladies show up in a group."

"He's always trying to find one who's all alone, no one to protect her."

"Maybe we can convince the streetwalkers to only work in groups of three or four. Tell them it's a matter of their own survival." Stebbel paused. "But I wonder if they would stick to that."

Dörfner shook his head. "They probably couldn't take the competition. You know: one whore offering a cut-rate price and snatching a john from her partner."

"Well, we certainly don't have enough hooks in the department to look after their well-being. That's for sure."

"Of course, we could always get the Imperial Guard to escort them around. The way I hear it, most of those ginks do nothing for most of the day, then do a little more nothing at night."

"Good point." Suddenly, Stebbel stopped. He looked up. "Yes – the Imperial Guard."

"I was only joking, Steb. There's no possibility that – "

"No, I don't mean that. It's … the Imperial Guard." He pushed back his chair and started tapping his desk nervously. He stared into space as if trying to focus on an image forming in the air. Dörfner just stood watching, a little concerned.

"Yes, that's it: the Imperial Guard." He spun around. "Now I remember where I've seen that face before."

"What face?"

"The one in the sketch. Herr Hitler's. It was the Imperial Guard."

"What??"

"A few years ago, I was at a special event at the Hofburg. There were several of us from the division there. When we got to the palace, they put us into this one room and assigned a handful of imperial guardsman to look after us, make sure we behaved ourselves. And … and one of those guardsman was, I believe, the man we've been looking for."

"You're shitting me!"

"No. No, I'm not. I'm most certainly not." Stebbel jumped up and clapped his hands in triumph, like a joyous child. He then started walking around the office excitedly. "Yes, the more I think back on that evening, the more I think we've found our suspect. Or at least we know where to find him."

"We just go and check out the Imperial Guard?"

"That's it. I think we've got our *big* breakthrough. Thanks to you, Herr Colleague. Thanks to you."

27

It was not at all difficult arranging an appointment to speak to the official Master of the Guards. Evidently, the palace itself had taken an interest in the case and wished to see everything cleared up as soon as possible. So when Dörfner explained that they needed to check on somebody in the guards, an appointment was set up with no further explanations needed.

They arrived mid-afternoon at one of the side gates. As they stepped in, a guardsman stepped out of his booth adjacent to the gate.

"Can I help you gentlemen?" he asked. But the way he said it, it came off as more of a challenge than an offer of assistance.

Dörfner knew this type all too well. He decided the easiest way to proceed was to show this fellow they actually outranked him. They opened up their police IDs and thrust them forward.

"Yes, we're from the Vienna Police Department. I'm Inspector Dörfner and this is Inspector Stebbel. We're here on privileged business. We have an appointment with Guido Albern."

This spun the gatekeeper around 180 degrees. "Oh, yes, right. You're ..." He picked up a sheet with various things written on it and read through too quickly. "You're Inspectors Stebbel and Doofner."

Stebbel stepped in here. "Stebbel and Dörfner. Would it be at all possible for you to hurry this up a bit. This is a very busy afternoon for us and we need to see Herr Albern urgently."

"We're investigating some very serious matters," Dörfner added for emphasis.

"Of course, of course. Indeed. Let me send you right along to Herr Albern." He then grabbed the tube whistle hanging from his shoulders, turned around and shot out an ear-splitting signal. This brought a young guardsman cadet trotting towards them.

"*Jawohl*, Herr Corporal?" He snapped a salute.

"Take these two gentleman to Herr Albern. And be quick about it, will you. These men are very busy and they can't afford for you to move at your usual drag-tail pace. They're here on important business."

"*Jawohl*, Herr Corporal." Then, turning to the two visitors. "Gentlemen."

He led the two visitors to a squat building sitting a short distance away, on a small hill. He guided them to the office of the Master of the Guards, Albern, tapped on the door and held it opened for the visitors when Albern responded.

Albern had been anticipating this visit, but he wasn't sure what the two inspectors wanted. Introductions and other preliminaries were kept to a bare minimum, and then the inspectors got down to business.

Stebbel pulled Hitler's sketch out of its protective envelope. He reached over and handed it to Albern.

"Do you know this man?"

Albern studied the drawing for a short time before speaking. "Brunner. Arnold Brunner." He looked up. "Is that right?"

"Actually, we have no idea who it is. That's why we came to you. All we know is that he was most probably in the Imperial Guard. You say his name is … Brunner?"

"Yes, Arnold Brunner."

"You're sure?"

"Sure? Well, not so sure that I'd want to bet my pension on it."
He took another look, his brow crunching tightly as he did. "But it
does look a lot like Brunner."

"No other member of the Guard that it could be?"

"None that I know of."

"Is Herr Brunner on duty right now?"

"On duty?" He gave a slightly embarrassed laugh. "No, of
course not. Brunner left the service about a year and a half ago."

"Oh?"

"He was dismissed actually. He had been caught drinking while
on duty several times and even got into a few fights with other
members of the Guard."

"I see."

"Yeah, one of his fights, the other man had to spend about a
week in the hospital. Well, you know, Brunner is a big guy, pretty
strong."

"Big, broad hands?"

"I guess so. Anyway, he's not someone you'd want to pick a fight
with. But according to the reports, Brunner himself started most of
those fights. Or at least took a tense situation and pushed it into a
good dust-up."

"So he was dismissed ... a year and a half ago?"

"*Unofficially* dismissed. The official records say that he received
an honorable discharge. On medical grounds." He sputtered out a
cynical laugh. "Yeah, I guess you could say he had his fair share
of medical problems. Not too many of his fellow guardsmen were
happy to hear that, I can tell you. They all thought he should just
be tossed out on his tin ear. But somebody up there decided that he
should go out with an honorable." He pointed towards the main
palace building.

Dörfner reacted immediately. "Someone in the emperor's inner circle?"

Albern shook his head. "I don't think they paid any attention to the matter." He leaned his head back and tried to recall the rumors spilling out at that time.

"No, I think they were saying it was someone in the Interior Ministry. The Imperial Guard comes under them, you know. Or else, it was somebody in the Justice Ministry ... or the privy council, some group like that. Anyway, our friend Brunner is sitting back somewhere collecting a nice pension that I'll probably have to wait twenty years to draw. Maybe I should start drinking on duty, then pound on a few of the cadets out there."

"Sitting around somewhere? Do you have any idea where that somewhere might be?"

"Excuse me?"

Stebbel stepped in. "Do you have a current address for Herr Brunner?"

Albern shook his head to show total ignorance. "I always assumed he went back to his home town. He was from Kärten originally. Give me a few minutes, I'll see if I can find an address for you."

He then stood, went to a shiny grey file cabinet and started looking for Brunner's file. While he was at that task, Stebbel and Dörfner exchanged charged looks. This interview was turning out even better than they had hoped. They both felt the investigation had taken a huge leap forward.

Stebbel pulled out his small notebook and started writing down a message. But before he could finish and slip it to Dörfner, Albern spun around clutching a file.

"OK, I found it. So let's see what we have." Settling back in his chair, he opened to the back of the file. His face grew intense as he read the yellowing sheets.

"Hmm."

That 'hmm' had the two inspectors sitting like patients waiting for a bad diagnosis from the doctor. As if Albern could sense this, he added another 'hmm'. And then another.

"It would seem that we have no address for former Guardsman Brunner." The faces of the two policemen dropped two storeys, in syncopation.

"It looks like everything has been sent to his sister."

He looked at the next sheet and nodded. "Yes, all official correspondence to Brunner was sent to his sister's address. We have no other address for him." He looked back up. "Sorry."

"Where does this sister live?"

Albern shrugged, as if the answer should have been obvious to anyone. "Here in Vienna. In the Geblergasse."

Both policemen immediately looked like they were men who had been drowning, then had a life preserver thrown to them and been hauled out of the sea.

"Could you please write that address out for us. That could prove very helpful in our investigation."

"Of course, of course." Albern grabbed a sheet of paper and carefully started writing down the name and address of Arnold Brunner's sister. Then, as if the question had come to him for the first time, he looked up and asked. "By the way – what are you investigating here?"

Dörfner took a deep breath. Stebbel stared at the muster master for two beats before thinking of the perfect answer.

"We're investigating people who may be cheating on government pensions – receiving more than they deserve."

As Stebbel and Dörfner reached the same side gate they had entered the Hofburg by, the guardsman saluted them and held the entrance gate for them. "I hope that your meeting was very successful, gentlemen."

Dörfner nodded. "Yes, very successful." They then returned his salute, and with ear-to-ear smiles, strolled out. It suddenly seemed especially bright that afternoon. Dörfner was especially cheery: he insisted they go to the nearby Demel's Café and celebrate.

28

Two days later, the two inspectors climbed into a police squad car with three other officers, street officers fully armed. They travelled to the Währing district, where Frau Katherina Keuler, the sister of Arnold Brunner, lived in a third-floor flat.

Frau Keuler was a widow, a status she had held for longer than she had been a wife. Her husband, a government railroad worker, had been killed in a freak accident during a storm some years earlier. Since then, his widow had been collecting a respectable pension from the state railway system.

The police came unannounced: if Brunner himself was up there, they wanted to catch him by surprise. But if he wasn't and they needed to interrogate his sister, they wanted to catch her fully off-guard.

They rang the front door bell, waited semi-patiently until Frau Keuler buzzed them in, and they all entered. The three hooks waited on the landing below, guns already drawn. Dörfner, who had told them where to place themselves, joined Stebbel and the two inspectors went to the door, rapped a few times, and were met by a confounded Frau Katerina Keuler. She was even more confounded when they introduced themselves as police inspectors.

"Police? But I have done nothing wrong."

"Of course not. But we just need to ask you some questions."

"I'm not very good at answering questions. Maybe you should

ask somebody else."

"Believe me, Frau Keuler, you are the best one to answer the questions we have." She nodded, with a deep measure of resignation.

Reluctantly, she invited them in. Actually, they invited themselves in and Frau Keuler acceded to their self-invitation. It was clear they had caught the poor lady totally off-guard and she was ready to accede to just about any request they made, as long as it was backed up by a badge.

Her parlor looked like a shelter for abandoned furniture and ugly knick-knacks. The furnishings reminded Stebbel of the flat where he now lived, back when it was the home of his aunt and uncle. The same kind of stolid and ultimately dreary stuff dominated the room.

Frau Keuler stood at an angle from her two unexpected guests, eyeing them cautiously. Stebbel fixed her with a sympathetic stare while Dörfner looked around the room and then peeked into the next room over, the dining room. To keep Dörfner in one place where she could keep an eye on them, she offered the policemen seats and then took one herself. Stebbel took his seat. but Dörfner first moved his slightly to the left so that the two men were now on different sides of Frau Keuler, with her square in the middle. This placement was strategic: by keeping her focus divided and then hitting her with questions from either side, they could keep the widow nicely off-balance. This gave them the best chance of squeezing out information that she might not be too willing to give them.

With their first questions, as innocuous as they were, it was clear that they had made the woman fully uncomfortable, even there in the sanctuary of her own home.

Stebbel felt bad about this whole process; he realized they were psychologically tormenting this obviously fragile woman, but he conceded that it was necessary. They needed to get all the information they could about her brother, especially where he was at that moment. The intense discomfort of this woman was of little concern when measured against the lives of any young woman out there on the streets who might become the strangler's next victims.

After a round of warm-up questions, they got down to the real task. Stebbel opened the probe. "Frau Keuler, we're here to find out about your brother, Arnold."

"Arnold? Is he in any trouble?"

"We hope not, but … that's why we need to ask these questions. He's not here right now, is he?"

"Here? No, of course not."

Dörfner then jumped in. "He is your brother, isn't he? You're on good terms with him, aren't you?"

"Yes, yes, of course. We only have each other now. Our parents are both dead, my husband … I've always got along with Arnold. I protected him when he was young. We remain very close."

"Do you know where he happens to be right now? Where he's staying?"

She looked from one inspector to the other. "No."

"No?"

"You're very close with your brother, but you don't know where he happens to be staying?"

She spoke very slowly, deliberately. "I … don't … know … where … he … is these days."

"OK, good. But when was the last time you saw your brother?"

"Oh, I don't know. A week ago … two weeks?"

"Do you get a lot of people coming to visit you, Frau Keuler?"

"No. I live a quiet life. I'm a widow."

"Of course. But if you don't get a lot of visitors, shouldn't you have a better recollection of when was the last time you saw your own brother – with whom you 'remain very close'?"

"Alright … two weeks ago. Arnold was last here almost two

weeks ago. A week and … a few days, I guess. We had dinner together. I made a *tafelspitz*."

"Oh, I love *tafelspitz*. My colleague, Inspector Stebbel, he loves it too. Maybe you should invite us over for dinner one night. Have your brother there, too."

Frau Keuler was clearly flustered by the impudence of this self-invitation. But the look on her face suggested that her embarrassment was compounded as she wondered if she had somehow invited this impudence. Riled but confused, she tried to show the policemen they weren't welcome for dinner at any time.

"We are private people, my brother and I. We don't have much social life. Very few guests."

"I see. Sorry."

By that point, they obviously had the poor widow squirming in a corner. They decided to press their advantage and hit her with a few more questions that might wring out of her just where her brother was holed up … or at least how often he came into Vienna. Unfortunately, they weren't able to find out much. But Stebbel then decided to pursue another tack.

"Frau Keuler, your brother is not married, is that correct?"

"Yes."

"Was he ever married?"

"No, he has always been a bachelor."

"Why is that?"

"He never found the right woman, I guess."

"Well, there is no right woman – or right man. You finally settle for what you can get. Am I right?"

"I am not an expert on these matters. You should ask someone else."

Stebbel continued, hoping to pin his theories, borrowed from Freud, onto that man Brunner.

"Frau Keuler, I have to ask you: did your brother have trouble with women? Did he have trouble ... building relationships with women?"

And that's where the inspectors hit the knot of resistance. Frau Keuler, until that moment utterly shy and defenseless, suddenly shot back with a sting in her voice.

"Gentlemen, I do not think this is a proper question to be asking me. Or asking any lady. This is a private matter, and you have no right to come in here and ask me such things."

"But if – "

"Gentlemen – if you are at all deserving of that name – we should go on to other questions or you might want to call it a day."

"Yes, you're right. Let's bring it to a close here. There's little more to say now."

The two inspectors stood. Frau Keuler looked as if they had both been standing on her chest and had just stepped off. She started resuming her normal breathing patterns. But Dörfner then momentarily knocked her off stride again.

"Excuse me, but can I use your telephone?"

"What?"

He nodded. "Your telephone. May I use your telephone? There's an important call I need to make." He pointed up at an old clock staring down into the room. "I should have made it ten minutes ago already. So I would be very grateful if – "

"I don't have a telephone."

"No telephone?"

"I'm a widow. I don't have much use of a telephone. But one of my neighbors upstairs has one. Or, if it's so urgent, the drapery shop right across the road has a telephone."

Dörfner smiled with artificial sweetness. "Oh ... it's not really that urgent, I suppose. I can wait till we're back at police headquarters to make the call." Frau Keuler nodded as a look of relief started flowing back into her features.

Stebbel now took the lead again. "As there's nothing else to ask you, I guess it is time that we took our leave." He paused. "But I think we should give you our official visiting cards."

They each had their cards at the ready, which they handed to Frau Keuler. "You'll find the telephone number of our office at police headquarters there. At the bottom. Now, if you have any more information about your brother, say if he contacts you, you should let us know as soon as possible."

"Immediately, I would say."

"Yes, immediately is the best way."

"And it is our duty as servants of the crown to remind you, dear lady, that withholding important information from the police is itself a crime. If you should hide anything from us, you will be subject to prosecution. And then probably a prison sentence."

"Prison?"

"Oh yes. But don't worry – it will be a woman's prison. I'm told that they are not quite as bad as the men's prisons."

Dörfner then took a pause, to allow the threat to seep into her heart. "But as long as you are honest and cooperative with the police, it's not something that you have to worry about."

"No, not at all."

"Anyway, you have our cards and our names. If your brother does contact you, please hurry upstairs to your neighbor with the telephone. And call us from there. We will be ..."

"Very grateful.

"Yes."

The two policemen then gave their most respectful head bows and started out the door. The not very merry widow stared at the cards and wondered what she should do with them. Stebbel was already on the landing and Dörfner halfway out the door when she called out in as loud a tone as her soft voice allowed.

"You have to understand … Arnold is not a bad person. He just sometimes gets into some trouble. It's not really him though. He had many problems as a boy. I often had to protect him."

Stebbel took two steps back to the doorway. "We understand, Frau Keuler. And we also want to help your brother as much as we can. We do."

The two inspectors then took another bow and left. They were down to the next landing when they heard the door close heavily behind them.

When they reached the next landing, where their backup waited, Stebbel put a finger to his lips and pointed down the stairs. All five policeman then headed to the front door of the building.

After they got outside, Stebbel informed the hooks that they would have to stand watch for an hour or two. They needed to be sure that Arnold Brunner did not pay a "surprise" visit to his sister in that time. If he did arrive, they were to hold him there, at gunpoint if necessary, and notify headquarters that they had Brunner in custody.

"And how will we know him, Herr Inspector?"

Dörfner answered. "He's … big. Bulky … strong. And he's got dark hair … dark brown probably." He turned for corroboration to Stebbel, who nodded. "He's not a bad looking guy, a bit on the handsome side actually. But it's an ugly handsome, if you know what I mean."

The three junior policemen shook their heads. Dörfner was at a loss to explain what he'd just said.

Stebbel stepped in. "That means he doesn't look very warm or friendly. He's not someone you'd strike up a conversation with in a café."

The two loupes then gave the hooks a few more instructions

about what to do if someone looking vaguely like that should appear at the front door of the building they'd just left. They also told the hooks they should keep the police vehicle with them and drive back when their reinforcements arrived. Stebbel promised to arrange a second shift of surveillance officers as soon as they got back to headquarters. The two inspectors said they themselves would take a taxi back to headquarters.

But on their way to find a taxi, they found a convenient café and dropped in for refueling and a post-mortem of the session. Along the way, they touched on the interrogation.

"Think she was lying?" Dörfner asked.

"Maybe. At least about some things. We'll just have to sift out the lies from the truth."

By this time, they had entered the café and started looking for a secluded place where they could conduct a summation of what they'd just discovered. Dörfner, already in a buoyant mood, was even more cheered when he threw a peek at the café's pastry chest and was greeted by an imposing four-storied chocolate cake with lush cocoa cream fillings. He rubbed both palms together and asked the counter staff to slice him a generous wedge of that delight. Wiley intimidation followed by chocolate cream cake – it was looking more and more like into an afternoon of one sweet triumph after another.

Dörfner and Stebbel took up their post in a corner of the café. "Well, that went quite well, didn't it? I thought we were really working as a team. Partners, you know. In perfect timing; like with a waltz."

"Yes, we were … rather effective there."

Dörfner gave an apologetic smile. "I know you weren't totally happy with how we managed to be so effective."

"I … had misgivings." He shook his head slightly. "I don't feel that comfortable using our position to bully a hapless widow."

"A widow trying to protect a brother who has this quaint hobby of killing women."

Stebbel sighed. "That's why I did it. We had to. That's why we worked together so well."

"The only problem now is that she might get to a telephone somewhere and call her brother."

"If *he* has a telephone."

"Good point. Anyway, I think we put a good fright into the dear lady. She might not even dare to call her brother, as much as she might want to."

"I guess we'll just have to see if blood is thicker than adrenaline."

"Adren ... What the hell is that?"

"Adrenaline is a natural hormone the body secretes at higher levels when fear strikes."

"Oh yeah? Did you study Chemistry at university?"

"Biology. Two courses. My first year at the university, I was a medical student."

"A medical student? No shit!"

Stebbel shrugged. "It was my father really. He wanted me to be a doctor. But by the end of that first year, I knew I could never be a doctor."

"Why?"

"I ..." Stebbel stopped, considered whether he should answer honestly, then chuckled slightly. "I couldn't stand the sight of blood."

"Couldn't stand the sight of blood? So you became a cop? And then you got yourself assigned to the Homicide Division?" Dörfner produced one of his large, full-bellied laughs. "You are really funny, Stebbel. You should sit down one day and write a book. A funny one. People like funny books. Yours will be a roaring success, I'm sure."

"Or maybe I'll just put all the stories together and go on the stage. I'll perform it in cabaret."

"I'd go to see you every night."

"So maybe that's just what I'll do that when this is all over. I think I may need a change of profession."

* * *

Back at headquarters, the two inspectors arranged for replacements for the surveillance trio they had left behind at Frau Keuler's place.

Stebbel then took out the casebook and the two loupes sat down to reconstruct the interview they'd just conducted as close to accuracy as they could. At the end of the reconstruction, Stebbel added an editorial commentary, as was his wont.

"Following upon this interview and everything that Frau Keuler said – and didn't say – I am now even more convinced that Arnold Brunner, one-time imperial guardsman, is indeed our vicious killer. I further believe that Herr Brunner suffers from severe personality disorders, and that these killings are a form of harsh revenge. He evidently blames women for some wrongs that were done to him years ago."

He finished the sentence and capped his pen. Dörfner, who had moved to the other side of the room to pour himself some mineral water, came back and asked to see what his partner had just written. Stebbel could hardly refuse him, as they were partners on this case and the reports in that book were supposedly opinions shared by both men. He slid the book towards Dörfner.

After reading the addendum, Dörfner nodded.

"Are you in agreement? With *everything* I wrote there?" Stebbel asked.

"Of course. As much of it as I can understand." He then squeezed out his impish smile. "One thing though …"

"Yes?"

"Don't you think you should, at the end, write 'with deep gratitude to Doktor Sigmund Freud, my mentor and idol.' " Dörfner's smile then exploded into a laugh. Stebbel managed a half-smile, took back the casebook, closed it tightly and placed it back in the drawer.

Now almost content, he leaned back in his chair. Outside their office, the sky had darkened with approaching rain, but Stebbel felt there were finally some rays of light streaming into the Spittelberg Strangler case. And in spite of whatever his highly opinionated colleague felt, Stebbel *was* deeply grateful for the assistance of Professor Doktor Sigmund Freud.

29

The surveillance at Frau Keuler's home extended into the early afternoon of the next day. Three different teams took up the watch in shifts. But the only male who appeared during that whole time was a late middle-aged man of meager build who lived in one of the flats above Frau Keuler. Stebbel looked over the brief reports of all three teams and clenched his lips.

"Do you think maybe she did get in touch with Brunner and warned him to stay away?" Dörfner asked.

"I have no idea. But it doesn't really make any difference, does it? All that really matters is whether we get our hands on him or not. And at present, we don't have him in our custody. He's still out there. Somewhere."

Dörfner shrugged. "Maybe he's been reading the same newspapers we have, and decided that these sidewalks have become too hot for his feet. Maybe he's already left Vienna, and he's holing up somewhere else. Maybe he even … caught a train, went abroad."

"Maybe. Though I think it's more likely he would have read those newspapers and felt quite flattered at those comparisons to Jack the Ripper. And now he's planning to become even more notorious than old Jack."

"What we need … what we really need is to get his picture posted in every police station in town, let every cop know who it is we're looking for. It can't be just the two of us running around with that one sketch, showing it to people who will forget his face ten minutes later."

"You're right. You know, you're all too right." Stebbel's mind was then working quickly. "Wait a minute – didn't our Herr Hitler say that was a copy he was giving us? That he still had the original?"

"Yeah, now that you mention it … I think he did. I think he did."

"OK, so we need to get in touch with Hitler and ask him to make more copies for us. As many as he can make. Remember, he said that it's easy for him."

"You think he'll do it?"

"We'll pay him. He says he's a professional artist. Well, he doesn't seem to be floating in a sea of financial success as an artist. So we'll offer him a fee for every copy he makes." Stebbel nodded at this own idea. "We have an address for him, right?"

"*Ja*, he's at the hostel there on Meldemannstrasse. Number 27, I think it is."

"I know the building. So we'll send someone around to arrange another meeting. We'll see if he can make those copies for us. Then we can distribute them here at headquarters, as well as at other divisions."

Dörfner agreed whole-heartedly with the plan. They then headed over to Rautz to clear the idea with him and then get him to requisition some funds to pay the struggling artist for his work.

*　*　*

Although he was fully unaware of the commission he was about to receive from the Vienna constabulary, it had already been an unexpectedly successful day for Adolf Hitler the artist. In the late morning, he had set up at the Danube canal and managed to sell several of his cheesy watercolors to tourists. In the afternoon, he had gone to see two of his regular clients and his success there was much more thrilling.

First he had gone to see Jakob Altenberg for his regular weekly visit. He knew Altenberg was running low of sample paintings and he expected to sell him a few. But much to his surprise, Altenberg asked for a dozen as his business had been brisk that week and he expected it to stay that way through the late spring home-remodeling period.

Hitler's next stop was to Samuel Morgenstern. Samuel and his wife Emma ran a popular glazier *cum* frame shop in the Liechtensteinstrasse. As Hitler entered the shop, Morgenstern gave him a friendly salute. He then came around to the end of the main counter while Emma and two assistants tended to the needs of the customers already there.

Business had obviously been good that week for the Morgensterns as well, and Samuel was in an especially buoyant mood. Though Hitler had just dropped in on a spec call to see if Morgenstern needed anything, his long-time client immediately said he'd like to see what Hitler had to offer. The young artist quickly pulled out the remaining pieces from his leather case. Morgenstern started going through the paintings rapidly, then selected seven of the ones he thought his customers would find appealing.

None of the customers of shopkeepers like Altenberg, Morgenstern or Herr Schiefer were actually purchasing the paintings as such. They were only buying the frames. The paintings of unknown and threadbare artists such as Hitler were inserted into the frames to let customers get an idea of what those handsome frames might look like when filled with a painting. But when they purchased the frames, they got the paintings as a little extra.

The shopkeepers didn't really know what the customers would do with those frame-fillers when they got home and put in the paintings that were actually hung in their homes. They suspected that many of them simply used the sample artwork to wrap garbage before disposing of it in municipal bins.

But that day, after selecting his seven frame-fillers, Morgenstern went through the other paintings Hitler had laid out on the counter. Three of them caught his eye; these he held up to a better light and inspected closely. He started nodding slowly and Hitler had no idea what was going through his mind.

Morgenstern turned back to his "house artist" and smiled broadly. "My friend, I would like to buy these three paintings from you. But not to put in the frames I sell here. I want to keep these for myself, for my own private collection."

Hitler didn't know how to respond. In fact, at first he thought Morgenstern was making a light joke at his expense. But then he read the face more closely and saw that Morgenstern was sincere: he actually wanted the paintings. He would hang two of them, Viennese street scenes, in his shop here and another one, a portrait of a young girl, in his home.

Morgenstern then explained: he felt that Hitler had made quite an advance as an artist. Hitler had always been known as a competent craftsman, but his paintings were always seen as hopelessly superficial. That was one of the reasons given for his two rejections from Vienna's art academy. But with these new paintings, which Hitler had actually done within the past month, he had clearly made a breakthrough.

"You've managed to catch something deeper here, my friend. These two street scenes … here you've found another dimension, a richer perception of the scenes. And in this girl's face, the way she holds her head and her shoulders … damn, I think you've really caught the soul of your subject. Most of your portraits, I must say, don't seem true at all. But here you've shown you're really able to plumb the human spirit and bring that into the painting."

Hitler was so exhilarated by this unexpected praise that he offered Morgenstern the three last paintings at a bargain rate. The shopkeeper accepted immediately and even threw in a few extra kroners to encourage this new turn in the young man's art.

As he left the shop, Hitler was bursting with joy and energy. In fact, he bounded down the street for the first few minutes and even did a little dance of triumph at one corner when he was sure no one would be looking.

As tragic as the death of that young woman in the Spittelberg alley was, Hitler felt that the whole experience – banging into her killer and then discovering her still warm dead body – had unleashed something within him. As Morgenstern realized, Hitler was now becoming the serious artist he always knew he was destined to be.

That, anyway, is what he thought on that day of one fine triumph after another.

30

The two inspectors decided it was time to share some of the latest developments with the husband of the first victim, the most powerful and wealthiest of the survivors.

They met again at von Klettenburg's *pied á terre*. But this time, it was in the secondary dining area just off the main salon. The *Geheimrat* had arranged for tea, coffee and pastries to be served.

"Do try the cakes. They're from Demel's – special order, prepared only this morning."

"Thank you," said Stebbel as Dörfner was helping himself to three of the pastries.

Small talk was kept to a minimum as they didn't have a common cache of topics. Most of what talk was passed about involved the pastries themselves and how delectable they were.

Finally, Herr von Klettenburg pulled back the curtain. "You said you had some news. Regarding the investigation, I believe."

Stebbel placed his cup back on the table. "Yes. We think we … may have a suspect in the crimes."

Von Klettenburg's cup stopped midway on its journey to his lips. He was obviously caught completely off guard by this. "A suspect, you say?"

Dörfner briskly nodded, almost spilling his plate as he did. "A member of the Imperial Guard."

"The Imperial Guard? At the Hofburg?" He took a full sip of his tea, almost as a way of helping to swallow this news. "What … What's the man's name? It's even possible I may have heard of him."

"I'm afraid we can't divulge that. Not just yet. As my colleague said, at the moment, he's just a suspect. He might not even be involved at all. So it wouldn't be fair for us to … name him yet."

"Of course. I understand. But what makes him a suspect?"

"There was a witness."

"A witness?"

Stebbel nodded. "To Frau von Klettenburg's murder."

"Someone saw my wife being murdered??"

"No, but he saw someone fleeing the scene. Had a collision with the man actually. So he happened to get a prolonged look at that man. Our suspect."

"I see. I see. This is all … so … remarkable. I … I'm so grateful that you came and shared this news with me.' He took a few troubled breaths. "I was beginning to harbor doubts that you would ever find the man involved. And now, what you're saying is … my dear wife may actually find justice. We may bring this fiend to justice." He rushed another swallow of his tea. "This is splendid news."

They then traded other bits of news and observations. Both inspectors turned down the offer of a second cup of tea. They also said they couldn't eat any more cakes at that point, but von Klettenburg insisted they take most of the remaining assortment along with them, to enjoy later. Stebbel obliged by having two of them wrapped up in a paper serviette. Dörfner enthusiastically agreed to take along the remaining half dozen or so.

This time, Von Klettenburg himself escorted them to the front door. As they shook hands and bade goodbye, the *Geheimrat* held onto the hands of both men a bit longer than even a well-trained Viennese gentleman normally would.

"And I want to thank you once again, gentleman. Both for having made a significant breakthrough here and also for taking the trouble to come here and share this news with me. I feel that two large stones have just been removed from me: one that was hanging around my neck, the other lodged around my heart."

A servant waited at the lift, and he escorted the two policemen back down to the main entrance. He made a modest bow as he opened the door and watched them leave. Their exit was more assured this time, suggesting two skilled craftsmen proud of the assignment they had just carried out rather successfully.

As they walked back the long way, through the park, Dörfner remarked on the fact that von Klettenburg did seem more upset about his wife's murder this time. He actually showed the wounds within. Stebbel immediately agreed.

"I think the first time we met him ... he still hadn't fully absorbed the loss. Didn't absorb it emotionally, I mean. He was still in a later stage of shock probably."

"A week after the murder?"

Stebbel nodded. "I believe so. It's possible that shock is ... the way we protect ourselves when the horror of an event would be too much if we took it all in at once. The shock acts like a drug, a sedative. After it finally wears off, we can deal with the full pain, the grief finally. And maybe sometimes it ... takes a few weeks for us to embrace the pain and swallow the grief."

"*Mein Gott*, Stebbel – you're beginning to sound like a crazy man. I think you've been reading too much of that Freud fellow. You'd better be careful, you know – reading a lot of that stuff can itself make you go mad."

"Nonsense."

"No, I'm being serious now. I was even speaking to some doctor once about something like this. He was the one who confirmed it for me: reading about all these crazy things and how the mind can get itself all twisted around eventually twists your own mind around."

"I'll remember that the next time I'm tempted to open one of Doktor Freud's books."

"Good." Dörfner snorted his snort of semi-victory.

"Anyway, I was glad to see von Klettenburg suffering there.' He shook his head. "I don't mean I was glad to see him suffering, of course. But he seemed ... I guess, more human today. I felt more sympathy for him. I could almost like the guy seeing him today."

"Yes," Stebbel said. "It's another new chapter."

"Now we only need to catch that swine who killed his wife."

Stebbel turned to his partner, but the only response he could provide was a slow nod.

31

The inspectors weren't back in their office for more than a few minutes when one of their assistants came in and reported that they'd conveyed the message to Herr Hitler and he said he would be in by four o'clock. Stebbel looked out at the clock in the corridor. That gave them barely an hour. But that was no problem, since they were just preparing a simple business deal. They doubted that the struggling artist would be willing, or able, to turn them down.

Hitler arrived a few minutes minute past four, flushed and his hair all a-muss. He apologized profusely for being late. The inspectors told him that he wasn't late and that they were grateful that he was able to turn up at short notice.

Neither Stebbel nor Dörfner found small talk with Hitler easy, so they moved quickly to the business at hand.

"Herr Hitler, you told us that the sketch of the killer you gave us was a copy from your original."

"That is correct, Herr Inspector."

"And you can make other copies, is that true?

"Yes, indeed."

"Excellent. We would like to commission you to make additional copies of the killer's face. You will, of course, be paid a reasonable fee for your work."

"And what ... do you consider reasonable, gentlemen?"

"Three kroners a copy?"

"Three?"

"Well then, let's say four kroners. Four kroners for each copy you give us."

Suddenly, a smile spread across Hitler's face as far as it could reach. It was the first time the policemen had seen Hitler really smile. Stebbel was just taking stabs in the dark with the price, but they seemed to have hit the right one.

"And how many copies would you like?"

"Oh, let's say ... at least six. Maybe as many as ten. Or even a dozen if that's possible."

Hitler started doing some quick calculations in his head. He shook his head in delighted disbelief. He was about to become a financially successful artist.

"And when do you need them by?"

"As soon as possible. We need them to ... distribute to other police officers. We think this will speed up our capture of this killer."

"Of course, of course. Yes, I see that this is an important assignment." Hitler paused for a few more moments as he finished up his calculations.

"Gentlemen ... considering the importance of this work, I am willing to push all my other commissions back so that I can concentrate on getting these sketches made for you. I will begin the work this very evening. I think it imperative that all of us do our part in capturing this fiend.

"You can rely on me, Inspectors. I will have your copies ready within a day or two." The two loupes looked quite happy to hear this. "How should I deliver them to you?"

They then worked out the details of delivery. Hitler was to drop off all his copies to the division. If Stebbel or Dörfner were in, he could hand them over personally. If not, he could simply leave them with the duty officer at the reception desk. He only had to stipulate that they were to be kept for either Stebbel or Dörfner. After they received the copies, they would issue a funds requisition form, and Hitler could pick up his fees two days later.

Everyone seemed satisfied with this arrangement, and the three shook hands on it. Hitler left the office beaming. His saunter down the corridor to the lifts was almost like a victory dance.

The inspectors were also quite happy; they felt that things were moving a little more quickly towards a resolution of the strangler case. They now knew that the sketch was not just some fantasy, that it had put them on the trail of the man who was, most likely, the brutal murderer who had become their obsession.

*　*　*

Stebbel turned the visitor's card over in his hands, as if there might be some clue, some further identification, perhaps something scratched into a corner at the back, or maybe written in invisible ink.

He read the name: Lorenz Bastian. It meant nothing to him. But the officer at reception insisted that the card had been left for him that morning. Also, the young man who had dropped off the card included a message: Herr Bastian would call the inspector at his desk shortly before noon.

Stebbel glanced up at the wall clock. It was now ten minutes to noon. For Stebbel, that qualified as shortly before noon. So when would this call be coming? He was starting to feel some pressure in his bladder, but was afraid to dash out to the toilet and not be there when the call from this Herr Bastian came through.

At two minutes to twelve, the phone on Stebbel's desk began to ring. He was about to grab it gruffly and answer. But he decided that the best way of playing Herr Bastian's game was to wait for the phone to ring four times, pick up the receiver and then bring the speaker slowly to his face.

"Inspector Stebbel."

"Yes, Inspector. So nice to speak with you finally. My name is Lorenz Bastian."

"I've seen your card, Herr Bastian."

"Then we should meet."

"If possible."

"Oh, I think you should make it possible. Shall we say … in an hour's time? At the west entrance to the Volksgarten? That is, I believe, not far from your office."

"Yes, that's correct. But let me ask you something before I agree to this meeting. Who are you exactly?"

"For the moment, let's just say a visitor from Berlin. Who has some information that you will find very interesting."

"What kind of information?"

"Very interesting. If we can meet there at the park at 1 p.m., I think you will definitely find the meeting valuable."

Stebbel looked up at the wall clock again. "Can we say 1:15?"

"We can. So, I shall see you there at the entrance to your Volksgarten in just over an hour."

"Yes. How will I know you?"

"I will be standing at the west entrance to the Volksgarten waiting for you." There was a teasing pause. "Oh, and I have a dark blue suit. And am, of course, extremely handsome." At that, Bastian let out a generous laugh at his own joke.

"OK. I'm sure I'll find you."

Stebbel arrived at the Volksgarten park, west entrance, at 1:10. As he approached, he saw a tall man in a blue suit. The man sported a large handlebar moustache looping over a well-rehearsed smile. He dipped his head in a slight bow as the inspector came closer.

"Herr Stebbel, if I'm not mistaken."

"You're not." They shook hands.

"Shall we take a bench and have a pleasant little chat. That bench right over there looks inviting; nice and sunny, you know."

"Fine." As they started walking, Stebbel asked, "Where are you from, Herr Bastian? You said Berlin?"

Bastian nodded. "From Duisburg originally. But now I'm a devout Berliner, through and through. And you?"

"From Innsbruck originally. But now, a Viennese, through and through. Or 'rotten to the core' as some others like to say."

"I can assure you, Inspector, I myself would never say something like that. I rather like your city."

A few moments later, they had found a secluded bench and seated themselves. As Stebbel had warned that he couldn't stay out of the office too long, niceties were kept to a minimum. After a few opening parries of polite questions, Stebbel asked what was this interesting information the Berlin visitor had for him. Bastian leaned back and smiled.

"There's a brothel in Paris ... "

Stebbel arched his eyebrows in mock amazement. "A brothel in Paris? The mind fairly boggles."

Bastian responded with a condescending smile. "Let me continue, please. You see, this is a very special brothel. For clients with very special tastes. The workforce there is exclusively young men. Young men who have been favored by nature in various aspects."

For Stebbel, the conversation was indeed becoming more interesting. "I see."

"Well, as it happens, your Herr von Klettenburg pays a visit to this establishment whenever he travels to Paris on business. Or whenever he travels there for any reason."

Stebbel nodded, now quite interested.

"We happen to have informants who operate in this brothel. They provide us with some detailed and valuable information on people like the *Geheimrat* von Klettenburg. For instance, we now know that Klettenburg has a number of … shortcomings in the area of sexuality and he likes this Parisian establishment because they cater to well-heeled gentleman with these kinds of problems."

"You're sure that these reports are valid?"

"Quite sure. Anyway, our informants assure us that your Herr von Klettenburg is one of those who enjoys the charms of young men as much as he enjoys women. So even a young, very pretty woman such as his late wife was clearly not enough to keep him satisfied." He now turned to face Stebbel fully. "And I think you're aware of how a man who has known a life of such privilege can find ways of getting exactly what he enjoys … whenever he can get it."

"Yes, I am … certainly aware of that."

"So, I was right, yes? This is an interesting bit of news for you. You might even find it valuable one day."

Stebbel nodded. "Perhaps."

"And why am I telling you all of this?"

"That was to be my next question," Stebbel replied.

Bastian's face twisted into a sour expression, as if he'd just bit deeply into a lemon. "We don't find this Klettenburg fellow very reliable. And we don't think you people here in Vienna should find him reliable either. We wouldn't want him and his machinations to interfere with our good relations."

"Yes, you keep saying 'we'. You sound like the pope. Just who is this 'we', Herr Bastian?"

Bastian turned back again. "I work in the Intelligence branch of the government of his Imperial Majesty, Wilhelm II."

Though it shouldn't have, this revelation jolted Stebbel. "You're working for the Kaiser's Secret Service?"

In answer, Bastian merely smiled. "Getting back to von Klettenburg's visits to that Paris brothel. There's this one young Russian lad there who von Klettenburg is especially fond of. He requests his favors on most of his visits. An extremely handsome fellow, we're told, and richly well-endowed below the belt."

He then drew a long breath. "We have reason to believe that this Russian lad is a plant, that his real business is actually something other than the flesh trade."

"He's a spy?"

"The Czarist secret services are ravenous for any information about the political situation in this region. And our sources in Paris tell us that the handsome young Russian is quite fond of conversation, both as foreplay and as a post-coital stimulant. And as I said, we consider your *Geheimrat* most unreliable."

"But you have no evidence that – "

"Evidence is just suspicion with a very nice haircut. Hard-and-fast proof, now that's quite another category. But no, we do not have any proof of that nature. Not yet."

"Well, should you ever get that sort of proof, I'm sure that people in our Interior Ministry would be very happy if you shared it with them. But I work in the normal police force, in the Homicide Division. Espionage is not my field."

"Of course. But as Herr von Klettenburg is connected to your major investigation at the moment, I thought you might like to know some of his peccadilloes."

Stebbel sat back and mulled this over for awhile. He had nothing to add or to ask.

"And now let me give you my official card." He handed it to Stebbel. "As you can see, this has all the contact information for my office in Berlin. Should your investigations ever turn up something interesting about the *Geheimrat*'s international ... connections, we would be very grateful to hear about this."

He again beamed that smile of noxious affability.

"Wouldn't it be better if you kept in touch with the people here who are responsible for espionage matters?"

The Berliner shook his head. "Your military intelligence office is also not entirely reliable."

Stebbel gave an inquisitive stare. Bastian replied with his rehearsed smile. He then pulled out his pocket watch, an elegant gold affair, and checked the time. "Hmm. I rather think I'd like to try one of your famous Viennese coffees. And perhaps indulge in one of those pastries I always hear so much praise for. Any particular establishment around here you would recommend?"

"The Prückel is quite popular. Here, it's not too far out of the way to my office. I'll take you there."

"Thank you. I am always so impressed with your Viennese hospitality. A refreshing change from our Berlin manners: up there, we're gruff ... but highly efficient."

32

The next few days were spared of any squalid – or even sober – reports of the strangler's misdeeds. Stebbel and Dörfner were hoping against hope that their fantasy might actually be true: that Brunner had left Vienna for a time and was laying low, miles away from the capital.

But the brief respite was shattered on a pleasant, warm evening in early May. A university student, Elisabeth Grettin, was returning from late research at her department. Having just missed one tram, she decided to cut across the upper Ringstrasse to another tram stop, then catch a streetcar that would bring her close to her home in Lainz. But to get to this other stop, she had to pass through an area noted for its heavy presence of streetwalkers.

Not wishing to be seen in this company, Frau Grettin decided to slip into one of the back lanes where prostitutes and their clients rarely ventured. Being unfamiliar with the area, she proceeded cautiously. Suddenly, someone called out to her.

"Fräulein, you seem to have dropped something back here."

Elisabeth turned. Right behind her stood a tall, bulky man, holding up a book.

"Oh, thank you, I must have – "

Before she could get out another word, the man slammed the

book into her face, smack on the nose, stunning her. Seconds later, he had taken her by the throat with two large, calloused hands.

She briefly tried to fight back, but was no match against the much stronger man. A full minute after the light of life seemed to have gone out of her eyes, he was still choking her. He then lowered her slightly before letting go and watching the body thud to the ground.

He bent down and picked up one of the books she had dropped after being hit in the face. He skimmed through it rapidly until he found Chapter Five. He then placed the book, still open to that chapter, over her face in a tent-like position. Standing back up, he surveyed the scene, then hurried out the slip-road exit Frau Grettin had been looking for moments before her death.

* * *

This fifth murder unleashed a storm of outrage across the capital. It was not only the stepped-up brutality (which the press had somehow gained wind of), but also the victim herself. As Werner Heissluft of the *Wiener Morgenstern* newspaper wrote the following day: "Not only do these grisly murders continue, spreading a corrosive fear throughout the city, but now the choice of victims has moved beyond the poor girls who sell their bodies to nameless lovers to the most delicate and innocent flowers of Viennese society.

"Frau Elisabeth Grettin, an excellent third-year student at our justly renowned university, has now given her life to the sub-human rages of a totally depraved criminal mind. This lovely young lady, who promised to contribute so much to our beautiful city and our beloved country, has now been brutally stolen from us. Yes, from all of us, and we all feel the deep loss of this tragic victim. And it is not too early to ask once again why the pampered and pompous police force of our supposedly great city seems powerless to bring an end to these murders."

And the Heissluft barrage was not even the most overwrought article that the latest murder had set loose. The front page of the *Weiner Mercur* carried the following headline, in towering type: IT'S ALL EVEN NOW! JACK THE RIPPER – 5, THE SPITTELBERG STRANGER – 5.

Inspectors Stebbel and Dörfner were forced to see first-hand the brutality that Frau Grettin had undergone. Early the next morning, they made their now too-frequent visit to the police morgue to view the victim. Doktor Gressler provided a more detailed commentary as he showed them the body.

"Again, the same bruises on the neck, though wider and more intense this time. You can still see it from the colors of the bruises: note how those bruises are an intense purple, the red is still flaming, the blue is – "

Stebbel cut him off: "Yes, yes, it's clear that our killer is getting more diligent in his work"

Doktor Gressler nodded sadly. "Of which, there were other indications. We seem to have found a slight fracture in her nose. Evidently, the strangler hit the young lady with a hard object before or after the actual killing."

Dörfner shook his head. "Maybe just before. To knock her off-guard, make her less able to defend herself from the choking?"

"Yes, that's very possible. You'll have to ask the killer about that, however. The only other witness to that moment is no longer able to speak." He spread his hand to indicate the cadaver.

"We have many questions to ask this fiend when we get him," Stebbel said. "That one will be somewhat low on my list," Dörfner added.

"Oh, one other thing about the attack that I almost forgot. This time, the victim had blood running from her mouth. That came from a broken windpipe sustained during the strangulation. We surmise that he spent longer on this murder, perhaps continuing to strangle her even after she was dead."

Stebbel turned away at this point. He felt ill. When Dörfner turned to see his partner, he noticed what he thought was a glint in the eye. Was he actually tearing?

Dörfner's own hands had clenched and unclenched several times during Gressler's account of the injuries and how they were most likely sustained. He felt an urge to get his own hands around the neck of the strangler and let him know what it felt like to be strangled. After staring at the corpse for a short time more, he turned and joined Stebbel. He patted him on the shoulder, trying to ease his distress.

The two inspectors threw a few more questions at Gressler as they were wrapping up the briefing, then thanked the doctor and made their way out. They remained in stoic silence as they walked down the corridor. Suddenly, just before they reached the *paternoster* lifts, Stebbel spun around and let forth an outburst.

"Alright, we pay Frau Keuler another unexpected visit. No, better still, we bring her in here, throw her into one of the interrogation rooms and lock the door. We get her to talk. Tell us whatever she knows. We'll … we'll put a lit cigar to the palms of her hands, the soles of her feet. We'll break her fingers, starting with the little one and then working our way to the thumbs if we have to. Whatever it takes – we will get her to tell us everything she knows about her brother. We have to find out where Brunner is, where he's hiding, and get him before he kills again."

Dörfner was stunned, but also quite amused. "My dear colleague! And where have you been keeping this raging tiger you have inside you? You're sounding like the cop I was always afraid I might become someday."

Stebbel took a long, cavernous breath. He closed his eyes and slumped against the wall. Moments later, he opened his eyes and straightened up.

"Sorry; I didn't mean any of that. Of course, we can't torture that woman to get any information. It probably wouldn't be reliable anyway, whatever we forced out of her. It's just ..." He turned and slapped the wall hard in frustration.

"I know, I know."

"We have to find him, Dörfner. It's getting to be too much. We can't let this monster strike again. He has no right to be sharing the air of this city with any of us. He's given up his right to enjoy life. We have to get him and stop these murders."

"What, you think I'm going to argue with you? Offer a rebuttal? I want to get that swine as much as you do. And we will get him, we will."

Stebbel looked his partner deep in the eyes. He held this look for about ten seconds without saying anything. Then: "Will we?"

In answer, Dörfner turned and looked down the corridor, towards the morgue. At that moment, the corridor looked even drearier than ever before.

* * *

Back in their office, the two sat almost shoulder-to-shoulder at Stebbel's desk. Stebbel had pulled out the casebook and was starting to write down the highlights of what they had seen, what they had been told, down in the morgue. But a few sentences into the report, Stebbel slapped the pen down and shoved the book away.

"No, we have to get out there now. I can't bear to see Rautz and Schollenberg this morning. Especially Schollenberg. Let's get out there and start scouring the sidewalks. I'll ... I'll go and see if I can get any useful information from the victim's family." He rubbed his left temple, where a tension headache was settling in. "I'll have to go back and ask Gressler what time they came to identify the body."

"And what should I do?"

"Why not ... Why don't you go to see the Turk. Find out if he knows anything about this Brunner. See if he ... if he can provide us with any help in this matter. Maybe he can get some of his people, the really hard ones, to serve as patrols on the streets. Make sure that if Brunner turns up again, he won't be able to kill anyone."

"Alright. I'll see what I can do. I have a few IOUs for favors there, so I'll tell the Turk I'm expecting some repayment now."

"Good. But let's get out now, before Rautz can discuss this latest killing with Schollenberg. Our peerless District Commander usually doesn't like to entertain any bad news until he's had his mid-morning coffee and pastry. Let's be long gone from here when he starts bellowing for action."

"I couldn't agree more"

The two then exited the office together in a rush. Dörfner headed immediately for the *paternoster* while Stebbel went to consult the preliminary report by the pulley police to get the address of the victim's family.

33

The Turk was not on duty at the Ottoman embassy, nor was he at his main shop in the Tichtelgasse. But Vlatko was there. When Dörfner asked the assistant where his boss was, the underling said he had no idea and also had no idea when he might be back. His reply had a spiteful echo, blending insincerity and truculence, so Dörfner decided to ask him one more time.

"Oh, I don't think you remember who I am." He reached into this jacket and pulled out his ID plate. "I'm Inspector Dörfner, that good friend of your employer."

As he said that, he thrust the plate towards Vlatko's face with a hard right jab. This time though, he stopped just short of the underling's nose. Vlatko flinched to avoid the punch and swallowed some musty air.

"So, you remember now? You might also recall that I'm the fellow who has a distinct distaste for false information."

The flunky then came up with a new story. He really did not know where the Turk was, but he knew that he had an appointment at eleven. Something that he couldn't miss. So he would probably be back at the shop by 10:30, 10:45 to get ready for that meeting. If it wouldn't be too much trouble for the inspector, he could come back then and see if the Turk could fit him in.

"Oh, don't worry," Dörfner said as he eased his ID plate back into his jacket pocket and started back towards the door. "He will be able to fit me in. Remember, we are very old and dear friends. You do things for friends. Maybe one day you'll learn that – and acquire a few friends of your own." And then he made his exit, closing the door carefully as he left.

Dörfner returned shortly after 10:30 and was told that Bahadir himself had returned a few minutes earlier.

"Excellent. Now, go back there and tell your boss that his dear friend from police headquarters is here to see him. I just want to take a few minutes of his time. He'll understand."

"*Jawohl*, Herr Constable." Vlatko did a military spin and headed to the back room.

The Turk emerged several moments later, flustered at seeing Dörfner there. "My friend, my friend … You must always alert me beforehand when you come to visit. I don't have any tea *or* coffee ready to serve you. Nor do I have any pastries to offer. You embarrass me by coming in unannounced like this. Could we perhaps – "

"No need really. I appreciate your generosity, but I just came from a second breakfast at the local café. I was actually here about an hour ago, before you arrived, so I treated myself to a poppy seed dumpling and a small pot of coffee to kill the time."

"Well, please let me show you my appreciation for your visit the next time you come. Not having anything to offer you, I feel almost like I'm standing naked here. And that's a feeling I find so embarrassing – except, of course, when I am entertaining charming women."

The Turk then waved Vlatko off to another part of the shop and escorted Dörfner into the back room.

Dörfner was pretty sure that Bahadir's embarrassment stemmed not just from the fact that he had no refreshments to offer, but mainly because he had that other visitor coming in soon, and he did not seem eager to have Dörfner meet this visitor. This embarrassment was actually a benefit, as the two got down to business immediately.

The inspector asked if he had heard about the latest murder. The Turk said he hadn't, and he looked and sounded sincere when he said it. Dörfner then quickly recounted all the details of the crime that he felt it safe to share with the Turk. Bahadir actually seemed upset at hearing just the details Dörfner was able to provide.

"This is very bad, you know; very bad indeed. It just poisons the air we all breathe in this otherwise wonderful city. It affects all of us negatively. I'll tell you, it's even bad for business. We have noticed that women are less willing to come to the shop and look at our excellent wares because of this murderer.

"And my friends who do their business in the skin trade, they tell me that their business has fallen off considerably in the last few weeks. Girls aren't showing up for work, and the clients are reluctant to venture out for their carnal pleasures because there are so many of you police patrolling the streets."

Dörfner picked up on this and told his friend that one of the problems they faced is that they didn't have *enough* police to patrol the streets. Their coverage had gaps, far too many gaps. This murderer seemed to be operating without much fear of getting caught – especially as he had just widened his field of operations beyond Spittelberg.

"And how could I help with this situation? Are you collecting donations so that you can hire more policemen? I would love to help you, but – "

Dörfner cut him off and announced just how he could help the police – and, of course, all the citizens of Vienna. He was hoping that the Turk could offer the services of his employers, the muscle division, to patrol those streets the police themselves couldn't cover.

Only until they caught this murderer, of course. And they hoped to do that very soon.

The Turk mulled this request for several moments, then asked how many men Dörfner was expecting to get from him. The inspector decided to aim high: at least twenty, he said, and they should be there from nightfall until the first streaks of morning light appeared over the city's easternmost district.

The Turk was taken aback by the number Dörfner was asking for. He gave a barking laugh, as he always did when mildly embarrassed. He then mulled this over for a half a minute, and admitted that it would be very difficult – but it was something that he was willing to do for a friend.

Dörfner smiled and gave a slight bow of gratitude. "Thank you. I knew you were the man to come to when I found myself in a moment of such duress."

"Of course, of course. I would be insulted if you thought of anyone other than myself. But one further thing, please: it will be difficult to get all of these fellows together and then out there on the streets of the redlight districts.

"Plus, I must convince them to do so despite the dangers they are putting themselves into. I will certainly do it as a favor to my very dear friend, but then I must ask myself what favors my dear friend is willing to do me in return."

"Well, Turk, I think your dear friend has done you a number of serious favors recently, and now he's just asking that you repay some of those favors. In fact, a few of the favors you might not even know about."

The Turk straightened up in his chair. "Oh? Such as?"

"You know, just last week, there was a small package sent to this shop. From somewhere in Anatolia. In that package were a number of the dolls that you sell in this shop. But it was funny – when several of those dolls were cut accidentally with a knife, you know what was inside?"

"I can't imagine. Doll stuffing?"

Dörfner smiled amiably and shook his head. "A rich cascade of heroin. Can you imagine? Very pure product, too, I've been told. Now one of my colleagues in the drug division, who also happens to be another good friend of mine, told me about this embarrassing shipment. It seems he was just about to come over here, arrest some people and then close the shop. Maybe close it in a very messy way, too."

"Oh."

"Yes, but I convinced this colleague that it must certainly have been a mistake putting the address of this shop on the package. It must have been intended for some other address."

"Of course. I would not wish to see anything like this in my shop."

"I told the colleague that myself. It took some convincing, but I was able to keep him from coming into this shop with a squad of ungentlemanly policemen who would have spent a good few hours going through this whole shop just to make sure there was nothing else like those dolls and their contents here. And then leaving with a number of people in handcuffs.

"So you see, my friend – I do favors for you even when you're not aware of them. And especially when you very much need such favors."

"Which is why we are such good friends, isn't it, Inspector? And that is why I will certainly help you out this time. But then, I hope you will remember this whenever you have the chance to do me a favor again."

"I will indeed. You need not worry about that." And the meeting wrapped up rapidly from there. Dörfner explained what would be needed for the patrols and said he would send over written details in the late afternoon. Then he thanked his friend for the cooperation and made a quick exit. After all, Bahadir the businessman did have another visitor coming in very soon.

34

When Dörfner returned to headquarters, he was excited to tell his news about the temporary street patrols he'd apparently secured. But even as he stood at the office doorway, he could feel the morose mood within.

Stebbel was sitting at his desk, pen in hand, casebook opened. But he wasn't writing anything; he was just staring out blankly. Dörfner's own mood dropped at seeing this.

"What is it, Steb?"

"I was just over there at the home of the victim. Frau Grettin. I saw her family, was asking them questions. Her mother, her father, a younger sister."

"I see."

Stebbel shook his head. "It was terrible. She was the pride of the family. An honors student, the first one in the family to go to university. They had so many hopes for her. It seemed like there was so much future for her.

"You know how people say they could actually feel the pain in a room? Today, I could feel the pain in that room. It was surrounding me, pushing in at me from different sides. I couldn't take it after awhile. I could barely breathe. I finished up quickly, didn't even ask all the questions I should have, and just got out of there."

"I can imagine what it was like."

"No, you can't. Sorry, but you can't." He looked up. "And I felt like I was partially guilty for that pain. As if I had let those people down. If I could have done a better job at catching the killer – or at least scaring him away for a few weeks – Frau Grettin would still be alive today."

Dörfner pulled his own chair closer to Stebbel and looked straight at him, though Stebbel continued looking the other way.

"You can't feel that way, Steb. It's not your fault. Also not mine. It's just that we don't have the resources, don't have the time … don't have the luck."

He tried looking Stebbel in the eye, then realized why Stebbel was looking away: he seemed to have tears in his eyes. Also, he didn't seem to be listening anymore.

Dörfner thought to himself that maybe this was the wrong profession for Stebbel. It seemed to be getting to him too much. Maybe when this was all over, he might mention it. But certainly not now.

Instead, Dörfner suggested they go for a drink. A brandy or something. It would be Dörfner's treat. When Stebbel finally turned and looked at him, Dörfner repeated the offer. Stebbel capped his pen, put away the casebook, and they went off for a well-needed break.

By the afternoon editions, most of the city's leading newspapers had managed to scavenge more details of the murder as well as the particulars of the victim. Front-page articles highlighted the most grisly details, and follow-up pieces inside just pumped up the gore factor. And, of course, the would-be poets and novelists who were stuck in poorly paid journalism posts were taking advantage of the continuing story and the poignant tale of the latest victim to churn out stories that relied more on exaggeration and outright invention than allegiance to the facts.

The morning editions the next day were even more livid. One paper, *Die Volkstribüne*, actually started running a contest: a prize of 50 kroners to the reader who could guess the exact date on which Vienna's strangler passed the official kill count of Jack the Ripper. When Dörfner was shown that bit of inspiration, he felt the urge to travel over to the paper's offices and punch out the chief editor and publisher.

But it had been a quiet night. Street police and journalists both noted that there seemed to be fewer people out on the streets of the First District that evening. It was almost like a holiday. Or rather, a day of mourning. One senior journalist said it reminded him a little of the dark evenings that followed the assassination of the beloved Empress Sisi.

Stebbel and Dörfner kept wondering when they would be called in again to face District Commander Schollenberg. And they wondered what they could say when they were called in.

The worst thing that happened in those first two days came when they sent a few pulley cops to Währing to bring in Frau Keuler for more intense questioning. When the police arrived, they were told that the lady had left the day before. She said she was going for a short vacation and asked one of her neighbors to collect her mail and newspaper while she was away. But she made no mention of when she might be back.

35

Adolf Hitler had been enraged when he read about the murder of Elisabeth Grettin. In fact, while reading, he had crumpled the bottom corners of the *Wiener Morgenpost,* even though the paper actually belonged to the hostel's library. When he realized what he'd done, he looked around and then furtively tried to smooth out the pages with the flat of his hand.

After reading a few more accounts of the crime, Hitler decided it was time for him to take a more active role. The police did not seem to be doing enough. He was starting to think that they didn't believe him about having seen the killer. Maybe they just didn't take him at all seriously. He would have to rectify that.

That same evening, he showered, slicked down his hair, put on his good jacket and set out for Spittelberg. Being perhaps the only one in Vienna who had seen the killer face-to-face and lived to tell about it, he was now determined to find that man, to confront him, and to help bring him to justice.

His plan was to wound the criminal, probably by stabbing him in the leg, and then run off and report the catch to the nearest police officer. Before leaving the hostel, he reached into the pocket of his jacket to check that the knife was still there. It was. He rearranged it so that the handle was standing up, ready to grab. He was determined to be a hero tonight, and he knew that a certain amount of preparation always helps when you want to be a hero.

As soon as he reached Spittelberg, he began searching diligently. He had been there for about 15 minutes, covered many of the streets, peered into several doorways and was starting to feel frustrated when he saw him.

The man was about twenty meters ahead of Hitler on the Bandgasse. Hitler could only see him from the back, but he was tall and burly and he had the ominous gait of the man he'd seen when the killings began. This, he felt, was indeed the man he was looking for. Now it was his task to stop him before he struck again.

Hitler increased his stride, quickly closing the distance between himself and his prey. Then, chance stepped in: the man was approached by the lone prostitute on that street, and he seemed interested in what she had to offer. He planted himself in front of the hooker and started to discuss business terms.

Within seconds, Hitler was upon him. By this point, the woman was leaning against the wall and smiling seductively. The man put his hand out and started rubbing her shoulder. Hitler was sure this was just the preliminary to strangling the girl. Having already slipped the knife out of his pocket, he positioned himself right behind the fiend.

"Stop! Take your hands off her. You're finished!"

The man spun around, obviously irritated at being interrupted just as he and the girl were about to close the deal. As he spun, he brought a large hand forward. Hitler reacted with great speed, swinging the knife at the man.

As he did, the blade sliced the palm of the hand. Within a second or two, blood started flowing profusely from the wound. The man clutched the lower part of his hand and glared at it with fear and shock. He then turned back to Hitler with rage in his face.

Even with his features distorted like that, one thing became clear to Hitler: this was *not* the man he had seen coming out of that alley. In fact, this face was completely different. He actually looked like a foreigner, probably a southern Slav or an Oriental. Hitler had made a rather unfortunate mistake.

Despite his wound, the man started to move towards Hitler. In response, Hitler lunged the knife at him; not far enough to pierce the man, but enough to frighten him. The man backed off, slowly edging further away from his assailant. He again checked his hand and saw that the lower part of his shirtsleeve was a deep red. Also, he started to feel faint.

At that moment, the whore, having recovered from the shock of the assault, started screaming. It was time for Hitler to leave. Seeing a passageway not too far away, he moved there as quickly as he could. He then headed for the Burggasse. He kept thinking that he could hear heavy footsteps pursuing him, possibly police or even the wounded man himself. But it was just his fear-fueled imagination. There was no one behind him, and he was fortunate enough to make a clean escape.

As he approached a tram stop, he pulled out his handkerchief, wiped off the blood, then squeezed the bloody cloth through a sewer grating. He thought of tossing the knife into the sewer as well, then decided not to. He knew he was taking a major risk keeping the weapon, but he was sure he would need it again sometime soon. He slipped it back into this jacket pocket, as deep as it would go, and trotted to the tram stop.

Within a minute, a tram arrived. He wasn't even sure where it was going, but he boarded nonetheless. The only important thing now was to get as far away from the scene as he could, as quickly as he could.

* * *

Dörfner walked into the office the next day reading a one-page police report.

"There was another attack last night in the red-light district."

"*Mein Gott, nein*! Two nights in a row? He's getting more determined now."

"No, it wasn't the Strangler this time. An ordinary knifing. Some guy slashed another guy's hand. The victim ... was rushed to General Hospital where he was treated to fifteen stitches."

"And what did he do to earn the slashing?"

Dörfner was silent as he started reading further in the report. A minute later, he nodded. "OK, here it is: the victim claims he was just out for a pleasant evening stroll, somehow got lost, suddenly noticed he was in the streetwalkers' district, and tried to get out as quickly as possible."

"I don't doubt a single word," Stebbel said with swirling dose of sarcasm.

"Who could?" Dörfner replied. "So while this poor innocent was trying to find his way out, he was attacked by some wild-eyed, knife-wielding madman who set upon him for no reason at all."

"Of course. Happens all the time." He sighed. "So ... another jealousy drama. Some fool saw that fool with a girl he considered his own and tried to make his point with a knife."

"You know, I really miss those days of jealousy stabbings. They were so understandable, easy to solve."

Stebbel then thought a moment. "Wait a minute – didn't the Turk promise to put a lot of men on the streets in that district? Why didn't they step in to stop the knife-wielder, or at least apprehend him right after his assault?"

"He said it would take a few days. They should be on the streets tonight."

"Well, I'm sure the press is going to have a great old time fitting this tale into the Strangler saga."

Dörfner then looked at his partner sympathetically. "Are you alright?"

Stebbel stopped his sorting of papers. "If I were alright, that would be a matter of some concern. But at least I'm better than what I was yesterday."

"Well, that is really good to hear."

"Still … I'm sure we're going to hear about this stabbing when we go upstairs to see Schollenberg."

"Oh yes; our beloved District Commander is going to see this as another one of our failures in this case."

"The question is: how many failures will it take before the people upstairs decide it's been one failure too many?"

36

On the third day after the murder of Frau Grettin, the two main inspectors were called upstairs. But it was not to District Commander Schollenberg's office: this time, their presence was requested at the office of the *Polizei Präsident* – the police commissioner.

Shortly before the 2:30 appointment, Schollenberg, Rautz, Stebbel and Dörfner arrived at the top floor of headquarters and headed down the corridor to the corner office where the Commissioner held court.

A secretary appeared and told Schollenberg and Rautz that they could go in. A polite smile informed the two junior inspectors that they should take seats on the bench next to the office door and wait.

The wait seemed to last twice as long as it actually was. But ten minutes after the two seniors had gone in, Rautz peeked out and asked Stebbel and Dörfner if they would like to join them inside.

When the two loupes entered, Rautz and Schollenberg had just moved their chairs to the outside. Rautz then pulled up two chairs in the middle for his men. This was more for intimidation than courtesy: with the new arrangement, the junior inspectors were flanked by their seniors and sat facing the Commissioner directly.

But the Commissioner was not actually facing them. As they took their seats, he was still reading from four different sheets of paper spread across his desk. Stebbel and Dörfner sat down nervously. Dörfner turned to Rautz and Schollenberg for some clue as to what was to come, but both remained poker-faced. Stebbel also threw Rautz a look, but the senior inspector merely shrugged.

Stebbel had a strong inkling of what was about to come down: he quite expected that the Commissioner was going to take them off the case because they had failed to catch the culprit and now the popular press and the smart café chatter had turned the whole thing into a macabre game.

Stebbel was actually split about being removed from the case. One part of him was actually relieved. No case in his six-year career as an inspector had taken such an emotional toll on him, and he sometimes felt it could only end by breaking him.

On the other hand, it was a slap in the face to be told he and Dörfner were being shunted aside because they had failed. Stebbel had no idea which of these emotions – relief or bitterness – would come out on top when the axe fell in a few minutes. And then the moment arrived: Commissioner Gutschirm finished his reading and drew a sour sigh.

The Commissioner then offered a smile that looked as fake as that of a Carnival effigy. He clapped his hands together and said, "Well, we have a real mess here, don't we?"

The two junior inspectors agreed immediately. The Commissioner pointed across the room to a table covered with a stack of newspapers. The two inspectors knew these were the latest editions, with rivers of purple prose flowing through them.

"The press is taking us over the coals on this. Well, what could we expect – most of them are controlled by Jews, pan-Germans and socialists." Stebbel thought this was an unusual yoking together of disparate forces, though he joined Dörfner in deferential nodding.

"Here on the top floor, we usually refer to the press as syphilitic rag-dealers. We have no respect for these mongrels. None at all. But … the general population reads this garbage and believes what they read there, so we have to take them far more seriously than they deserve." He then drew another sour look, as if he had just bit into something unpleasant.

"Anyway, as I was just telling the District Commander and your senior inspector, I had a phone call from the mayor this morning." He nodded in confirmation. "The mayor himself. And late this morning, I had a meeting with the mayor's top assistant and a senior assistant to the Minister of the Interior. Yes, this case has reached the highest levels. Everyone in Vienna is enraged about these crimes."

"The mayor's office has suggested that we issue an immediate prohibition of street solicitation, and the Interior Ministry agrees; they're ready to implement all the necessary statutes. We pull the whores off the streets, and this monster won't have any victims to prey on. What do you two gentlemen think of that plan?"

Stebbel, who knew this "question" was actually the polite Viennese way of telling them this was an order, decided that he would have to risk the wrath of all three seniors in the room and say why this plan wouldn't work.

"With all due respect, Herr Commissioner … this last victim was not a prostitute. She was just a university student who apparently got lost somehow. Neither was the very first victim a prostitute. She was … returning from the theatre when she was attacked.

"Plus, the latest attack was outside the Spittelberg district. If we really wanted to deprive the killer of available victims, we'd probably have to impose a strict after-dark curfew on all females, and all the way across the city."

The Commissioner started mulling this over. The look on his face suggested that he thought that might not be a bad idea really.

But then, Dörfner jumped in. His partner's act of minor

insubordination had emboldened him to add his piece. "Actually, my colleague has an excellent point there, Herr Commissioner. If we just sweep the streets of the prostitutes, that would mean that the killer will start going after the more respectable women of the city. And you can imagine how the press will react to that."

This seemed to hit the Commissioner at his core. He looked away and drew another long sigh.

"Alright. I might be able to postpone the order for a few days. No more. If you can't guarantee the safety of our fairer sex by then, the streetwalkers will have to go. And we may even have to consider that blanket curfew you just suggested."

Stebbel made a slight face. He was suggesting the absurdity of that solution, not suggesting that it be implemented. But he wasn't ready to argue with the Commissioner any further.

"So what progress have you made on this case anyway? I'm going to have to give the mayor's office and the Interior Ministry something, or we're all going to catch flaming hell."

Stebbel took a deep breath before speaking. "We do have a prime suspect."

This caught the Commissioner by surprise. "You do? Who is it?"

"We think it's the killer. We have a witness who thinks that he saw the killer right after the first murder. We even have the name of the suspect, and we checked his background; there's a good possibility this is our man."

"Then why haven't you arrested him, for God's sake? Just go to his home with as many armed officers as you can manage and bring the bastard in."

"We don't know where he's staying at present, Herr Commissioner." The Commissioner's eyebrows ascended sharply at this. The gesture demanded an immediate explanation.

"He left his last registered address over a year ago. He has not officially registered any residence since then."

"What??" And then the Commissioner slapped his palm hard on the desk for punctuation.

His reaction was strange; it was as if he was saying it's bad enough this brute goes around strangling defenseless females, but the fact that he hasn't bothered to register his current address with the authorities is just a bit too much.

"But we do have a number of good leads," Stebbel added mendaciously. "And we think we're moving in on him. We hope to end this terror ... soon."

Dörfner then added his own bit. "Plus, we have stepped up our patrols in the Spittelberg area as well as the theatre district. We have the two major red-light sections covered much more thoroughly now."

"You do?" Dörfner nodded convincingly. "Well, that's good."

Both Dörfner and Stebbel were glad that Gutschirm did not ask for any details. They would not have been comfortable telling him – or Rautz and Schollenberg – the regular patrols had been augmented with a contingent of toughs provided by one of the city's major pimps, smugglers and drug dealers. But all three seniors left it like that.

At this point, the Commissioner seemed to have become exhausted with the whole subject. He looked like he wanted to wrap up the meeting quickly, which is just what he did.

"Anyway, I've heard good reports on the work you two have done so far." He pointed at Rautz and Schollenberg, indicating they were the sources of these good reports. "Just continue doing good work – only better, much better. We need to deliver a head to city hall and the Ministry as soon as we can. And we don't want any more murders in the meantime." He then sat up fully straight.

"Our Spittelberg Strangler can't be allowed to match the record of Jack the Ripper, gentlemen." He fixed all four men with a warning stare as he said that. All four nodded in agreement, even though they knew he had already matched the Ripper's tally.

After they left the Commissioner's office, District Commander Schollenberg said he had to visit another office down the corridor. He would meet up with the other three some time in the next two days to discuss what was said in that meeting with the Commissioner and where to go from there. Stebbel, Dörfner and Rautz all thanked him for his continuing support and headed to the *paternoster*.

There were no words, only looks, exchanged until they got there. As it was dangerous for three people who were not quite nimble to climb into a single carriage, the two juniors deferred to Rautz. "I'll see you below," Rautz said as he stepped on.

Stebbel and Dörfner let the next carriage go by, then hopped into the next one. Rautz was waiting for them when they arrived on the fourth floor.

"So ... not as bad as it could have been, right?"

Stebbel even managed a smile. "I actually thought my partner and I were going to be removed from the case. I kept thinking that almost until the end of the meeting, when the Commissioner slipped in that little bit of praise."

Rautz had a surprised look when he heard this. "Remove you? Who else could we assign this case to?"

Both of the junior inspectors beamed at this endorsement. But then Rautz added a sprinkle of sour to the compliment. "Who else would want to take the damn thing at this point?" And then he turned in the other direction and headed down to his office, leaving his split compliment stinging the air.

Once they had returned to their own office, Stebbel and Dörfner breathed in a more relaxed manner. But that lasted only for a minute or two, as Stebbel pulled out the casebook. Then he turned to his partner.

"OK, we find out where Frau Keuler has gone on her vacation. Somebody must know. And then we get the police there to haul her back here."

"So how do we proceed from there? Should we each take turns breaking alternate fingers, or do you want to interrogate while I do the breaking?"

Stebbel gave an appreciative laugh. He was starting to like working with Dörfner more and more.

"I don't think we'll have to take it that far. But we sit her down in an interrogation room and we scare the holy spirit out of her. If she's not pissing herself after five minutes, we won't be doing our jobs right."

He drew a relaxing breath. "Besides, if we find out where the widow Keuler is hiding out, I wouldn't be surprised to discover her brother is hiding out there with her." Dörfner nodded. He, too, felt that the meeting upstairs had breathed now energy into the two men.

* * *

Nothing much happened over the next two days. The police were still not able to determine where Frau Keuler had escaped to, and even the eight extra sketches that Herr Hitler had provided weren't able to help locate her brother. (Two of the new sketches stayed in their division, while the other six were distributed to other stations across the city.)

There was an enlarged presence of foot patrolmen in the red-light district. Some of them were the Turk's auxiliary force, looking suitably unpleasant. The increased patrols actually did have the effect of reducing the corps of streetwalkers. They were either afraid of being taken in for solicitation (still officially a criminal offense) or were just intimidated by the appearance of the Turk's men. But there was no new headline material for the newspapers in those two days.

Even so, Dörfner and Stebbel realized that they were just buying time, not making any real progress. They still had no idea where Arnold Brunner was, even if he was still anywhere near Vienna. And, truth be told, they weren't really sure they weren't just chasing down a false lead with Brunner.

As Stebbel reminded Dörfner, the only evidence they had that Brunner might be involved in any of these murders came from that Hitler fellow, who – they had to admit – may not have been in full possession of his sanity. But they had nothing else to hold onto at that point, and they desperately needed something to hold onto.

37

It was the third day after their meeting with the Police Commissioner. Late afternoon had passed into early evening. Stebbel was still at his desk. Spread out in front of him were the files of the five victims. He had each one opened so that the morgue photos were at the top.

He examined each face, trying to imagine a life, a whole world, that had suddenly been brought to an end.

He briefly touched each of the photos, as if he could recreate the lives behind these now lifeless faces: the young innocent from Galicia with a toy lion in the room where she serviced clients; the abandoned wife trying to keep her home and her sanity; the honors student working hard for a future that never came; the confused woman from the east who took refuge from her confusion in the deeper fog of opium. And, of course, the grace, warmth and generosity of the first victim, Frau von Klettenburg.

He started to close the files. He felt so useless, unable to help the dead. And probably unable to help those soon to be dead.

Dörfner walked in, his evening bag slung over his shoulder. He was ready to call it a day. He wanted Stebbel to join him for a drink. The senior partner at first politely turned him down, but Dörfner persisted. He told Stebbel that he really needed a break and a drink; they both did. Stebbel was just about to relent when the phone on their desk started ringing.

"Don't answer; it's probably Rautz or Schollenberg."

"But it's also officially after-hours. Let me see what they want. Maybe they just want us to pick up something tomorrow on our way in." He slipped the receiver off its switch-hook and answered.

"Inspector Stebbel here."

"Ah, Inspector Stebbel. Yes, Inspector, I'm so pleased to finally have the honor of speaking with you. I have some very valuable information for you."

"Who is this, please?"

"I'm a friend of justice. And I'm very concerned about the strangler case. The one you and your partner are buried in right now."

"Oh?" Stebbel gave Dörfner a look that nicely expressed his confusion at that moment.

"Yes. Anyway, I happen to know that you're looking for someone right now. Your prime suspect. A certain Herr Brunner."

"Yes …?"

"If you want to find him, I think you and your partner should go to the Ebersdorfer Bridge tomorrow evening at around nine. Right under the statue of Saint John of Nepomuk."

"I'm not too familiar with that location."

"It's the only statue on that bridge."

"Then we shouldn't have too much trouble finding it."

"I think you'll be very glad you went there. Your prey will be waiting there, though he'd be very shocked to discover he's waiting there for you."

"How do you know this? And, if it's not too much to ask, could you please tell me who you are."

"A friend. As I said, the Nepomuk statue on the Ebersdorfer Bridge. Tomorrow at nine. Oh, and be careful: he will probably be carrying a weapon. He is, as you may know, a former member of the

Imperial Guard."

"Yes, yes, we're aware of that. But could you please just – "

"Good bye, Herr Inspector." And with that, the caller clicked off. After a few moments, Stebbel hung up the phone and turned to Dörfner slightly blanched.

"Who was that?"

"He wouldn't say. But he claims to know ... that Brunner will be waiting somewhere tomorrow evening. He says we should go there ourselves if we want to make Herr Brunner's acquaintance."

"What??"

Stebbel nodded. "The Ebersdorfer Bridge. There in the middle."

"Just like that? Oh sure; we've been turning this town upside down for weeks and weeks looking for Brunner, and then someone calls and serves him up to us like a strudel on a shining plate." He threw up his hands in exasperation. "It just can't be that easy. There's definitely something sinister behind this."

"I think we should go."

"No! It's all a hoax. And probably a dangerous one at that."

"I think we have to go. Remember 'pursue every lead, no matter how flimsy'? And what if we don't go there and this swine kills another girl? And then another one, and another one after that. Would you be able to sit within your own skin after that? I know I wouldn't. We'll go, just to say we went, we tried. But first, we'll tell Rautz about the call. And we'll try to get as many people to go there with us as we think wise."

"Can't be too many."

"No, that's why I say as many as we think wise. But I don't want to walk into this without some backup, some support there. Though you're right: not so many that the killer thinks there's a police parade marching through the area. We'll discuss it with Rautz, see what the optimal number is. But we have to go and see what we can find. To tell the truth, I think the whole thing's a fraud myself. But we have to be there to say that it was a fraud."

Dörfner took a deep, grumbling sigh. "OK, I guess you're right. But we need that backup. I think this is probably a set-up and the only way we can avoid a nasty surprise is if we go in there with more firepower than they have."

"They? And who do you think this 'they' is?"

"Whoever."

38

That next morning, the pace of activity on the fourth floor was achingly frantic. Stebbel and Dörfner first had to hunt down Senior Inspector Rautz and inform him of the call and the message the caller had left.

Rautz was also fairly skeptical about the reliability of any new information coming from some anonymous caller, but agreed that they needed to pursue the lead. And pursue it with all available energy and resources.

The first order of business: to put together a task force to be sent to the bridge and confront the killer – if, in fact, he even turned up there that evening.

"So how much do you know about this suspect anyway?"

"We know that he was a member of the Imperial Guard," Stebbel answered.

"The guard?"

"Stationed at the Hofburg."

"Oh, *Gott in Himmel* … So what else?"

"The anonymous caller said that he would probably be carrying a weapon tonight."

"And we already know he's good with his hands," Dörfner added. Rautz nodded unhappily.

After discussing their next moves a bit more, the three were unanimous that Inspector Prenger should be part of the team that went to the surprise party for the killer. Both Stebbel and Dörfner trusted Prenger, and he had more experience on stakeouts than the two of them put together.

They also decided that they needed the best possible shooters with them. Rautz went to see Captain Farber, who was in command of the department's hooks. He said he needed the names of the best marksmen amongst the hooks. Farber, who looked like he had just been woken up, agreed and said that he would put the word out. He should, he promised, have some solid recommendations in a few days.

"We need them one hour from now."

"One hour? That's just absolutely impossible."

"Well, you have to find a way to make it possible, Herr Colleague. Honestly, I wish we had more time, but we don't. And if you want to discuss the matter further, you'll have to speak with District Commander Schollenberg … and the Commissioner."

After twisting a scowl around his face several times, Farber nodded. "Alright. But let me tell you something, Rautz. You better take a few days off after this. Maybe even apply for a rest spa. You're getting rather obsessive. I've heard you're all getting pretty obsessive down at that end of the corridor." He then sat back, took a deep breath and tried to calm himself down. "So you need our best marksmen?"

"And we need men with strong nerves. Men who won't panic. Even in a situation when any normal human being would panic."

Farber heaved a long sigh. "How many do you need?" Rautz smiled and held up four fingers.

Farber said, "I'll try to have four good men report to you in an hour's time."

Rautz thanked him, patted him on the shoulder, then rushed off to make other arrangements.

As they plotted out their strategy, they also brought in one Sergeant Király from the Morality Police division. Király was a decorated officer whose beat in the early days had included the area around the Ebersdorfer Bridge. (The south bank there had once been a popular place for impromptu sexual encounters.) Király briefed them on the geography of the area and how they could work out the capture.

With a district map spread out in front of him, Sergeant Király indicated some key places. "Right here on the corner, at the south side of the river, there's this café. A nice place, with a small seating area out front." Dörfner's eyes widened at this piece of information.

"The problem is, I don't think the café stays open that late. Otherwise, it would be a perfect surveillance point."

Rautz waved this concern away. "It will be open tonight. I'll take care of that myself. I'll send a few people over there, including someone from the Health Authority. If they don't want to help us, we'll just threaten to find some obscure violation and close them down for a week. They'll be cooperative."

"Good," Király continued. "Then you can station a few men there. It can give you a decent view of the bridge, at least from this point to around the middle. About here.

"Now on the north side of the river, there used to be a number of benches facing the river bank. I hope they're still there."

"We'll check that as well," Rautz said.

"Fine. Now, if they are still there, you can put two men right here." He pointed to a spot. "This provides an even better view of the bridge and anyone mounting it. You are all going to be undercover, right?" The four inspectors nodded. "Then there shouldn't be any problem. And the sweetest thing is that no matter what side of the bridge the suspect enters from, one of these lookout posts will be able to see him and alert the others."

Prenger then stepped in. "And because it's a bridge, we'll have him automatically boxed in. If we have officers advancing from both the north and the south, he'll have nowhere to flee."

"Except maybe jump into the river," Stebbel noted.

"I hope he's a good swimmer then," Prenger responded.

"You mean, you hope he's a bad swimmer."

"Yes; that's exactly what I meant."

This part of the planning session wrapped up quickly from there. Sergeant Király headed back to his own division after receiving hearty thanks from the four inspectors. They were all satisfied with a job well done.

Shortly before noon, the four lower-rank marksmen arrived and the group moved to a larger briefing room. Assignments and overall strategy were gone through in tight detail. Stebbel and one of the marksmen would be sitting at an outdoor table, posing as customers. Another marksman would also be there, pretending to be their waiter.

Prenger and his partner would be on the north side miming a pleasant evening chat on a bench. Dörfner and the youngest member of the team, Officer Esslin, would be stationed on the south side, diagonally across from the café, and they would advance as soon as the suspect appeared.

"But he can't see us," Dörfner said. "We have to stay out of sight until he arrives."

"Or blend completely into the background," Stebbel added.

The briefing ran smoothly and efficiently. Rautz stood back while Stebbel, Dörfner and Prenger outlined the operation. They then asked for questions. One of the sharpshooters from the street patrols raised his hand.

"When do we use our weapons?"

"We will try not to use our weapons," Stebbel replied firmly.

"We want to take this man alive, and in good health. We would like to ask him questions about these murders. Many questions."

The young cop raised his hand again. "But what if he pulls out a weapon?"

"Then we shoot," Dörfner interjected. "Without hesitation. We try to wound him, but if necessary ..." He paused and looked at Stebbel, who completed the thought.

"If necessary, we do what is necessary."

39

The team gathered in a special room in the headquarters canteen for their *Vespers* meal, a light supper of bread, cheese, sliced meats and pickles. No alcohol was allowed. "I'll treat you all to a good drink at the end of this evening's assignment," Inspector Rautz said as he raised his glass filled with mineral water. Then he offered a toast. "To a complete success."

The other officers all lifted their glasses. "To complete success."

Shortly after eight, the team was taken to the area of operations in two police vehicles. After dropping off the members of the team, the vehicles drove off; they didn't want the suspect to see two police cars sitting together and get suspicious.

The group then broke up into its three components: the café, the bench north of the bridge, and just south of the bridge. By 8:40, they were all in place, guarding their positions as if guarding a patch of sacred ground.

Inspector Rautz, however, took up his post in the café itself, towards the back. He had decided to supervise the operation from a safe distance. But he served another important function there, as he explained to the front-line officers. He had to sit there with the café owner and keep him calm, assuring him as often as need be that his establishment was safe, that there would be no gunplay in or around the café.

While there had been anticipation, even excitement, from the time they first left for the Ebersdorfer Bridge until they had taken their places, as nine o'clock neared, the mood had changed radically. At about ten to nine, it was a free-floating uneasiness; five minutes later, this uneasiness had increased considerably. Then, as the minutes squeezed ever closer to the top of the hour, it swelled into raw tension.

Stebbel could read it in the face and neck of Officer Koubek, the young cop chosen to stand post with him. He also noticed that Koubek was doing flexing exercises with his right hand, the one he used to fire a gun. Was this a good sign for a sharpshooter? Or just the opposite?

He then noticed that his own hand was shaking. When he turned and saw that their "waiter" was also flexing his hands and fingers, he decided to do likewise.

Not too far from where Stebbel was sitting, Dörfner felt his old army injury acting up. This sometimes happened when he was extremely tense, but it was especially unwelcome then. The inspector knew that he might need to move quickly and deftly when the suspect appeared, and an old pain throbbing in his leg was the last thing he needed.

But that wasn't the only pain he felt. His neck was also starting to ache, something that occurred only when he was extremely tense. He rubbed his neck vigorously, hoping to work out the ache. When he gazed over at his own partner, Officer Schildhauer, he saw extreme nervousness in his face. He also saw his lips moving and then realized that Schildhauer was praying. Dörfner himself then made the sign of the cross, closed his eyes briefly, and asked for guidance in the task to come.

Then it was nine o'clock, the time the caller claimed Brunner would arrive. But as the bells tolled nine in a nearby church, no one had come. No one at all. All the policemen breathed a sigh – a sigh equal parts relief and impatience.

There was no heightened tension from the previous high level until another five minutes had passed – and no suspect had come by. In fact, no one at all had come by. Another five minutes later, Brunner was still a no-show and when 9:15 arrived and there was still no prime suspect, the entire stakeout team was nearing the breaking point.

Inspector Prenger started counting backwards from thirty. When he reached zero, he turned to his junior, Officer Kern, and said, "Well, he's now officially fifteen minutes late. *Das akademische Viertel.* If this were a classroom, we could leave immediately." Then, with a wry smile: "Don't you wish you were back at school?"

From the back of the café, Senior Inspector Rautz gazed at his watch for about the fortieth time in the last twenty minutes. He had seen no movement from the three officers outside, so he could only assume that the suspect had not appeared yet. Gingerly, he moved a little closer to the front window and craned his neck to see what he could see. What he saw was a quiet evening scene, dimly lit, with no one in view other than Inspector Stebbel, Officer Koubek and Officer Griesser in waiter's dress.

Rautz then looked at his watch again, the second time in less than a minute. He decided that if this Brunner person did not show up in the next five … well, maybe *ten* minutes, he would call the action off. He didn't want to waste the time of his own best people and the highly praised street policemen they had with them.

There would always be other opportunities, he decided. This whole thing had probably been a very mean, tasteless joke by someone who did not have the proper respect for Vienna's police force and its men.

Across the river, Prenger had just bent over to check a security rope placed under the bench when Officer Kern tapped him lightly on the shoulder and cautiously pointed towards a figure approaching along the river bank.

Within moments, it was clear this figure was a male. A fairly tall and burly male. At the bridgehead, the man stopped, looked around, then started onto the bridge. About ten meters in, he turned ... looked around again. Prenger and Kern, facing each other, pretended to be involved in a heated discussion. As Prenger's back was now turned to the bridge, he whispered to Kern, "Tell me if starts coming back."

"No," Kern replied. "No. In fact, now he's started walking again, towards the middle."

"Then let's count to five, get up slowly, and join him."

Both officers pulled out their revolvers, index fingers pushed against the triggers. They were ready for any thing that might happen, expected or unexpected.

Meanwhile, Dörfner and Schildhauer started moving across the bridge, on the opposite side from the large man. The man had now reached the middle of the bridge and taken up a position in front of the John of Nepomuk statue, as had been forecast by the anonymous "friend of justice".

When he saw this pair approaching on the other side, he turned and pretended to be looking into the Danube, admiring the view. Across from him, Dörfner briefly turned and pointed towards the river. This was the signal for Stebbel and the two sharpshooters at the café to commence their advance.

Meanwhile, Schildhauer clutched a small rock he had brought along and threw that into the river, as close to the north side as possible. A quarter century before the invention of the walkie-talkie, this was the way police and military personnel communicated with each other on operations such as this one.

But Prenger and Kern had already vacated the bench and started across the bridge, treading the same side as the late arrival. As soon as he saw them out of the corner of his eye, Dörfner whispered to Schildhauer, "Now!"

Both officers spun around, guns drawn. Dörfner barked out: "Herr Brunner – it's the police. Please turn around, raise your hands and put them high in the air."

The man across the way spun around abruptly. For the first time, Dörfner saw his face. And he could see that, except for the cold fear now etched there, it was the same face as in Herr Hitler's sketch. He also saw that the man had moved his right hand to his chest, the fingers just sliding under the jacket. He shouted once more. "Brunner – raise your hands. High! Right now!"

Instead, the man started back in the direction he had come from. But after just a few steps, he saw the other two officers advancing on him, guns drawn. He stopped and leaned against the railing as a smile spread slowly across his face. And then, he started humming. A waltz tune, with the smile on his face broadening as he hummed.

He then started swaying his shoulders, in rhythm to the tune he was humming. Dörfner tightened the pressure on his trigger. His throat almost painfully dry, he managed to yell again. "Herr Brunner – last chance. Raise your hands. High!"

Instead of following this order, Brunner reached into his jacket and started to pull something out. There was no possibility they would wait to see exactly what he was pulling out. Dörfner shouted, "Open fire!" At almost the same moment, he heard Prenger shout the same order.

By the time Dörfner had taken aim, the suspect had swirled just as the first bullets, from the guns of Prenger and Kern, tore into his left leg. He let out a scream of pain and fell awkwardly against the bridge railing. But even though wounded, he managed to pull out what looked like a gun.

Dörfner again barked: "Fire!" He and Schildhauer started firing, one right after the other, as if taking turns in a shooting gallery contest. Four bullets ripped through the left side of the man's chest; a large blotch of dark appeared where they had entered.

A look of shock filled that face Dörfner had seen repeated times in roiling dreams and the man pitched forward. Seven policemen quickly converged on the large figure, now sprawled over the walkway. Stebbel, Koubek and Griesser had rushed up, but got to the action just as the shooting had ceased. By the time they arrived at the scene, Schildhauer and Prenger had turned the man over, onto his back. As Stebbel approached, he peered at Dörfner. Dörfner nodded.

"Brunner. It is Brunner." Stebbel looked down at the figure on the ground and nodded in agreement. "He's gone. It's over. It's all over."

The two partners then knelt down and stared closely at the face of the man who had obsessed their lives over the last few weeks. His eyes were wide open, staring upwards.

Dörfner pointed down at the face. "Look at those eyes. Like he still sees something. It looks like he's ..."

Stebbel finished the thought. "Like he's staring out at something terrifying." Dörfner nodded.

As they rose, they stared at each other. Dörfner then spontaneously reached over and put both arms around his partner and lowered his head against him. "We got him, Steb. We got him. The whole mess is over." Stebbel squeezed him in return. The other five officers on the detail looked away for a few moments, allowing these two men who had spent so much energy and emotional capital trying to capture this killer have the moment to themselves.

But it lasted little more than a few moments. Stebbel and Dörfner then broke their embrace and stepped away, both of them embarrassed at this spontaneous show of stored emotions. Prenger stepped over and gave a comradely pat on the shoulder to both men.

And then Stebbel croaked out a downbeat note.

"But I wanted him alive. I wanted to interrogate. There were so many … things left unanswered."

"We had no choice, Inspector," Prenger said. "He drew his gun. He was not going to give up. It was his life or ours." Stebbel looked at Dörfner, who nodded sadly.

By this time, Inspector Rautz had made his way out of the café and was moving as quickly as he could to join the others. He still had no idea what had gone down, but he saw a body sprawled across the pedestrian walk. He started counting the men standing around the body. Five … six … seven. It wasn't one of his men; he was exulted.

He finally reached the group and put his arm around Stebbel's shoulder.

Stebbel then shook his head, still awash in regret. "But I wanted to interrogate him. I had questions. I had so many questions I needed to ask him."

Staring down at the face, Prenger said, "Don't worry: it looks like wherever he is now, he's being called upon to answer some very difficult questions."

40

As promised, Rautz took the entire team out to celebrate their triumph. He chose one of his favorite cafés, the Blauer Stengel. As they entered, Rautz signaled the head waiter, then whispered something into his ear. The head waiter had one of his subordinates show the party to a large table near the rear of the main salon as he himself headed off to the kitchen.

After a short time, three waiters approached. The first set up an ice bucket just to the left of Inspector Rautz, the second carried a tray with eight glasses on it, and the third toted a bottle of champagne.

When each officer had his glass filled to the brim with bubbly, Rautz stood and prompted a toast. "To every man here – for their sterling work this evening. There were so many things that could have gone wrong, but you all proved yourselves to be total professionals. And – dare I say it – you are, each of you, heroes for your actions tonight."

To this, they all raised their glasses and sipped the champagne. Rautz then tapped a spoon on his plate and offered a second toast.

"I want to say that there are three of us here at the table who deserve special praise, for tackling this case right from that first dark morning. We put untiring energies into pursuing this monster, who tonight was finally given his bitter dose of justice.

"So – to my brave and resourceful colleagues, Inspectors Stebbel and Dörfner, who were my right-hand men in solving this case." The other policemen all raised their glasses to Stebbel and Dörfner and took deep drinks. Those two sneaked a look at each other and arched their eyebrows at Rautz's puff of self-praise.

Later, generous slices of cake were served, which the men washed down with the remaining champagne. Rautz signaled for the three inspectors to lean closer while he imparted some important information.

"I have to go soon. Those damn newspaper reporters will be flocking to headquarters to get some details. For the morning editions, you know. We can work on the full report tomorrow, so you three can just go on celebrating. But I will need some details for when the journalists ask me."

"Of course, Herr Inspector."

Rautz then slid the receipt for the celebration to Stebbel and asked him to write down the name of the killer, so that he would have the exact spelling. While Stebbel was carefully printing the name in large letters, Rautz asked other key questions. "OK, so the killer, he did really have a gun with him tonight, correct?"

"*Jawohl*, Herr Inspector."

"And he did pull it out, which is why we had to shoot him?"

"Yes, we had to consider the safety of every member of the team. Knowing him to be a vicious murderer – '

Rautz was already writing something down. "We couldn't give him the chance to kill one of our own."

Prenger then added a detail. "The gun this Brunner was carrying was a Remington Star." Then, in a softer voice, he added an editorial note. "Not a very good firearm actually. Even if it was only one of us facing him down there on the bridge, he wouldn't have had much of a chance."

Dörfner snorted. "A much better chance than he offered any of those girls he murdered." The other three inspectors tapped their fists softly on the table to show their full agreement.

Rautz left a short time later. Before departing, he again thanked all those on the capture and warned the young hooks that they shouldn't stay much longer, as they had to get up early again tomorrow for duty and they "all needed their beauty sleep". He then leaned over to inform the three inspectors that they could take the whole morning off, at full pay. Just make sure they were in by mid-afternoon, he added; they would probably be called upstairs to receive congratulations from the District Commander, maybe even the Commissioner.

*　*　*

Following the celebration at the café, the three inspectors headed off to a late-night tavern to continue with their celebrations. On their way, these three men who had planned and overseen the operation looked back at the end of the mission.

Stebbel turned to Prenger. "So that gun he used, it wasn't very good?"

Prenger shook his head. "An old model, and one that always had problems. I'm surprised he even showed up with such a relic."

"So why do you think he didn't just … give himself up? He was outmanned, outgunned, out-everythinged."

Dörfner had an answer to this. "He knew he was facing the noose anyway. And he was a military man. There's a code in the military: if the cause is lost, you still go down fighting. Keep shooting and hope you take out as many of the other bastards as you can before they take you out. He was just following the code."

Prenger shifted uneasily in his seat, then turned to the other two loupes. "There's one other big question dangling."

"What's that?"

"Who was Herr Brunner expecting to meet there tonight?"

Dörfner had no idea. He turned to Stebbel as the only one who might have an answer. But Stebbel simply shrugged. "A friend of justice?" he said.

Though they got lost several times along the way, the trio finally reached the tavern. It was not too long before they had become darlings of the owner and the staff. One tall carafe of wine was not even finished when the trio called for the next.

Dörfner poured himself another glass and took half of it down in one deep swallow. He then smiled through his self-imposed fog and tapped the wood to get the attention of his two colleagues at the table.

"I, Karl-Heinz Dörfner, being of sodden mind and unwound body, do hereby declare that you two fellows are the most valuable friends one could find in the entire Viennese police force."

"I second that motion," added Prenger, hoisting his glass high.

Stebbel likewise raised his glass. "For what it's worth."

"Great friends. The kind you can rely on. The kind who you can put your hands in their life. I mean, you could put your life in their hands." He paused for a minute to go over that last sentence again, making sure he had gotten it right this time.

"Yes, great, great friends. Especially this guy." He pointed at Stebbel with his glass. Stebbel smiled and raised his own glass in gratitude.

"And let me tell you, I am going to take care of both of you guys when I'm running things around here."

Prenger pursed his lips. "Oh. And when is this going to be?"

"Before long. Very soon, in fact. Soon, soon, soon. Here, feel this." He then put both of his hands on the table and with a head gesture, prompted his two colleagues to do the same. They duly joined him.

"Do you feel that? That's the big roulette wheel. And I mean the *big* one. Spinning faster and faster. And that wheel is going to going to take another big spin, and when it stops, my side will be on top."

Stebbel smiled. "What? You're going to win a bundle at some casino? Remember me when you do."

"No, that's nothing. Crumbs from the stinking rich. I mean, when the wheel stops and the workers are finally in control."

Prenger thumped his palm on the table in a mock show of triumph. "Ah yes. Attention, gentlemen and cops: we are now about to hear an inspiring speech by Charley the Red." He turned to Stebbel. "You know Dörfner is a Red, don't you?"

"What?"

"*Ja, ja* – he's a deep-red socialist. Can't wait for the ruling class to be overthrown."

Stebbel was incredulous. "Is this serious?"

Dörfner nodded and raised his glass high. "To the working class and their true allies. When we're running things, things will run right. Finally."

Prenger grabbed the wine carafe and refilled Dörfner's glass to the brim. "Come on, let's get him mumbling drunk before he can give us his whole theory of the coming revolution."

Dörfner folded his hand over the top of the glass even though it would have been impossible to pour in more than a few drops. He was in a buoyant mood and he had what he felt was an important point to make.

"Let's face it: the Habsburgs are finished. Old Franz-Josef doesn't even know what century it is most of the time, and he probably needs four assistants to help him sit down to shit. Forget about him trying to run the empire.

"Franz-Ferdinand? OK, I grant you he doesn't seem to be that bad. Some people tell me he's even clever, and sympathetic to the common folks. Like us. But the old fool Franz-Joseph has already declared that none of his offspring can ever inherit the throne. Why? Because his wife is not from the ranks of the upper aristocracy. Marrying out of that group is the only way to produce kids that aren't natural-born idiots, but F-J doesn't want that. And why? Because he only feels comfortable with idiots like himself running the country.

"And who would be next in line after Franz-Ferdinand? Karl! God help us! Give him six months on the throne and the whole Habsburg farce will fold up its tents and leave the scene as fast as they can get out."

Prenger again raised his glass and spoke in a mocking tone. "To the new order! And to Karl-Heinz the First! The leader of the empire's proletariat."

Dörfner clutched his own glass and hoisted it high, spilling about a third of its contents on the upward trajectory.

"To us! And especially the three of us sitting right here. Here. We will be there among the leaders of the first Workers Republic of Austria-Hungary."

Stebbel then raised his own glass. "To a better tomorrow!"

They all clinked glasses. Prenger took a swallow, then turned again to Stebbel. "You really didn't know that our Karl-Heinz was a socialist agitator? The worm within the rotten apple?"

Stebbel threw his hands up. "I ... This is the first time I ever hear of this."

Dörfner nodded. "Stebbel and I are good at keeping secrets. We keep our secrets away from criminals, informants, newspaper guys, and even each other." He swallowed most of the wine left in his glass. "Yes, Herr Colleague, there are a lot of things you don't know about me yet."

Prenger smiled. "And there are probably a lot of things you don't know about Julian."

Dörfner's head lolled from side to side, which was all he could manage to serve as a nod at that point. "Absolutely. Now that we're big heroes though, and we rely on each other so much, we'll have to learn more."

He then leaned over, cupped his hand and pretended to whisper to Prenger. "I do know some of his secrets though. For instance, I know he writes poetry."

Prenger turned to Stebbel. "You do?" Stebbel smiled and shrugged.

"And very good stuff, let me tell you – if only I could understand any of it." Dörfner leaned back and smiled at his partner. "He even writes it in the office, I think. I find it sometimes in the desk. In that drawer that we both have a key to. He hides it under other papers and a few notebooks. I was looking for something one time, pulled out all the papers and found that poetry. At first, I thought it was the confessions of some half-crazy criminals. But then I recognized Steb's handwriting. I was so proud right then to have a real poet as a partner." He hoisted his glass high again. "To Julian Stebbel – the Goethe of our age."

They all laughed and guzzled wine, though Stebbel's laugh was half embarrassment. And then he tried to switch the conversation to another topic entirely: the way the press would treat their triumph of that evening. And as both Dörfner and Prenger were more sozzled than he was, he managed to get them to that topic and keep them away from any personal matters until they left the pub not too long afterwards.

41

Inspector Rautz was right about Stebbel and Dörfner being called into District Commander Schollenberg's office the next afternoon. Schollenberg congratulated them heartily and told them they could expect a little bonus in their next pay envelopes. He was seeing to that himself.

Schollenberg then noted that the Commissioner was too busy right at that point to see the two heroes, but he did send along his congratulations and was hoping he could shake their hands personally early the next week.

The Commissioner was also having a Certificate of Highest Commendation prepared for the two, and was trying to have a stamp and a signature from the Interior Ministry next to his own at the bottom of the certificate.

Later that afternoon, two large boxes were delivered to the inspectors' shared office, each one carried by two younger policemen. Affixed to the top of the boxes was an envelope with the inspectors' names carefully inscribed.

Inside the envelopes were letters signed by *Geheimrat* Karsten von Klettenburg.

He thanked both men for their courage and hard work in finding and bringing to justice the man who had murdered his dear wife, along with the four other innocent victims. He said he would never be able to express the sense of release this fiend's demise had brought him, but the two inspectors could rest assured that he would be in their debt for as long as he was able to draw breath.

The accompanying cases were a small measure of his gratitude for the peace they had brought him. It was a sample of some of the best products by one of his French business associates. He hoped they would appreciate this gift and also his undying thanks.

Dörfner pulled out a large pair of scissors and ripped open the top of his own well-sealed case. He then did the same for Stebbel's case, though more carefully and deftly this time.

Both men folded back the top flaps and peered within. "Wine. It looks like wine," said Dörfner.

Stebbel pulled out a bottle, while Dörfner pulled out two and examined them to see if there were any differences. "Huh – it is wine."

"Yes; remember that the *Geheimrat* was off in Bordeaux on business when Frau von Klettenburg was murdered. I guess this is one of his businesses."

"Looks good," Dörfner admitted. Most of Dörfner's own experience with wine was the fresh product served at the *Heuriger* taverns, so he deferred to Stebbel's judgment on this.

"You think it's good stuff?"

Stebbel had just pulled out another two bottles and seen that they were all the same. "Yes. Yes, I think this is quite a nice wine," he said as he read the label: Lafite Rothschild.

* * *

It didn't take the Viennese press long to join the parade of praise for the successful conclusion of the Strangler saga – probably not much longer than it takes to rip one half-filled sheet of paper from a typewriter and scroll in another. The same papers that had spent weeks denouncing the Viennese police as incompetents, laggards, almost complicit in the last three murders made a sharp 180-degree turn. Now they were heaping adulation on the brave, stalwart and resourceful policemen who managed to bring the Strangler's killing spree to an abrupt end.

Much of that praise was directed towards Commander Schollenberg and Senior Inspector Rautz for their "steadfast leadership in tracking down the killer and then dispensing instant justice" there on the Ebersdorfer Bridge. Not coincidentally, Schollenberg and Rautz were the only two police officials who had spoken directly to the press. But a number of newspaper reports also mentioned Inspectors Dörfner and Stebbel and the important roles they had played in the pursuit and killing of the Strangler.

The palace had discreetly requested that the press make no mention of the fact that the fiend was a pensioned former member of the Imperial Guard. A few editors acceded to this request for the first editions, but most of the tabloids duly disregarded the request. Brunner's ties to the palace, however tenuous, gave the story a slight whiff of scandal, and scandal was what sold papers.

However, none of the city's journals were able to obtain a single photo of the killer. The Imperial Guard refused all such requests, while the police said their photos were all taken right after the shootout and were thus too grisly. (Many a Vienna journalist clenched their fists in frustration when they heard how grisly the photos were and were then told they could not get their hands on them.)

Frau Keuler had retreated to her hometown after the shootout and was beyond contact. But her location made no difference: she would have sooner shared nude photos of herself with the press than any photos of her late brother. So the only images of the killer the public got were the written accounts that described him as nasty, brutish and tall. And almost mythically strong, if you were to believe the panting reports of the yellow press.

Arnold Brunner's body was released to his sister after a week of intense forensic investigation. The University of Vienna had requested the removal of his brain for further study. The plan was to work with pathologists in the police department to determine if there was something in that organ which disposed the man to such horrible crimes. However, Frau Keuler appeared nauseous when a professor from the university simply began to explain their intentions and adamantly refused to allow her younger brother's cadaver to serve the interests of science.

The remains were brought back to their small town, where Brunner was given a private burial, closed to the public and the press. There was no wake before the burial and no priest at the graveside. No one from the palace, the Imperial Guard, or the Vienna police force attended the funeral.

* * *

Two days after the Vienna police had closed the chapter on the Spittelberg Strangler, Stebbel and Dörfner returned to headquarters from a long lunch. A long lunch was just one of the privileges the two loupes had earned from their successful pursuit of the strangler. They were also permitted to come in a bit later in the mornings, and mid-afternoon reconnaissance missions to a favorite café were not frowned upon.

As they returned that day, Henninger, the reception officer, called them over. "Inspectors – that gentleman is here to see you again." They turned to see Hitler sitting stiffly on the visitor's bench, in almost the same spot he occupied on his very first visit. He did not look very happy.

The inspectors were, of course, surprised by this visit. Dörfner leaned over and half-whispered, "What's this all about?"

Stebbel shrugged. "Let's ask him." Dörfner reluctantly agreed.

The two inspectors walked over to the bench. Hitler, who had been staring straight ahead for some time, turned and attempted a smile when he saw the two. He stood and dipped his head slightly in greetings.

"Inspectors, I apologize for coming in once again unannounced, but I did have one small matter of some urgency I need to discuss with you.

Stebbel was receptive. "Of course, Herr Hitler. What is it?"

Hitler took a deep breath before answering. "The reward. The reward for information leading to the capture of that vicious murderer. I believe that I am now entitled to some of that reward.

"But I was just at the department responsible for this, and they told me that I have no valid claim. I was told it was the report of an anonymous informant that led to the killer. The officer there said only that anonymous person can claim the reward."

The two inspectors exchanged confounded looks, and Dörfner then tried to explain.

"Actually, Herr Hitler, it is true that an anonymous caller – " He didn't even finish his sentence before a hostile look filled the visitor's face.

Stebbel quickly intervened. "To be fair, I think that Herr Hitler also has a legitimate claim here." He tilted his head towards Dörfner. "If it weren't for his excellent sketches, we would not have been able to make significant progress in the apprehension of Herr Brunner. Isn't that true?"

Hitler gave Stebbel a nod of gratitude for this interjection, then turned to Dörfner and flashed a smile steeped in smugness. Dörfner floundered in getting out another reply.

"Yes, but I think …"

"You're quite right, Herr Colleague, but I do think there is a way for us to get *some* reward money for our friend, Herr Hitler." He then turned back to Hitler and, with the sincerest look he could muster, added, "But you realize, sir, that you must share that reward with the anonymous hero who provided us with the essential information. And your share will be significantly smaller than his."

Hitler mulled this over for several moments, then conceded the point. "I guess from a certain perspective, one could argue that's fair." He considered the whole thing for a few more moments. "But how much money are we talking about, gentlemen?" Stebbel thought for a moment. "Perhaps … two hundred kroners." Dörfner made a choking sound. "No more than that I'm afraid."

Hitler seemed to be making some quick calculations. Then he nodded. "Yes. Two hundred kroners. That would be … adequate. And when might I expect to receive this amount?"

"Well, we must go through some official channels and … In a few days perhaps. Maybe … Thursday."

Hitler smiled. "What time on Thursday?"

"Oh, the afternoon would be best. Shall we say … three o'clock?"

"Three o'clock. I will be here, gentleman. You can rely on that."

The three men stood and Hitler extended his hand to shake on the deal. Both inspectors shook his hand, and noted that it was the reassured handshake of someone who felt he had just won a fight for justice. They then escorted Hitler to the front desk, where another young officer was called over to escort him to the *paternoster*.

As they watched those two saunter off, Dörfner spilled out a light laugh. "I guess we'll have to arrange to be called off on official business Thursday at three o'clock." Stebbel turned to him with an admonishing look.

"Not at all, Herr Colleague. I really believe we owe Hitler something for his assistance. And he could certainly use the money.

Let me speak with Schollenberg."

"You think the District Commander is going to part willingly with any of the department's treasure?"

"Not willingly, but I'll make a good argument why he should be able to take 200 kroner from that reward pot and give it to our friend. He should see the wisdom of my reasoning."

"Maybe you should just threaten to lock him in a room together with Herr Hitler for an hour or two. That should do it."

Stebbel smiled broadly and nodded. The two inspectors then returned to their office to look through the afternoon's mail, much of it something in the nature of fan mail.

At 3:30 on Thursday afternoon, there was a rap on the inspectors' office door. Stebbel answered it and was told that they had a visitor who wished to see them. They had a good idea who it was.

Looking down the corridor, Stebbel saw that Hitler was already there. He invited him in. All he could imagine was that Hitler had encountered more problems picking up his reward money.

But just the opposite was the case. As Hitler entered the office, he was wearing a smile so big, it could barely fit on his face. When he held up a bloated brown envelope, they knew exactly why he was smiling.

Hitler then assailed the two inspectors with enthusiastic handshakes and thanked both for their help in securing him the reward.

"And now, gentlemen, I have something for you. A gift. For each of you." He reached into the leather case lodged under his arm that whole time and pulled out two large sheets of paper. He looked at each sheet warmly, almost as if he hated to part with it. Then he handed one to Dörfner, one to Stebbel.

"Gentlemen, as a memento of our fruitful work together. I hope this will help you to remember me."

The two officers inspected the gifts: two sketches, one of Dörfner, one of Stebbel. The loupes carefully inspected the drawings. Not very good either, but both men nodded appreciatively.

"Well, thank you, Herr Hitler. This is so thoughtful. And so … impressive in its artistry."

All three stood and shook hands again.

"We wish you all the best. Perhaps we'll be able to work together again on some project."

"Perhaps. But I am going to make a short trip to Munich in the near future. There's some business I must attend to there."

"I understand. Anyway, again, all the best. We wish you continued success with your artwork."

This seemed to flip a switch deep within Hitler. "You really like it, do you? You think I'm that good? A true artist?"

"Yes, of course, of course." Stebbel held up his sketch and then pointed to Dörfner's. "And your sketch of Arnold Brunner helped us to track down that fiend." He paused just a moment. "You are truly a talented individual."

Hitler again smiled broadly, thanked both of the inspectors once again for everything, and made his departure. A young officer stood waiting near the office door to escort him to the *paternoster*. Stebbel and Dörfner traded looks of admiration as they glanced at the two sketches.

"OK, I admit that they are fairly good," said Dörfner with an expansive smile. "But he still wasn't able to capture just how handsome I am."

"But that's almost impossible, isn't it, Herr Colleague?" Dörfner shook his head and they both laughed freely.

42

In the next few days, Adolf Hitler tied up all the loose ends of his life in Vienna; at least, those that could be tied up quickly. He paid off several small debts to his closest friends at the Meldemannstrasse hostel – much to their surprise. He also paid off a few debts to a client who had advanced him money, and then collected on debts from two other clients.

He gathered together everything he thought important and worth bringing along to the next phase of his life. This mainly involved two valises of clothing and all his unsold artwork, packed into the leather case and then laid carefully at the top of one of his valises. In a large paper bag, he had stashed a number of odds and ends that he might need in the weeks ahead.

On the evening of May 23rd, Hitler went around to all the people at the hostel with whom he still enjoyed amicable relations and bade them farewell. He told most of them that he was moving to Munich. He had friends and family there, he said, and they had invited him to stay there for a while and pursue his career as an artist.

In point of fact, Hitler had no family or real friends in the Bavarian capital. He did have a few strong acquaintances from his days in Linz who had gone off to Munich, but he had never bothered to keep up with them. But there were other, much better, reasons for him to leave Vienna and seek a new base of operations.

As he admitted to his co-resident Josef Greuler, who shared Hitler's pan-German biases, he was simply sick of life in what he often called "this mongrel metropolis". He just needed to get to a "real German city" and "breathe clean German air' without all these foreign elements polluting the atmosphere.

What he wouldn't admit even to Greuler was that he had been dodging the draft for almost a year, failing to turn up for scheduled medical exams and induction calls into the Austro-Hungarian army. His years in Vienna had sewn a deep contempt for the sprawling, multicultural empire that was his homeland. As he put it, he had no stomach for serving in an army that protected and served "Serbs, Hungarians, Croats, Poles, Czechs and other Slavs, to say nothing of all the Jews and God knows what else had taken up residence within the borders of the empire".

Hitler believed it was only a matter of time before the authorities caught up with and arrested him for avoiding military service. This was especially true now that he had become well known within police headquarters for his role in catching that monster Brunner. Sure, he was a hero, but that would probably not protect him from prosecution – or, worse, being forcibly inducted into the army and then shipped off to some God-forsaken post in the far east stump of the empire.

Also, he was now afraid of being arrested for assaulting that man in the red-light area. Hitler felt no real guilt for this – the man truly deserved to get slashed for reacting the way he did. Besides, to Hitler, he looked like one of those foreigners looking to defile some lovely German girls – but he didn't wish to go to prison for that rash act.

He was also afraid that he might run into that man on the street somewhere, and as the swine was much bigger than Hitler, he might have given him a good thrashing for stepping in to defend the honor of the young girls forced into prostitution.

He thus had three good reasons for wanting to get out of Vienna. Now that he had his reward money, he was finally able to do so.

He had already bought his ticket, a one-way ticket, for Munich, and late the next morning, Hitler boarded a tram that took him to Vienna's *Westbahnhof*, or Western Railway Station. There he met up with Rudolf Häusler, a local pharmacist, who had also decided to relocate to Munich.

As the train lumbered out of the majestic station, Hitler moved to a window in the corridor, leaving Häusler alone with his copy of the *Altdeustches Tagblatt* newspaper. He stayed there, posted at the window, for the next twenty minutes, seeing for what he thought might be the last time this robust but horribly diseased capital of Habsburg grandeur. He drank in all the grandiose buildings, the wide boulevards, the swarm of people on the streets going about their late morning business.

He thought of the extravagant plans he had once nurtured for reshaping this city, of adding new layers of architectural grandeur to the imperial capital. He felt a slight lump in his throat and his eyes started to moisten briefly.

But then he remembered how this city had rejected him, rejected him over and over again, and he knew that his future lay elsewhere. Vienna would always remain a part of him, but even now, while still within the city's confines, he felt it was a part that had grown worn and useless.

Most of Vienna took no notice whatsoever of the departure of this lean young man who twenty-five years later would come back and alter the history, tenor and terrain of the city in ways no one could imagine in May 1913. For now, he was another barely noticeable dot in a sea of dots, and until he had assisted in catching its most notorious criminal of the pre-war era, Hitler had made little impression on most of the capital's residents.

Besides, most of the public's attention that had been seized by the Spittelberg Strangler was now riveted on the scandal around Colonel Alfred Redl, former head of the imperial military intelligence. The very next day after Hitler's departure, Redl committed suicide in an elegant hotel room.

It had been discovered by the same military intelligence operation that Redl himself had set up and developed that the colonel had, in fact, been operating for years as a spy for the Russians, providing the empire's arch-adversaries with vital military information.

Confronted with the evidence against him, Redl was offered the chance to avoid a nasty trial – with its torturous, drawn-out humiliation – simply by self-administering justice. He did so with a single bullet to the head. But now all of Vienna was asking how he could have deceived everyone for so long and just how damaging was the intelligence he had provided to the Russians for handsome payments. So one undernourished draft-dodger slipping over the border into Bavaria was of no concern to the Viennese public.

But as to the Redl affair, District Commander Schollenberg had offered the services of Stebbel and Dörfner to the current directors of military intelligence, to help in their investigations of anyone else who might be involved. Though the head of intelligence expressed his gratitude to Commander Schollenberg, he had to turn the offer down; they wanted to keep things in-house so as to control any further bad news that might seep out. Schollenberg understood completely.

43

Strangely, no one came forward to claim the lion's share of that reward money. Between the rewards offered by several newspapers and the one offered by the police and government, it would have added up to a tidy sum. All the principles at the police department were baffled that there was no attempt to collect the reward, except for a few all too obvious frauds hoping to snare a windfall from somebody else's anonymous tip.

The one most intrigued by this failure to collect the promised reward was Stebbel. At first, he – like everyone else concerned – was merely baffled. It was such easy money; why not drop in quietly, give the evidence of identity required, and walk out with the money.

But then he began to craft a theory as to why the informant had not presented himself: The tipster probably knew the killer too well. He may have been afraid that friends of Brunner would come after him. Or, he himself was an accomplice. By turning up to collect the reward, he could very well be incriminating himself.

* * *

The next two weeks ran rather smoothly for the two new stars of the Vienna constabulary. They received praise from many quarters, along with those special privileges. Within the department, they had become something like envied celebrities. But Stebbel remained uneasy with the new life.

One evening, shortly after the takedown of Arnold Brunner, he sat down at his desk at home intending to write a long letter to his wife. He had sent her a short missive right after Brunner was killed, but now he wanted to share more details about the case, how long and hard they had worked trying to solve it, and how much tension and sleeplessness it had cost him.

He would also squeeze in the perfunctory declaration of how much he missed her and a promise to come to Slovenia soon for another visit, an extended one, as soon as he could manage to get away.

But after writing just a few lines, he pushed the letter to the side and pulled out his journal. He opened it to the first empty page and stared at the white emptiness for about half a minute. Then he picked up his pen and again began to write.

He just couldn't pull himself away from the Strangler case. With the killing of the killer, the case was officially solved. The praise, the certificates of merit, the bonuses ... even the *Geheimrat*'s shipment of Bordeaux wine affirmed that the long nightmare was over. But for Stebbel himself, there were still several nagging, unanswered questions sticking out like thorns. And he kept pricking himself on those thorns – intentionally.

What *was* Frau von Klettenburg doing out all alone that night, and in that quarter frequented mainly by streetwalkers? And why was she dressed so provocatively, her makeup so ostentatious? Also, whose semen filled her vagina when she was murdered? They knew that her husband was hundreds of miles away in Bordeaux, so with whom had she been intimate just before her death?

Was it Brunner? Did they have sex – full sex, no caution – shortly before he murdered her? And was there something about their sex that threw a switch deep inside Brunner, that set him off to kill first Frau von Kletterburg and then four other innocent women? He wouldn't have sex with those other woman – couldn't perhaps – but was the act of thrusting his hands around a woman's neck, then strangling her, his substitute for intimacy.

Was there something shocking, disgusting, or humiliating about his sex with that wealthy woman who ranked far above him on the social scale that plunged Brunner into one of the darker caverns of his own mind? Did he perhaps find himself caught in a labyrinth of his own depravity that he simply could not find a way out of, even if he had tried.

Stebbel snapped the journal shut. Maybe Dörfner was right: maybe he had been reading too much Freud, sinking himself too deeply into his exotic theories. Perhaps he was becoming slightly mad himself, twisted around by those theories and how tightly they fit over the twisted world of the modern criminal.

He went to the window and gazed out onto the Währing heath and beyond. His Vienna, decked in full evening splendor, was indeed a beautiful place – so beautiful it was sometimes hard to imagine it also as a home to such horrors. But the horrors were as much a part of his Vienna as the staunch splendor, the august architecture, the rich cultural life, the patchwork of districts and social classes.

In fact, if it weren't for the horrors, would he have been so successful in his career? Maybe he would have ended up a mediocre *Gymnasium* teacher, here or back home in Innsbruck. More likely, he would have wound up behind a desk in some useless ministry, a dyspeptic civil servant processing papers no one had any real interest in. So, he admitted, in a perverse way he owed a measure of gratitude to those horrors. Without them, he would be fully useless to himself and others.

Stepping back into the dining area to retrieve his glass of brandy, he was seized by the feeling that his home had acquired a few more ghosts. Or at least one more. For the last week or so, his apartment – the spacious apartment for which others envied him – had become a rather uncomfortable place for the inspector as he felt himself being squeezed even more by these ghosts.

Fortunately, Stebbel had now grown honest enough to know that he had to speak to someone about these problems.

44

At 2.40, Sigmund Freud was already settled on the bench at the edge of the Liechtenstein Park, enjoying a cigar. Several minutes later, Inspector Stebbel arrived.

"Excuse me," Freud said with a generous smile, "but aren't you the famous police inspector, Julian Stebbel? Scourge of criminals from one end of Vienna to the other? Won't you join me." Stebbel returned the smile and took his seat right next to the good doctor.

Freud pulled out a cigar and extended it to Stebbel. "It would be an honor for me if you'd join me in a congratulatory smoke. For your fine work in catching that ruthless murderer."

"Thank you, but … I've been having some problems with my breathing lately. That respiratory condition I mentioned once? So I'm afraid I'll have to turn your kind offer down."

"That's a shame. A hero deserves a good cigar." To make his point clear, Freud took a deep draw on his own cigar and blew out a soft banner of smoke. "So, it must feel quite good having caught this … Bruning fellow?"

"Brunner. Yes, it does feel … fairly good. Everyone tells me how good I should be feeling about finally bringing him down." Freud nodded. "So why do I not feel as good as I'm supposed to feel?" He then looked at Freud in a way that told the doctor this was not a rhetorical question.

Freud took two shallow puffs from his cigar before answering. "Well, you've suddenly become a hero of sorts." Stebbel merely shrugged. "Maybe it's still too strange a role for you. After all, being a hero carries certain obligations with it. People expect a certain ... way about you. It takes some adjustment, I know. Perhaps you're still not comfortable with everything."

"Yes ... I guess that's a big part of it."

"Let me offer some advice: don't worry about how that hero's mantel fits you. Just think of all the young women's lives you may have saved by ending this Brunner's reign of terror. Think of all the relief you've brought to so many of this city's residents.

"Honestly, a number of my female patients tell me how much safer they feel now that the strangler has been removed from our streets. I've even been able to halve the dosage for some tranquilizers because the patients are so much more relaxed now.

He tapped Stebbel lightly on the shoulder. "You've accomplished so much by stopping this killer. Focus on that, Inspector. That should make you feel much better."

"Yes, I ... I think that might help."

"And if you need something more, I can always write you a prescription for something that will relax you. In your case, I don't know that I would recommend it, but if you think it would also help ..."

"Thank you, Herr Doktor. But ..."

"Yes?"

"I think ... a big part of my problem is that we did kill the killer. Before I ever got a chance to interrogate him. There are so many unanswered questions now. I wanted him to tell us the why. So many whys, actually. Now the mystery sits there forever." He shook his head, the sting of frustration etched deeply into his face. "If only I could have had him alone in that interrogation room for an hour, two hours maybe."

Freud shook his head sympathetically and patted Stebbel on the shoulder again. "My friend – and I am proud to think of you as a friend – I must tell you that these things are not that easy. People like this strangler may not know themselves the true motivations for what they do.

"I often have patients trying – trying desperately – to reach the caverns of their own minds, find the roots of their own fears, and it takes us many months, sometimes years, before they make that breakthrough and get to those roots.

"And, unfortunately, I think that would have been the case with this killer of yours. It's particularly true of people who do something awful: they lock their secrets so deep within their own hearts, they themselves have trouble digging them out again."

As Stebbel chewed on this, Freud pulled out his watch and threw a glance at it. "Sorry, but I do have to be leaving soon. I have this new patient, a challenging case, and I have to do a little extra preparation this time."

"Well thank you, Herr Doktor, for tending to this troubled soul."

Freud shook his head to demur. He then stood. But before leaving, he again pulled out that cigar. This time he squeezed it into the outside upper pocket of Stebbel's suit jacket. "For later. When you're breathing more easily again. After all, a hero deserves a good cigar."

"I'm sure I'll enjoy it when I feel more like a hero."

Freud gave him another sympathetic smile, turned and started walking back towards Berggasse. About ten paces away, he stopped. Stebbel thought he was going to come back and add some last bit of advice. But after that slight hesitation, he continued on towards his appointment without even turning around.

Stebbel continued sitting on the bench for a time, his arms folded, wondering how much of Freud's advice he would really be able to use.

45

Dörfner had invited Stebbel to join him for an evening out. He was planning to first go out for a nice dinner, then head over to his favorite brothel. "They have a number of new girls there. The spring line, I guess you'd call it. Real lookers, too.

"There's this one beauty from Galicia: red hair, fair skin, amazing blue eyes. Big boobs too, of course. They seem to come standard with those Galician girls.

"Anyway, I'm sure this beauty would love to share all her charms with the great Inspector Stebbel, the man who helped make this city safe for women everywhere."

Stebbel pretended to mull over this offer for a few minutes before declining. He told his partner that he had some business to attend to at home and, besides, he wasn't really feeling that well. But, he said, he was looking to joining Dörfner on a future excursion to that house of joy.

But after returning home, Stebbel decided that it was not at all a bad idea to go out that evening. It was the beginning of a long weekend after all, and he felt he needed to push himself to again engage with life. He had gone through a long series of negative events, in both his personal and his professional life, and he knew he had to move past them.

He bathed and then headed to a favorite café, where he took

a table on the outdoor terrace. He ordered a double brandy and a slice of apple strudel. Both tasted delicious, a sign that his emotional doldrums were coming to an end.

As he sipped at his brandy, he thought of all the things that had been troubling him in the weeks since he had become a "hero". Why did his triumph seem to have a lingering echo of failure about it? Was he just one of those people Freud and his group wrote about who can never really be happy, never truly satisfied? Had he somehow lost the capacity for full joy? Could he ever recover it, or was it lost forever?

He decided that he would have to jump back into life headfirst – into the life of the casual police inspector who took everything more easily. After all, he doubted that Rautz, Dörfner or the other inspectors in his office felt too often the way he'd been feeling of late.

And then he recalled the moments he had come closest to a full symphony of joy in the last few months. It was that hour he had spent with Carina, the Spittelberg streetwalker. He knew that it was just the easy delights of early infatuation, but it did bring him to something like emotional abandon, embracing (literally) a fantasy, and he realized that's what he really needed again.

He finished the brandy quickly and called for the bill. He knew that his next stop was going to be Spittelberg, where he would stroll around until he found this Carina – or whatever her real name was.

He caught a taxi and had it drop him off a few streets from the red-light section. He felt it somehow inappropriate to be dropped off in the district itself; walking into the streetwalker's area was somehow more fitting, he thought. Well, when in Rome...

Within minutes of reaching the zone, he felt better. The district's cobble-stoned streets, framed by the subdued elegance of Biedermeier-style buildings, had a wayward charm that helped lift his mood. And, of course, there were the streetwalkers themselves.

A number of these women really were quite pretty, he now

realized, and the late spring breezes lapping the picturesque lanes just made the whole atmosphere more pleasant. He politely turned down every offer of a good time as he strolled past and just enjoyed the feeling of being approached by so many available young women. But he was looking for one specific woman.

He had been sure he would see Carina again. After all, this was Friday, which had to be a working night for her.

He had it all planned out: after their meeting, she would take him to her room. He would pay her for two hours. For the first half hour or so, they would talk and he would find out what she had been doing lately. He wondered if she would know that he was one of the officers responsible for ending the Stranger's killing spree. Then, after their conversation, they would make love, talk some more, and then see what the time and mood would allow.

But though he kept walking and looking intensely now, searching out every face, Carina was not to be seen. Perhaps she had another customer who had already bought a few hours of her time. As he considered this, he felt betrayed, then realized how foolish such a feeling was.

He noticed that as he prowled some of the lanes a second or even a third time, he was getting funny looks from some of the working girls as he passed them again. He suddenly wondered if this is the way Brunner had operated, cruising aimlessly until he found just the right girl, one standing all alone with no witnesses around.

At the end of one lane, he saw a figure in a lemony half-light. She then stepped forward a step or two, just enough that he could see her better. "Are you looking for someone in particular, mein Herr? Maybe I can help you find her?"

Her voice was soft and mellow, the way Carina's voice had been. It wasn't Carina, and she wasn't quite as pretty as Carina. But she had that look of barely tarnished innocence that he needed that evening. Not much makeup, and her hairdo was what you might expect from a university student. Also, she was dressed seductively, showing just enough to make the promise of seeing the rest hard to negate. Suddenly, Stebbel felt a surge of lust. He stepped very close to her and the lust surged more.

His opening line was strange. "Where are you from?" he asked. Her room was just a few minutes away, she said. "No," he said. "Where are you from originally?"

"From Moravia. A small town. You've probably never heard of it, being the educated and sophisticated gent you obviously are."

That answer was enough for Stebbel. He then asked how much. She came back with the standard lines: "Ten kroners. Is that too much?"

"No ... not at all," he replied, and a short time later they were in her room. Stebbel had removed his hat and his jacket, then stepped to the side and watched her undress. She had removed her shoes and her flimsy dress. She sat on the bed and started to slip off her stockings, when something suddenly happened to Stebbel. He felt faint, slightly nauseous even. He took a few deep breaths, closed his eyes and leaned against the door.

"Are you alright?" she asked. Turning to look at her, he realized that most of his lust had disappeared. He could probably work at it and get some of that lust back, but it would be a foolish exercise to have sex with this girl. And a foolish exercise was not what he was looking for that evening.

He told the woman that he was suddenly feeling unwell. Something he had eaten earlier in the evening, he told her. He then pulled out the ten kroners. He insisted that she take the whole amount they had agreed on and apologized that he couldn't enjoy her charms. He then added that he really wanted to enjoy her, but he just wasn't up to it.

She shrugged and took the money. It appeared that men getting to her room and then realizing they were unable to perform was not that unusual an occurrence for her. And she did not seem to be too unhappy that she had not been able to sustain his lust, even as she undressed.

Stebbel grabbed his coat and hat, apologized again. But by that point, she had already pulled her dress back on and was easing her foot into one of the shoes. Stebbel wanted to say something else, a strong exit line, but nothing came to him, so he simply opened the door and stepped out, closing the door hard behind him.

He started down the steps, moving as quickly as he safely could. He passed two other couples going up the steps to fulfill their transactions; all four stared at this figure trying to squeeze by. He smiled and tried to gesture that everything was all right, he just needed to get out and get some fresh air.

As soon as he hit the street, he realized that he really had needed fresh air. He crossed the narrow street, stopped and just sucked in deep breaths for the next thirty seconds. Then he headed off.

He walked for the next fifteen minutes, not even sure where exactly he was walking. Not knowing what he wanted, he stared at the faces of the many girls he passed, the men who had come looking for their quick dip of sex, the louche types leaning against walls and staring back at him with suspicion. Those latter were probably pimps, but tonight Stebbel couldn't give a damn what their business was, just as long as they left him alone.

After a few streets, the faces, the bodies, the hazy lights, the whining doors opening and closing ... everything became distorted. He felt that this nocturnal journey had turned into a hallucinatory excursion. Every person he passed, every sound he heard, every smell – it all seemed like a series of hallucinations.

Finally, he found himself on the Mariahilferstrasse. He hailed a cab and climbed in. He started to give his address and then caught himself;

he didn't want to be dropped off right in front of his building. He told the driver to let him off at a pub a few streets from his place.

He decided to buy a bottle of cheap wine to take away, then walk back from there. The vintage Bordeaux waiting for him back at his flat was too elegant for his present mood. He wanted something coarse and unfocused to fit his demeanor. And if it made him really sick, so much the better.

As he shuffled home from the pub, Stebbel was feeling even more despondent than when the evening began. As he approached his building, he saw what seemed at first to be another hallucination: there was a young priest standing guard near the front door. To increase the hallucinatory effect, as he came a little closer, the priest trotted down the steps towards him and called out, "Are you Inspector Julian Stebbel?"

Stebbel hesitated for a moment. What was this all about? Did his guardian angel, repulsed by his visit to the whores' quarter, fly over to his local church and inform on him? Had this priest been sent out to force a confession of his sin? After all, he had sinned in thought and word; he only failed in the action segment.

Stebbel saw no way out of this strange situation other than telling the truth.

"Yes, I am Julian Stebbel. And why do you ask?"

The young priest first raised his eyes towards Heaven and whispered a short prayer of thanks. He then explained the reason for his mission: he was sent by his superior, a Father Wenzel, to find Stebbel and bring him to the Holy Savior Hospital as quickly as possible. But he had been sent over two hours ago and been waiting most of that time at his current post.

And why was he needed at the Holy Savior Hospital, Stebbel asked. A man, a man in critical condition, needed to see him. He had some confession he needed to make, and that confession had to be made to Stebbel. And only Stebbel.

Even though Stebbel was still dubious, even suspicious, he agreed to go. But first, he said, he had to go up to his place, drop off the bottle of wine and pick up something. "Of course," replied the priest, a nervous smile twisting his face.

As the anxious priest trotted towards the corner hoping to find a taxi, Stebbel hurried up the steps to his second-floor apartment. He turned on the gaslight, stuck the wine bottle into the umbrella stand next to the door and headed for the study. There, he went to his desk, pulled out his keys and unlocked the middle drawer, where he kept his personal revolver.

He pulled out the revolver and checked the barrel. Fully loaded. He also clicked off the safety. If this was a trap, if he was heading into an ambush, he would make sure that those waiting for him would get a big surprise of their own.

When he re-emerged, Stebbel saw that the priest had not only found a taxi, but that the taxi was waiting right out front for him, its engine grumbling, its driver looking irritable.

As Stebbel climbed into the back seat, he found the young cleric even more nervous than before. He seemed to be whispering a prayer as they drove off. *His superior must be a pretty tough fellow*, Stebbel thought.

In the taxi, the priest – who finally identified himself as Father Alois Meller – told Stebbel everything he knew about the call to the hospital. But "everything" didn't amount to much. All he seemed to know was that a certain gentleman had suffered a serious accident, was close to death, and he needed to talk to Stebbel about something. No clue as to what that something was. Stebbel remained in a thick, swirling fog.

46

When they finally reached the hospital, the priest rushed to the reception desk and made some inquiry. Half a minute later, he turned, grabbed Stebbel by the arm and pulled him towards the *paternoster*.

"It's Room 424," he said. "That's fourth floor, you turn to the right when we get off and then all the way down to the end of the corridor." He breathed heavily. "And by the grace of God, I hope we're not too late."

When Stebbel arrived at Room 424, he found a gangly priest with a pinched face waiting near the door. The priest nodded and addressed him.

"Are you Inspector Stebbel?"

"That's right, Father. And you are …?"

"Father Andreas Wenzel. I just heard his confession and gave him absolution. But he's still not completely healed. Healed spiritually, I mean. He still insists on making a further confession. To you."

"Yes, that's what I've been told." But the inspector was no less perplexed than before. Before he could ask why this patient insisted on seeing him, the priest gave a pained smile and opened the door for the visitor.

As Stebbel was about to enter, the priest laid a hand on the crook of his arm. "Oh, his name is Oswald Zingler. He says you may have heard his name before." Stebbel shook his head, then stepped around the priest and into the room.

Inside, Stebbel found the patient, Herr Zingler, staring at the ceiling from the slump of his bed and generally looking terrible. He didn't seem to be aware of Stebbel until the inspector took a seat right at the bedside. Zingler then turned and found a smile somewhere.

"You're Inspector Stebbel, aren't you?"

"Yes, I am." He gazed at the heavy bandaging across the chest. "You've been wounded."

The patient gave what started out as a laugh before it caved into a cough and then a gasp. Finally, he managed to speak. "Yes, self-inflicted. With a gun. I aimed it at my heart, but apparently I missed and only managed to pierce a lung."

He stopped to take two gulps of breath. "They don't tell you how difficult it is to shoot yourself in the chest. You'd think it would be very easy, but it's not, is it?"

"I don't really have any experience to speak of."

"Well, it's not. Now I'm in terrible pain. Terrible. It was a foolish mistake. I should have jumped off a high roof. Next time, that's what I'll do. Anyone you know who wants to kill himself, tell them that's what he should do. The roof."

"Yes, I will." He took a slow, long breath. "You wanted to see me, Herr Zingler? To make a confession?"

"Yes, I need to do this in order to die in anything close to peace."

"Anything I can do to help you. But I don't really – "

"I was responsible for those deaths. The five young women, beginning with Frau von Klettenburg. That was my doing."

Stebbel now thought this poor man was fully delusional and wondered why he had been called here in the middle of the night to deal with him. Just another sad, troubled mind confessing to some crimes he didn't commit.

"No, I think you're innocent. We found the killer. He's paid in full for his crimes." And just to be sure, Stebbel took another look at the man's hands. Although they were now clenched and feeble, he didn't think they were ever capable of those brutal murders that he himself had viewed the end results of.

"No, I don't mean that I actually committed the crimes. Brunner did that; that's clear. But I was responsible. I was the one who contacted him … who paid him … who told him what to do."

Suddenly, this confession rolled back into the realm of the vaguely possible. Stebbel leaned forward, his ears perked up.

"You … you paid Brunner to kill these women? Why?"

"My client paid *me* to do it. He was the one behind it all. All five of those souls are ultimately on his conscience."

"And your client was …?"

"The *Geheimrat. Geheimrat* von Klettenburg."

Stebbel was stunned. "Is this true?"

"Yes, yes; so terribly true. He ordered the death of the first four women. And then the last one, the student, we were both responsible in a way for her death." He suddenly started breathing heavily and seemed to pull away from the conversation.

"Please, please – I need some more explanation. Why would von Klettenburg want all these women dead?"

"It was all because of his wife. She had gone too far. Truly."

"Too far?"

"He didn't mind her affairs when it was kept discreet, when it was within the bounds of decency. But then she started seeking adventure … excitement … danger. And that made it dangerous for the *Geheimrat*. And then … well, it all came to a head with Leopold Scherling."

That name sounded familiar to Stebbel, but he couldn't make an immediate placement. He quickly gestured for Zingler to continue with his recital.

"Yes, Scherling was one of her lovers. And he played all her very dangerous games with her. He'd meet her on the streets, she'd take him to a hotel, he'd pay her money, they would ... you know. And then he would pretend to beat her and steal the money back."

"This was their game?"

"Yes; she had all these very sick fantasies, and she needed men who would help her live out these fantasies. She sought them out, actually."

"I see."

"But even that sort of sickness would not have been too much for the *Geheimrat*. But then ... then Scherling decided that he could profit from this. He was in serious debt, you see, his business was about to go bankrupt."

Suddenly, the name snapped into place for Stebbel. "Yes, I remember the case now."

"So he came up with this plan to get a lot of money and save his business. He contacted Herr von Klettenburg and blackmailed him. He said that if he didn't meet his demands, he would expose the whole sordid game Frau von Klettenburg was playing. With him and several others.

"Of course, the *Geheimrat* was outraged ... and worried. He then came to me and asked me to arrange the murder of his wife. He wanted her removed so that she couldn't ... disgrace him and his respected name any further."

Everything was now starting to come together for Stebbel. "And then the two of you decided to kill Scherling as well ..."

Zingler nodded. "He was a very stupid man, Scherling. No wonder his business went under. After her death, he came to see the *Geheimrat* and actually raised his blackmail demand. Can you imagine that?

"He had figured out that her murder was no chance occurrence. He realized that she'd been killed because of that threat to the von Klettenburg world her secret fantasies had caused. He told the *Geheimrat* that if he didn't pay his demand – an outrageous sum, actually – he would go to the police, to you probably, and tell them everything he knew. That same evening, he joined Frau von Klettenburg in eternity."

"Brunner smashed him in the head and then tossed him into the Danube. Staged it to look like a suicide."

"Exactly."

Stebbel took several deep breaths. Though he'd been a policeman for over six years, he was shocked by the audacity, the ruthlessness of the whole thing. While he'd had suspicions, right from the start, about the depth of von Klettenburg's grief, he never imagined that he would be capable of such a thing. But there was still a huge gap in the explanation.

"Alright, I see his motive for wanting to get rid of his wife and her greedy playmate, but what about the other four girls? Why did they have to die?"

Zingler took a deep breath. "That may be the thing I feel absolutely worst about. After we had taken care of Frau von Klettenburg and Scherling, the *Geheimrat* started to get worried. The police – you and your people, in fact – started putting so much energy into the case.

"He reckoned that if you were looking only at her death, you might eventually chance upon his motives and follow the bloody threads back to him. I ... I agreed with him that this was very possible. So then we discussed what we could do to keep you away.

"We started planning out diversionary tactics. Things to really pull you off the right path. And we decided that the safest way to keep you far from the truth was to make you think that Frau von

Klettenburg was not a specific target. We wanted to make it look like a random killing, part of a string of random murders of young women. As Herr von Klettenburg put it, 'They will be like a row of lovely pearls on a string.'

"When we had a second murder, and then a third, maybe a fourth, it would look like they were all unfortunate victims of a sick killer. Our own Jack the Ripper, isn't that what the newspapers called it? So instead of a finger pointing directly back at the *Geheimrat* from his wife's dead body, she would seem to be the first unfortunate victim of that random killer."

"So you instructed Brunner to go out and find some more victims."

"Yes. I feel so terrible. We let him go after whoever he could find. It didn't matter; all we needed was follow-up victims. But we did … we did insist that those victims should be streetwalkers."

"Why?"

Zingler started to give a heavy shrug, but the pain in his chest was so sharp that he stopped the gesture halfway through. "Well, they were only whores. We didn't think it would be as bad as killing decent women." Stebbel turned away slightly and winced at this. And for the first time during this confession, he felt the urge to strangle Zingler himself.

"But … but after the third one, we started to feel bad, even if they were whores. At least I did. Herr von Klettenburg seemed to be more … objective about the whole thing. The important thing: we did order Brunner to stop the killings for a while. We said we all needed to take a pause to see how our strategy was working and how we should proceed from there."

"And Fräulein Grettin?"

"That was Brunner working entirely on his own. Entirely. The three of us sat down together right after that. The next day, in fact. And you know something – that was the first time Herr von Klettenburg sat face-to-face with Brunner since the evening we first talked about removing Frau von Klettenburg.

"We were very upset with Brunner. First of all, he had gone and killed another girl after we had insisted that he take a pause. And second, the victim was a complete innocent, a university student. We were disgusted and … He received quite a tongue-lashing from the *Geheimrat*, let me tell you."

"That must have been devastating for him."

"The frightening thing was, he sat there and started defending why he had killed that fifth girl. And … and there was something like joy in his face, in his voice as he talked about it.

"As he spoke, his hands – the instruments of these murders – those hands started dancing around in the air, tracing the method he had used to kill the girl. It was like a … a strangler's waltz."

Zingler stopped and Stebbel looked over to see if he was all right. Now, for the first, he saw tears rolling out of the man's eyes. "He seemed to enjoy it. He seemed to find pleasure in the act of murdering a completely innocent stranger. And …"

"Yes?"

"And he told us that he had to top Jack the Ripper. He needed to kill at least one more so that he could become more famous than the Ripper."

"So you decided to halt his attempt at eternal fame by tipping off the police to where he would be that evening we caught up with him?"

"Yes. He had really become a liability. That's how Herr von Klettenburg described it. He said that in business, you always incur some liabilities and you can accept them for a certain time if they are somehow linked to your assets. But at some point, your liabilities threaten to destroy everything you've built up. And that's when you have to just dispose of them."

"It's good that Herr von Klettenburg is such a shrewd businessman."

"Oh, that he is, that he is. The biggest mistake that Brunner made was right there in that room: he wanted more money for killing the fifth girl than he had received for the previous three. He actually insisted that the *Geheimrat* pay him more for a murder that he didn't even want. He said things were getting very dangerous out there with the police increasing their work, so he should get more money.

"Well, the *Geheimrat* felt that this was just the beginning, that he'd soon be blackmailing him openly, and for much more money that that idiot Scherling had demanded. So he said we had to bring an end to Brunner and his killings."

"Stop the music and end the strangler's waltz."

"Yes. That was it, pretty much."

By this time, Stebbel had stood up and was pacing about the room slowly, deliberately. He tried to maintain a veneer of civility despite all the raw anger churning up inside him. It was almost incomprehensible: a member of the imperial privy council coming up with a diabolical scheme and then providing the funds to see it carried out. Five women murdered to shield his pride. To keep the family name unblemished.

Stebbel was filled with loathing for von Klettenburg – and for Zingler as well. This loathing wiped out any earlier feelings of sympathy he'd had for this older man lying in the bed, severely wounded. He didn't even want to look at him again, so deep was his disgust. He only did so when Zingler called out to him. "Inspector …"

Stebbel summoned up some last scrapes of sympathy and did turn to face Zingler. "Yes?"

"Do you think God will ever forgive me for what I've done?"

Stebbel shook his head slightly, not quite believing what he'd just heard. "I think the priest standing outside the door there is better qualified to answer that than I am."

"That's just it. He swears that God can forgive me; will forgive me. He says I only need to show true remorse for my sins. But I don't know if that's true. I feel that what I've done is so terrible … Well, maybe thousands of years in purgatory, and then I can …"

"As I said, Herr Zingler, this is not really my territory. You'd do best to ask the priest again."

Zingler suddenly had a hurt look on his face, as if *he* were some kind of victim. "Would you forgive me? If the decision were left to you, would you ever be able to forgive me?"

Stebbel looked at him for several moments, then turned and started walking towards the door. But just before he reached it, he heard Zingler's strained voice calling out.

"Inspector?" Stebbel could hear the intense pain of his wounds in that voice. He stopped at the door and turned around again.

"I'm sorry. I don't really know what forgiveness could mean in a situation like this." And then, as an afterthought: "You should never ask a policeman about forgiveness anyway; we don't deal in that commodity. I have to go now."

A few seconds later, Herr Zingler was again all alone in his bed with his tortured conscience.

As Stebbel came out, Father Wenzel approached. He seemed to be wearing the same pained smile he had assumed when Stebbel headed into the room. Stebbel's face was filled with anger, contempt and confusion. The priest read these feelings from his face, then again reached out and took his arm.

"Inspector, we have to realize that sometimes justice escapes us in this world. But there will be full justice in the next world, and those who have done terrible things will pay for them there in the next world."

Stebbel closed his eyes briefly, then shook his head. "Father, I need justice in this world. That is why I'm a policeman." He gently lifted the priest's hand from his forearm, gave a polite nod and started walking away. The corridor now reeked of rancid pity and seemed twice as long as when he was on his way to hear Zingler's confession. The inspector picked up his pace to get away as quickly as he could.

Father Meller stood waiting for Stebbel at the *paternoster*. He saw him down, hurriedly found him another taxi, and paid the driver in advance for the fare back to Stebbel's home.

As they drove along, Stebbel stared glumly at the half-lit streets flanked by formidable buildings, the manicured parks, the yawning squares, those imposing statues, all of it filled with sullen shadows. The city was a masterpiece of imperial pomposity.

He suddenly realized that his feelings for Vienna, the place he'd spent such an important part of his life, had become like a love affair gone bad. You wouldn't even notice those first signs of alienation, the disappointments, the slights. Then, at first slowly, you started slipping further and further apart. And then you suddenly realized, as Stebbel did there in that taxi, that the love was largely drained, replaced with something like a snug contempt. He tapped his fist against the window in anger. The taxi driver turned slightly, then raced on through the darkness without saying anything.

47

Stebbel was thoroughly exhausted, but even so, he lay there in his bed staring up at the wall, unable to tumble into what he had hoped would be a healing sleep. Where did all this leave him? The case was now reopened and had become messier than it had ever been in its messiest moments before now.

He closed his eyes and wished for some kind of oblivion. He was exhausted but not capable of sleep; he was hungry, but without any appetite; he was aching, but with no desire to lose the aches. And he couldn't straighten out his thoughts to come up with a way out of this new labyrinth.

Eventually, Stebbel did sink into sleep, but it was more like sinking into a dank swamp: a troubled sleep, tossed back and forth through all the concerns, obsessions and doubts that he'd lived with over the last month. He woke shortly after five a.m. and realized he wouldn't be able to get back to sleep. But it was still hours before he was expected at the office. He rose, washed, and dressed. After downing his third tumbler of water that morning, he headed out.

His ultimate destination was the Lange Gasse, where Dörfner's boarding house was. However, when he arrived, it was still too early to rouse his partner. So he strolled over to the Café Kettner, arriving just as the bleary-eyed staff was opening the doors. He ordered what he suspected would be the first of too many coffees that day, and drank it with a bitter expression despite the three spoonfuls of sugar he'd added.

He lingered over that *kleiner Brauner* coffee, then downed another. Finally, he decided it was almost a decent time to call on Dörfner. He had to talk to him before they met up at the office.

When Dörfner opened the door, he was caught completely by surprise to see Stebbel standing there. Stebbel had only come to Dörfner's place once or twice since they'd become partners, and never first thing in the morning. Even stranger, this was a free day for both loupes, supposedly the beginning of the long holiday weekend.

Dörfner was still in his bed clothes, just wrenched out of an alcohol-aided sleep, so his invitation to Stebbel to come in was awkward and mumbly. He just managed to ask Stebbel the reason for this surprise visit while moving towards the small toilet cabinet.

"I had a meeting with our mystery caller last night. The self-proclaimed 'friend of justice'."

This report jolted Dörfner fully awake within seconds. He told Stebbel that he'd get ready and be with him in just a few minutes.

Stebbel had to wait at a table near the front door while Dörfner finished with his morning ablutions and his dressing. When he reappeared, Stebbel flashed a broad smile: his partner was wearing a fancy new suit. *These are a cop's trappings of success when you solve a major case*, Stebbel thought. And he wondered what changes in demeanor would fold over Dörfner when he heard the news Stebbel had come to share with him.

Stebbel suggested they have breakfast together and Dörfner agreed. The two then shuffled over to the Café Kettner. The waiters greeted Stebbel like an old customer who commanded special attention.

After they'd placed their orders, the senior partner began to tell his junior about the confession at the hospital the previous evening. He spoke even more slowly than usual as he deftly pulled out every detail of the evening, from the time he was met at his own front door by Father Meller.

He tried to fully describe Zingler lying there in the hospital bed, his difficulties speaking, the fear and self-disgust he saw in the man's face. And he recounted the story in a way that made Karsten von Klettenburg seem even more cold-hearted and malevolent than he had appeared in Zingler's account.

Dörfner just sat and listened for most of the time, nodding to underscore his interest. He only asked one or two questions, slight clarifications. For the first part of Stebbel's narrative, Dörfner seemed astonished. Once or twice, he shook his head, as if he was teetering on that thin line between belief and non-belief.

When he heard the rationale behind the last four murders, he seemed to be glaring at Stebbel, almost like he was about to accuse his partner of having made this whole horrific tale up. But a short time later, the look of astonishment disappeared and was replaced by anger.

The anger was constant and almost reached the point of rage. As if to keep that rage safely bottled up, he clutched his tie and the front of his shirt as he leaned forward to whisper to Stebbel.

"You know, I always half-suspected our friend the *Geheimrat* was involved in this in some way. But never this deeply, the bastard. He makes Brunner look like an altar boy. Yeah, an altar boy just serving the dark priest of deception."

"I won't argue with you, Charley."

"And the worst thing is ..." Stebbel raised his eyebrows to encourage Dörfner to continue. "The worst thing is, he'll probably get away with the whole thing. Brunner dies, this other pimp in the hospital will probably die, and Herr von Klettenburg sails right along through all the turbulent storms. The swine will probably even get some honor from the Emperor, something for bravery or meritorious service or some shit like that."

He took a deep swallow of his coffee, as if to refuel his bitterness. "Yeah, justice rarely scrambles up to the top tiers of society."

Stebbel fixed him with a hard stare. "No, we're not going to let him get away with it. That's why I came to see you this morning. All last night, I was tearing myself apart inside, thinking that he would get off without getting a smudge on him. But then, this morning, I came up with a plan."

Dörfner was immediately engaged. "What is it?"

"We go to the office right now. We'll get in a little early, grab one of those typewriting machines, and write out a confession for Herr Zingler. We put down everything he told me last night. About all five murders. Well, six, actually, because we have to include Scherling. Now we know that was a murder as well, no suicide." Dörfner nodded zealously.

"Then we rush over to the hospital and we pay Herr Zingler a visit. We tell him the only way he can really earn full forgiveness is if he signs that confession. He has to tell the world what he did, and who else was really behind it all. I don't think he's worried about retribution from von Klettenburg at this point. So we get the confession signed, and then we go after the *Geheimrat*."

Dörfner looked ready to sign on, but a small sliver of doubt remained.

"Do you think it will work?"

"It's the only thing that can work. Otherwise, you're right: von Klettenburg walks off looking like a brave widower. He will have managed to commit the perfect crime – but only by killing five additional people to masquerade the crime."

Dörfner scooped out the remaining egg from its shell and stuffed it into his mouth. He nodded several times as he swallowed. "Alright; we'll do it. We're together on this all the way. Except …"

"Yes?"

"You'll have to type that confession. I have nothing but trouble with those typewriting machines. My fingers, you know." He held up his hands. "Every one of my fingertips smothers five or six letters at a time."

Stebbel chuckled. "Alright, I'll do all the typing. I'm no expert with that contraption, but I do have some experience. Mostly sad experience, but I can manage."

Dörfner then chomped down his half-eaten roll and picked up the remaining one on the plate. He paused, raised a hand and finished his energetic chewing.

"One other thing."

"Yes?"

"If we catch the bastard on this, do we have to give back all that wine?"

Stebbel sputtered a laugh and shook his head. "I don't think so."

"Good. I've already polished off half of mine."

They finished their breakfasts quickly, paid, and took a taxi back to the precinct.

48

Typing the confession proved as painful a task as Stebbel had thought it would be. But they kept the document short and blunt, without omitting any damning details, and an hour later, they signed out on the duty sheet and headed over to Holy Hearts Hospital. Checking to see that Zingler was still in the same room, Stebbel nodded, then led his partner to the *paternoster*. A few minutes later, they were knocking at the door of Zingler's room.

A nun with a wimple resembling an assault umbrella answered the door. When the two inspectors identified themselves and said they needed to see Herr Zingler urgently, the nun turned a light shade of fluster. Herr Zingler was unable to see any visitors, she told them, and advised them to speak with Doctor Reimann instead.

Dörfner said they understood why the hospital wouldn't want a crowd gathering inside the room and carrying on a long conversation with the patient, but this was different: they were high-ranking police inspectors on an important investigation and they really needed Zingler's assistance at that point.

The nun still refused to remove herself from the doorway, but she offered to take them to Doctor Reimann's office. It was just down the corridor, she said, and it would take no time at all.

Reimann's office was actually at the other end of the corridor, and during the trek, the nun kept apologizing for not letting the two inspectors in. She had strict orders, she told them, very strict, and if she did let anyone in, she could find herself in deep trouble. Stebbel and Dörfner put on their gracious faces and said they understood entirely.

Reimann's office was spacious, sunny and resolutely sterile. It looked like a place you would store medical specimens. Reimann himself was a tall man with an elongated face and small, unsympathetic eyes. After the introductions, the inspectors simply said that they were on important police business and needed to speak with Herr Zingler.

Reimann stared at them the whole time like a school principal listening to two students asking that they be allowed to violate some long-established school regulation. When they'd finished, he nodded sympathetically and told them it was not possible to see the patient right then. Herr Zingler had taken a turn for the worse during the night, he explained, and it would be highly irresponsible for him, as a doctor, to allow the patient any visitors.

But all they wanted, Stebbel interjected, was to have Zingler read through a short document, not quite a page-and-a-half, then sign it.

Absolutely not, Reimann replied. The strain of reading some official document was exactly the kind of thing he wanted to protect his patient from in this perilous state he was now thrown into. Plus, if this document was anything official, something intended to carry legal weight, it would not be very valuable with the signature of a heavily sedated man who was having trouble remembering where he was or what year it was.

The two inspectors nodded sadly. But before leaving, they did insist on one thing: the moment Zingler had recovered enough to entertain any visitors, they were to be informed immediately and allowed to show him the document in question.

In fact, they added a slight grace note of threat: if Doctor Reimann did not undertake to have them informed immediately, he could well be charged with obstruction of justice. Reimann assured them that they would be notified the moment any signs of recovery showed, and asked where and how they could be contacted.

The discussion ended on that sour note. Reimann saw them to the door, they exchanged mechanical handshakes, and the two inspectors went back to the office.

* * *

For the next day and a half, Stebbel and Dörfner worked on a missing person case and tried to keep themselves well informed of Zingler's progress. Finally, late Thursday morning, Stebbel received a phone call from the nun at Holy Hearts Hospital.

Sister Elisabeth said that Herr Zingler had passed away shortly after dawn. There were a "series of complications attendant upon his accident". His mortal body had been collected by the Froner Funeral Institute in Grinzing. A wake for the dead would be held there the next two evenings for friends and family wishing to see the deceased one more time. Requiem mass would follow on Saturday, at the Votive Church.

The nun ended by offering her condolences to Inspector Stebbel and his colleague; she could see how agitated they were when they came to visit Herr Zingler. The three of them must have been close.

Stebbel thanked the good sister and dropped the receiver into the hook with a clunk of despair. Dörfner, who had been watching him closely throughout the call, dropped his voice.

"Zingler?"

Stebbel nodded slowly. "His soul was taken up by the angels."

Dörfner looked like someone had just yanked a stopper and depleted him of enthusiasm. "I hope von Klettenburg is grateful to those angels. They just delivered the Herr *Geheimrat* from justice."

"Earthly justice. As the priests always like to remind us."

"*Tja.*"

Suddenly, Stebbel's mood lifted a few degrees. "Wait a minute. There's still a chance we can get the evidence we need. There is still that chance."

"How?"

"Remember, Karl-Heinz, that we're not even sure our Herr von Klettenburg was really behind these murders. Zingler could have been making that part up."

"Why?"

Stebbel shrugged. "Maybe he had a grudge against the *Geheimrat*. A deep, ugly grudge. They worked together for some years. That's a lot of time for a rich and arrogant man to sow some nasty grudges."

"*Ja*, maybe." He took a contemplative snort. "So what's this chance to find out the full truth?"

"From a man who has his sights set beyond mere earthly justice."

Just after noon, Inspector Stebbel entered St. Bartolemus Church. He hesitated before going further, dipped his fingers in the holy water fount, looked towards the altar and genuflected. Then he hurried down the side aisle where he found Father Wenzel rearranging hymnbooks in the middle pews. His approach obviously surprised the priest.

"Good afternoon, Father."

"Oh yes. Inspector ..."

"Stebbel."

"Of course. What can I do for you, Inspector?" Stebbel hesitated for just a moment. "I take it that you've heard about the passing of Herr Zingler." Stebbel nodded.

"I was there at his side at the end. I gave him the last rites."

"I thought you did that the first night."

"I did."

"What, does the absolution wear off after a day? You have to keep on applying it?"

Father Wenzel gave a reluctant smile. "Who knows how he might have sinned in thought over the next two days." He then smiled more easily, as if preparing to share a secret. "Anyway, the final sacrament, especially administered repeatedly, is often more for the dying person and his family than for the forgiveness of God."

"I see."

"But I don't. I am pretty sure that you didn't come here for a lengthy discussion of the sacraments."

"What did he tell you, Father? When he was confessing his crimes. Did he tell you who else was involved? Did he go through the details of the crimes?"

"You know I can't reveal that. You are a Catholic, aren't you, Inspector?"

"From time to time."

"Then you are well aware of the absolute seal of confession." Stebbel nodded. "Everything that Herr Zingler told me about those crimes was conveyed during the sacrament. I am bound by the rules of our Church to keep those details secret. Even unto and beyond death."

Stebbel stared at the priest hard. "Father, I suspect you know this doesn't just involve our Herr Zingler. There may be someone else involved in those horrible murders. Someone who was actually the man pulling the strings. And that man may just walk away absolutely free, never pay any price for those crimes. He will, in fact, profit from all those crimes."

"What does it profit a man to gain the whole world but lose his soul?"

"You have no regard for earthly justice?"

"That is your responsibility, not mine, Inspector. I must think of the next world." He paused for a moment. "We all should think more about the next world."

"Thank you, Father. I may see you at the wake." Stebbel turned and started walking angrily back down the aisle. The priest took a deep sigh.

About ten meters down the aisle, Stebbel stopped and turned back.

"Father, would you give absolution to that other man? The one pulling all those strings? The man who pulled the strings that strangled five innocent women?"

"It is my duty as a priest to give absolution to anyone who comes to me in full contrition."

"So, no justice in this world or the next, as long as the swine comes to you before dying and pretends to have contrition?"

"There is always purgatory. There, we are still bereft of the presence of God, and the punishment for all our sins, even those forgiven in confession, will be rendered from the judgment of the one flawless judge."

"I see."

He turned and started walking away again. A few steps along, Father Wenzel called out to him. "Inspector!" Stebbel stopped and half-turned. The priest walked up to him quickly. "Inspector, I have the sense that you have many things that are troubling you. Things that go beyond the body and into the soul. If you should ever like to make a full and profound confession … I would be honored to serve as your confessor."

"Thank you, Father. I will keep that in mind."

Stebbel then turned one last time and strode out of the church. The priest watched him until he disappeared into the vestibule, from where his footfall carried echoes of deep resentment.

49

An hour later, Stebbel and Dörfner were sitting in the Café Henslich. Dörfner was halfway through a tall Dobos torte; Stebbel, who could only manage a few nibbles from a cherry strudel, had just signaled for another Franziskaner-style coffee.

"So you weren't able to get anything from this priest?"

Stebbel shook his head. "Anything of importance that Zingler had told him was given under the seal of confession. The priest was bound to silence."

"The seal of confession? Oh, hang on a minute – isn't that like the seal of silence between a perverted psychiatrist and his perverted patients?"

Stebbel cracked a slight smile at Dörfner's sardonic twist of their earlier discussions. Dörfner then slipped back into his morose tone. "So, he couldn't tell you anything?" He expressed his frustration by spearing a chunk of the Dobos torte.

"Couldn't ... wouldn't. The important thing is, my trip was totally wasted. I think he *wanted* to tell me that von Klettenburg was involved, but he ... couldn't."

"So that where it stands. And that's where it ends too. I guess." He shoved the chunk of torte into his mouth and swallowed it after two rough bites. "The rich bastard gets away again." He grabbed his coffee cup brusquely, spilling some out of the side as he did.

"I guess we should console ourselves with the possibility that he wasn't really involved after all. Maybe Zingler was lying."

"There on his deathbed? Calling you out there in the middle of the night to make a final confession? And then he's going to lie about the swine who was behind the whole thing."

"Not very likely, of course. I just said it was possible."

"Well, as far as anyone else knows, the case is closed. We caught the killer and he paid for his crimes with his own life. It all ended very clean, neat and efficient, as Rautz would say. Just the way he likes to see a case wrapped up."

Stebbel gave a look halfway between a wince and a smile. "Very neat and clean indeed. Too damn neat and clean."

"Well, I guess we can't really complain: we're heroes, and Rautz is a model senior inspector and ..."

"And Karsten von Klettenburg is a grieving widower whose terrible grief has been at least partly assuaged by our heroic work finding his poor wife's murderer." He shook his head sadly. "So, it was all too true what he told us at that first meeting: his wife also played the game, but not as well as he did."

Dörfner had just gobbled down the last piece of his torte and tossed his fork onto the plate. "I would like to know for sure though. That it *was* von Klettenburg behind everything. For sure, without that shadow of doubt scraping at the back of my head." He stared over at Stebbel, who seemed swallowed up in his own thoughts. He then glanced down at the plate in front of Stebbel.

"Are you going to finish that strudel?"

He slid the plate across the table. "No, no; you have it." At that same moment, he came out of his private thoughts and his mood seemed much brighter.

"You know ... you know, there may be a way that we can find out. We can trick von Klettenburg into telling us himself."

"Really?"

"Yes, I think I may have just come up with a way."

"I think I would be happy with that. Just to have him tell us himself."

"And that may just be within our grasp."

50

On the morning of Oswald Zingler's funeral, Mother Nature showed no measure of sympathy for the occasion. The weather was completely out of sync with any funereal mood. It was, in fact, a glorious day, the most beautiful so far that year as full-bloomed spring showed off all its powers.

Not far from the graveside where an Augustinian priest was reciting the prayers of burial, groups of children ran around cheerfully, using tombstones as shields while they played tag and pass-the-waffle.

At the sleeve of the hill overlooking the service, the sun shone off rows of tombstones and a modest mausoleum, making each one look like a thick gem lodged in the ground.

Inspectors Stebbel and Dörfner waited a respectful distance away from the service, trying to calibrate the feelings of the mourners. After the priest threw the required handful of dirt into the grave, the funeral attendant guided the mourners to the grave one-by-one so they could toss their roses into the pit and give their final farewells to the departed.

Geheimrat Karsten von Klettenburg was the first after the family members to be escorted to the grave. He threw in his rose, bowed his head, made the sign of the cross, turned and headed back to his motorcar where his chauffeur and another servant waited to help him in and then back to the center of town.

As soon as he had left the graveside, Stebbel and Dörfner moved quickly. They intercepted him about ten meters before his waiting car. The *Geheimrat* was thoroughly surprised to see the two loupes there.

"Inspectors. Did you also know the deceased?"

Stebbel spoke. "No, not really. We're here on some official business."

"Oh ... indeed?"

"But you yourself ... was the deceased a friend or a business partner?"

"Both actually. Our relationship had started out on a strictly business basis. But then certain dealings brought us closer together. By the end, we had become quite close in many ways."

"Ah, so I can understand your feelings of sorrow then. And you've certainly had more than your fair share of sorrow lately."

"Yes, that's very true. So if you don't mind – "

"He shot himself, didn't he? Why do you think he did that?

Von Klettenburg took a deep sigh. This was going to drag on a few more minutes, so he had best make the best of it.

"Well, he had actually been rather depressed for the last few years. Following the death of his wife. And he did apparently have some serious health problems. He was often in considerable pain these last months. It pained me to see him suffering. And that was every time we got together recently. I imagine everything just came together and became too much for the poor man."

He turned to look back at the burial plot. Those at the tail end of the mourner's queue were tossing their flowers into the grave. "But now he's together with his beloved wife. And I console myself with that thought: that he has found a level of happiness which he was lacking over the last several years."

"And no one knows better than you the pain of losing a beloved spouse. Especially when that spouse is taken away so abruptly, so ...

cruelly."

"Yes, that's very true. And now I lose a long-time friend. So if you don't mind, I really would like to get back to my home and – "

"Of course. We'll let you get on your way in just a few minutes. But as I said, we are here on some official business. We were hoping you might be able to help us. In fact, it involves the loss of your dear wife."

"Oh?"

Now Dörfner spoke for the first time in the trap round. "Do you happen to know this man?" He pulled out one of Hitler's sketches of Brunner from a thin folder he'd been holding since their arrival.

Von Klettenburg took the sketch and looked at it. He was obviously taken aback, very much so, at seeing Brunner's face there. It was clear that he knew immediately who it was. But that's not what he said.

"No. No, I have no idea who this man is."

"Are you sure? Are you quite sure you've never seen him before?"

Von Klettenburg's look of mild shock now morphed into one of exasperation. "Look, I'm a businessman. I have the bank and several other enterprises. I also meet many people at various functions. I can't possibly remember all of them. So it is conceivable that I may have met this man at some point or other. But if I did, he clearly did not make any lasting impression on me."

He took another sigh, this one a relaxed sigh; he felt he had wiggled out of an uncomfortable corner. "But for all practical purposes, we can say that I do *not* know this man."

"Oh, that's too bad. We were hoping you might be able to help us identify him. You see, we have reason to believe that this man may have been an accomplice in the murder of your dear wife."

"You …" He pointed towards the sketch. "But that is … I mean, I thought you had already caught the killer. Hunted him down and made him pay for his crimes."

"Oh, we did. But this fellow here is still out there somewhere. And we have sufficient reason to believe he was an accessory to Brunner in his crimes. That's why we want to find him now and bring him in for some heavy questioning."

Von Klettenburg suddenly looked very confused, fully disconcerted. It was clear to the two loupes that he recognized Brunner from the sketch, that he knew him all too well, that he was shaken by the recognition.

The two loupes had all the proof they needed of his central involvement in the murders, so they wrapped up their questioning quickly, then escorted him to his car. They thanked him for his patience and his cooperation and extended their condolences for his loss of a good friend.

Von Klettenburg was helped into the back seat of his car by the second servant as the chauffeur climbed into the front. Stebbel and Dörfner started walking ahead, barely concealed smiles on their faces as they walked. Their trap had worked beautifully.

As von Klettenburg's car drove past, the *Geheimrat* stared out at them, a stiff anxiety etched in his features. The car then picked up speed and the two inspectors watched as it raced off into whatever refuge the deeply privileged could still rely on.

"So it was him," Dörfner said.

Stebbel nodded. "Nobody who didn't already know Brunner would have recognized him there. The press never published any pictures."

"I'll tell you, I almost broke out laughing when we told him we suspected the man in the sketch was 'an accomplice'. That confused look on the bastard's face: like a rat stuck in a maze, half his tail up his ass." And at that point, Dörfner did break out in a deep, triumphant laugh.

"I never had too many doubts. Not since that night at Zingler's bedside. I just wanted to be sure. I needed that."

Dörfner shook his head sadly. "Doesn't do much. Our being sure won't stand up in court and get him convicted."

"Not at all. He wouldn't even be indicted. But at least we know. That's worth something. And he knows we know. That's worth even more."

Dörfner nodded. "Right."

They started walking off to the front gates of the cemetery, where a police motorcar was waiting for them. The day seemed to have become even brighter, the air more luscious.

But suddenly another consideration clouded Dörfner's bright mood. "Yeah, he does know, doesn't he? And that might not be too good for us."

"Why is that?"

"Well, we know this swine is not above hiring killers to get rid of people he wants to get rid of. We might be his next targets, don't you think?"

"I guess we'll just to sleep with one eye open for awhile."

"For the rest of our lives?"

"We're policeman, Dörfner. We have to get used to little inconveniences like that. After awhile, we may even find it hard to sleep with both eyes shut."

"Just what I've always dreamed of."

They walked on in silence for about one hundred meters. Just before they reached the cemetery gates, Dörfner spoke. "So this is what earthly justice feels like?"

Stebbel shrugged. "It's a taste of it. Just a taste."

"*Ja*; something like a thin soup," Dörfner suggested.

Stebbel nodded. "Wait till we get to dessert."

Dörfner shrugged. "Alright. But I'm afraid it's going to be a long wait."

51

All the loupes were gathered in the briefing room for their weekly rundown from Senior Inspector Rautz. The senior went through all the past week's crimes, latest police department business, and asked for questions. Then, as the briefing seemed to be ending, he added one last morsel.

"One other thing, gentlemen. I know that several of you got to know the respected *Geheimrat* Karsten von Klettenburg recently because of the tragic murder of his wife. I think a number of us were moved by the sorrows this man had to endure, losing such a wonderful woman at such a young age, and under such horrible circumstances.

"Well, there's one more bit of sad news to tie up this saga. It seems the sorrows finally became too much for the *Geheimrat*. He was found dead late last night in the park near his home on the Shubertring. A suicide, it seems. From a self-inflicted bullet wound in the head."

Rautz pointed his own finger to the side of his head, just east of the ear, and mimed pulling a trigger. "Bang! One shot, clean through, no chance for second thoughts."

He then took a deep breath and seemed to be stifling a giggle at the same time. He re-imposed his somber look before speaking again. "I'm sure that our thoughts and prayers are with this unfortunate gentleman and his surviving family and friends. The only consoling thought out of all this is that Herr von Klettenburg is now probably reunited with his beloved wife. They have their peace and can resume their relationship in another realm.' He then took a somber snort. "Any questions?"

Inspector Delling raised his hand. "Was there any suicide note?"

"Nothing that we've found so far." Rautz shrugged. "But I guess none was needed. The reason for the suicide was so clear in this instance. There's just so much sorrow and stress any one man can shoulder. At some point, it just brings us crashing down."

Rautz then dismissed the group. The inspectors finished gathering up their things and started heading out the door. Rautz threaded his way back against the stream going out the door and approached Dörfner and Stebbel. He discreetly asked them to stay just a few minutes after all the others had left.

When it was just the three of them in the room, Rautz began the extra briefing with his telling nod.

"I know that the two of you had more to do with Herr von Klettenburg than anyone else in this team. You probably got to know him a bit, certainly more than me or any of these other fellows.

"I just wanted to say that you shouldn't blame yourselves for his death. Nobody can say you didn't do everything you could to solve that case as quickly as possible. I think you made his pain a little more bearable for awhile, and then ... Well, who knows how the human soul operates."

"*Jawohl*, Herr Inspector." Dörfner stood and Stebbel was about to when Rautz extended his hand to stay them for another few minutes.

"There's something else I wanted to share with you two. Nobody else in the division knows this, and I don't want you to ever tell anyone else." The two junior inspectors looked puzzled.

"I mentioned that no suicide note has been found. That's true, there was nothing quite like that. But there was one note discovered near the *Geheimrat*'s body. It was an anonymous note, crumpled up, lying where he must have dropped it. Or thrown it.

"It seems whoever wrote that note accused the *Geheimrat* of having an affair. But not any normal, healthy affair ..." He shook his head as if he didn't know how to say this.

"It was a ... sexual relationship with ... a young man. Worse, this young man was apparently a Russian, and even worse than that, he was apparently a spy for the Russian secret service." He took a swallow of sour breath. "Very messy, very messy.

"Now whoever wrote this letter said he was intending to bring his evidence to some of the scandal sheets in the city and ruin the *Geheimrat*'s reputation completely. That may have been the real motive for his suicide, I don't know." He tapped his chin three times, each tap a *mea culpa* for how little he knew. "But we do have that note."

"The main reason I'm sharing this with you is that I want you two to take care of this. After all, you were the ones who handled the Frau von Klettenburg murder, and eventually solved it. I'll see that you get the note, but you make sure that no one else ever sees it. We don't want to tarnish the reputation of this fine man, especially now that he can no longer defend himself."

The two inspectors said they would take care of the matter completely.

"I knew I could rely on you. Oh, one other thing: the gun that von Klettenburg used to kill himself ... it was a Steyr-Hahn M11."

Dörfner sniffed. "The one we use."

"That's right; standard issue. And this one had a serial number suggesting it may have once belonged to the Vienna constabulary." He looked around, just to be clear there was no one else there, maybe lurking outside the doorway.

"Now, I want you to be very discreet about this. *Very*. Snoop around, see if any firearms have gone missing recently. But don't make a big thing about it, just see what you can find.

"The most important thing: wrap this up neatly. At the moment, it all has a nice, neat narrative to it. A murder, grief, the murder gets solved, the grief doesn't go away, and then a suicide. Very neat, just the way I like things. See if you can keep it that way."

Rautz then dismissed Dörfner and Stebbel, thanked them again for all their fine work and walked out just ahead of them.

As they headed back to their office, Stebbel was silent, his eyes focused straight ahead. Finally, Dörfner broke the silence.

"Funny thing there, that von Klettenburg would use one of our pistols to do himself in."

"Yes, I guess so."

"You know … they can't be too easy to get, those police pistols."

He and Stebbel turned to face each other fully. After ten very long seconds of gauging each other, Dörfner nodded. "It only proves once again those rich bastards can get anything they want. *Tja*, everything's easier for them." He gave Stebbel a wink. "Come on, let's go for a drink. I'm inviting you."

"It's only 10:05."

"Who cares? It's a lovely morning, and I think we have something to celebrate. Besides, I always like to have a nice drink with my dessert. And I would say we were just served dessert."

He tapped Stebbel on the shoulder to underscore that last remark. The two then nodded to each other like full partners and headed for the *paternoster*. It had never looked so inviting as on that beautiful June morning.

Read more in the Vienna Noir Quartet

Volume Two of the Vienna Noir Quartet takes place in early 1919. Having lost not only the First World War but also its once sprawling empire, Austria has been reduced to a small, land-locked country and Vienna has lost over half of its population. The blow to the national psyche is immense.

But at the Vienna Police Force, Inspectors Dörfner and Stebbel are still the most respected investigators on the force, relied on to solve the city's most difficult cases. It's not long before they are thrown into a case that is quite baffling and challenges even their highly respected skills.

A man is found in the Vienna Woods, his throat slashed in a deliberate and strange design. Inspector Stebbel recalls a similar design on the throat of a murder victim several months before. Does Vienna have another serial murderer on its hands, this one a connoisseur of artistic throat slashings? More important: were the victims chosen at random, or were they targeted? And if the latter, *why* were they targeted?

As Dörfner and Stebbel pursue the few leads they have, they find themselves drawn ever deeper into the labyrinths of Vienna's occult underworld. Were the two murders, and those that soon follow, just a part of some bizarre occult ritual, or is there some even more sinister rationale behind them?

Sigmund Freud is again called upon to lend his expertise to the investigations, and key appearances are also made by such Viennese notables as F.A. Hayek, Gustav Mahler and Arthur Schnitzler. As we discover, Vienna's importance as a political capital may have greatly diminished by 1919, but its status as a world cultural and intellectual capital is as strong as ever.